DRAGON'S ROOK

DRAGON'S ROOK

CAROL L. DENNIS
& RICK DENNIS

WILDSIDE PRESS

Published by Wildside Press LLC
www.wildsidepress.com

To our daughters
Shayla Erin Taylor
Tammy Anne Montagne

Who taught us so much about little girls

To our special editors and advisors

Pepper Hume
Richard King
and
Andrew Taylor

PROLOGUE

Baloo, the young energy-being, stretched to form his bright, silvery shape into an arrow as he left Achaea's sun. He had slept for years after Mirza, his human friend, had sung him to sleep. Now he was ready for some excitement.

He rippled as his mind searched for Mirza. One of the things he loved about her was something interesting always happened around her. He liked her husband, Jarl, the Dragon's Knight, and their sons, Seren and Argen, as well.

As he searched, Baloo became aware of a wrongness on the rim where the stars lay so far apart it took him a few minutes to pass from one to another. Something out there threatened his human friends and frightened him. He fled closer to the center of the Milky Way Galaxy. Here the warm suns were easily accessible to mind and body.

He started to call to Mirza for comfort, but he decided she might sing him back to sleep, and he didn't want that. His great intellect, though young, had immense strength. He began searching through space for the powerful mind that belonged to the human, Mirza. At last, he found her on the world of Realm, standing outside a circular gate's granite surface with her husband, Jarl. Baloo slipped into Realm's sun so he could eavesdrop. Mirza had told him before that it was not nice to listen to others without letting them know he was there. His aura became pink with what passed among the Bright Ones as a chuckle. He wasn't a baby any more. His powers had grown while he slept. He could listen undetected.

* * * *

"Going away on a vacation is a major change," Mirza said. "You are forgetting Murphy's Law. Anything that can go wrong always does and at the worst possible moment. This trip is a double challenge to the status quo."

"You agreed to a vacation." Jarl materialized a showy white Stetson on his head and shouted, "Ya-hee!"

Out in space, Baloo looked on in admiration. Using pure energy, he created a hat like Jarl's for himself and whispered, "Ya-hee!"

With a wave of his hand, Jarl produced a proclamation out of the air. "Read this," he said, handing it to his wife.

Mirza plucked the scroll from his fingers and started reading. She lifted her head, distracted by the energy crackling around the portal she and Jarl planned to use.

Baloo carefully shielded his energy flow so it would no longer excite the gate. He didn't want Mirza to discover him now. His aura flared in amusement at the luggage, which formed a high pile inside the twenty-foot portal. Baloo found it odd that humans took so many possessions. He could travel from one place to another with a thought. Anything he needed he could create with his mind. For a moment, he considered hiding in one of the pieces of luggage. He could imagine their surprise when he jumped out at their destination and said, "Hi!" He was about to do so when Mirza's words caught his attention.

"Why is this proclamation necessary? I know Seren is older, but why put him in charge instead of Argen? Seren isn't here. He has chosen to live on Earth. He's been in the military there for the past fifteen years."

Jarl eyed his wife. "You have the position of head gate keeper, but as Dragon's Knight I get everyone's problems. While we are gone, someone has to have the authority to act in case of trouble, which I don't expect."

He scowled at her outfit. "Without your robe of office, that pleated skirt and walking shoes make you look nondescript." He nodded his head and changed her clothing to a short skirt and scooped-neck blouse.

"Jarl Koenig, you stop that!" Mirza's face turned pink. "You're the one pushing this vacation, remember."

She pointed her finger at him and his dark clothing became cowboy garb, complete with jeans and a plaid shirt that closed with mother-of-pearl snaps. "I always think you look so handsome in those western shirts," she told him. "No changing. If I wear this immodest outfit you selected for me, you keep what I chose for you."

Baloo spun inside the sun in delight. He especially admired the pearl snaps. Could he hide in something that small?

"All right," Jarl agreed. "I don't know if I like being duded up like some belt-wearing rodeo star."

"What a good idea!" Mirza said, materializing a huge belt buckle with a Texas star design on his snakeskin belt.

Jarl sighed. "I should have known better than to get into a competition with you."

"May we return to the discussion about Seren? I still don't understand your choice of Seren over Argen."

"The proclamation gives Seren the authority to handle problems in my name."

Baloo noticed Mirza's frown. Jarl hadn't answered her question.

"Honey, picture Seren and Argen walking into a room. I'm not being a proud father when I say Seren has command presence. It's hard to believe Argen and Seren are brothers. Argen would trip over the rug, and his socks seldom match."

Baloo realized that while he slept, the boys he had played with as children had grown into men. He was tempted to riffle through Jarl's mind to see what Seren and Argen looked like now, but knew it would alert Jarl to his presence. He could wait. He would search for the brothers later. He continued listening.

"Argen isn't going to like this." Mirza shook her auburn curls. "I hope his pride won't be hurt. Don't you feel the least bit guilty dumping all these potential problems on Seren without a word to him beforehand?"

"Do you remember anyone warning me before I came to Realm with the dragonmage, Wyrd, wrapped around my wrist as a bracelet all those years ago? It's not my fault that Seren never comes home to visit us. We always travel to Earth to see him. I doubt he realizes that people from all the known worlds have brought their problems to Realmgate for resolution since Wyrd left."

Baloo watched as Mirza crossed her arms over her chest. He knew what that meant. Jarl had better be careful!

"I agree once we are gone on this vacation, something is bound to happen. This document provides guidance," Jarl explained as he duplicated the proclamation and posted it on the castle wall where anyone entering or leaving the gate could see it. "I've already sent one to Argen. He'll contact Seren if necessary."

"What worries me is that Seren doesn't have a dragon companion," said Mirza as she magically lengthened her skirt by two inches.

"Neither does Argen. The dragon Flame, who is ruling now, has a relationship with Seren. They'll work together." Jarl kissed Mirza and shortened her skirt with a blink. "Besides, Love, handling all the other worlds' problems will make a player out of him."

* * * *

"Do you know something I don't? I thought the reason we were going now was because everything has been calm for so long."

Jarl shook his head. "All those years on Earth away from Realm playing soldier haven't necessarily made a man out of our oldest son."

"Darling, Seren's almost thirty-five. Don't you think he's adult enough already?"

Jarl smiled and guided her to the surface of the gate.

Mirza balked. "Perhaps we should leave word with the gatekeeper about where to find us. She waved at Librisald. "No one knows where we are going."

"That's the point, dear. We agreed not to have an itinerary or schedule." Jarl hugged her. "We haven't been on our own for years. Seren will do all right if there is a problem."

Jarl placed his arm around Mirza's shoulders and pulled her closer to him. "Argen probably won't come out of the library long enough to notice we're gone, let alone get his feelings hurt. Trust me. You don't see much of the world with your nose forever in a book."

"You may have something there. After all, what could happen?"

"Finally," Baloo heard Jarl mutter under his breath.

Baloo watched as Mirza took Jarl's hand. They stepped onto the surface. Baloo had waited long enough. He gave the gate an energy boost. The two travelers disappeared in a blinding flash of light, luggage and all.

Librisald rubbed his eyes until he could make out the log book. All he could do was note the strange departure. He still couldn't see the portal. It remained a blind spot to his eyes.

The energy being condensed into a small, bright light and hung over the gate. He had stayed behind because Seren would need help. Baloo had catnapped for years waiting for this chance. What should he do first? He must find out what was happening on the rim. Whatever it was, Seren could take care of it. Adventure beckoned! It was time to light up the gathering shadows. What fun he would have! With a loud "Yee-ha!" that startled several birds in nearby trees, the light that was Baloo winked out with a crack, adding a headache to Librisald's partial blindness.

CHAPTER ONE

The wind blew though the open doorway to the balcony, moving the golden drapes and ruffling the edges of the bed canopy. Mari felt chilled and groped for a cover. A loud banging on the heavy bedroom door caused the leprechaun queen to stretch and raise her head, cracking one eyelid open. The position of the moon through the long vertical windows told her it was past midnight, but far from morning light. The shape of a form indented the bed next to her, but no Rory, her part-time consort. She wondered if he had disappeared when the noise started. Rory always put his pot of gold first. Finally, Mari managed a sitting position. "Enter," she commanded, exasperated.

Instead of the usual servant, her leprechaun chief-of-staff, Padraic, stuck his head through the door. "A thousand pardons, Your Majesty. The Sidhe are in an uproar."

Mari snorted. Padraic had disapproved of giving the Sidhe refuge on the richly forested world of Eyre. His remark sounded suspiciously like an I-told-you-so. She glared at her current tormenter before Irish humor overcame her temper. His robes of state were pulled haphazardly over his pajamas.

Her mind darted back to her world's guests—silly fairies wanting to be called by that old Irish name. Most people couldn't pronounce it, and the spelling was atrocious. Few knew enough ancient Gaelic to say "Shee" for Sidhe.

"Come in. I'm halfway decent. Even if I wasn't, I doubt I have any charms you haven't seen." A little temper reasserted itself. "Do you have a reason why this couldn't wait until later in the morning?"

The leprechaun edged into the room, concentrating on the artwork on the walls, his eyes averted from the fancy bed. Mari's anger caused his embarrassment to give way to fear. "One. One of their males teleported into their palace on an energy beam conjured by something, semiconscious, cut to ribbons, with large holes, maybe bites, covering him. He keeps gasping about a multitude of huge black things as he drifts in and out of consciousness."

"All right. Send a servant to help me dress. Locate Rory. The three of us will visit the Sidhe enclave to see if we can find out more about this." Mari waved her hand in dismissal.

Padraic hurried from the room, eyes still averted.

A few minutes later, Mari swept into her throne room. Only her chief-of-staff, his ministerial robes straightened, but still over his pajamas, awaited her.

He shrugged. "We couldn't find Rory anywhere, Your Majesty."

That sounds as if Rory left before this uproar, Mari thought.

The room shimmered and Mari felt herself abruptly seized by a magical spell. The majesty of her palace dimmed, and then vanished in the silvery mist. She appeared in the magical forest throne room in front of Arthurian, King of the Sidhe. Mari stamped her foot in anger, recognizing she stood below his throne so that he could sit above her.

"An unsafe world you've got here," started Arthurian, his silver eyes blazing down on her. "We've lost another male. We can ill afford that. After all the skirmishes trying to capture other worlds, there aren't many Sidhe remaining." He held up four fingers.

Mari was surprised that the Sidhe were reduced to four males. She knew Arthurian resented the fact that leprechauns were numerous compared to the Sidhe. "Unsafe indeed. You didn't have many choices left after your behavior on other worlds. Remember, I allowed you to settle here on Eyre," Mari snapped, her eyes glaring.

Unpleasant and stiff-necked though he might be, Arthurian was her kingdom's guest, she reminded herself. "I suppose from your complaint, your injured subject died. Did you learn any more about the attack?"

"No," sighed Arthurian. "He died without regaining full consciousness. We are so few," he repeated. His doleful manner indicated more anguish over his peoples' racial loss than concern over the individual who had died. "Your subjects outnumber the Sidhe by a hundred to one. You are a mighty host by comparison.

"So, what do you intend to do about the menace that killed him?" demanded Arthurian.

Frustrated at being on the defensive, Mari shot a mental bolt at Arthurian. *Menace? What menace? You don't know any more about what happened than I. I'm going to do what you're doing.* Relenting at the sight of Arthurian holding his hand to his head in pain, Mari noted her guest's unusual lack of stoic pride. Typical Sidhe fixation, the loss of breeding stock outweighed all other dangers.

"Doing what? I am presenting the facts to the proper authority," said a puzzled Arthurian.

"You're passing the buck. I'll make that my plan, too. I'm off to Realm. I'll dump this mess where I take all problems, the Dragon Knight's lap. Care to come along?"

Arthurian recoiled in horror at the idea of leaving his palace. "Deal with humans? Never!" He finished talking to empty air. Mari had vanished.

* * * *

Mari used gate travel rather than make the trip to Realm using her own magical powers. The distance was too great without a wizard's boost.

When she came through the portal at Realmgate, she noticed that the ancient human, Librisald, and not the head gatekeeper, monitored the impact zone. She thought the frail Librisald had retired to run the dragon's library on Realm years ago. Then she remembered that Argen had recently seized control of that library leaving Librisald only the university library.

"Where's Mirza?" she asked Librisald.

"Gone."

"I need to see the Dragon's Knight. Where can I find him?" Noticing Librisald's blank look, Mari stamped her foot in frustration. "You know who I'm talking about—Jarl."

"Gone!" repeated Librisald and turned to leave.

"What is this, an echo chamber? Where are they?" Mari demanded. She grabbed Librisald by the arm and turned him to face her. "If they're not here, who's in charge?"

Librisald shook himself free and looked down his nose at the foot-high leprechaun queen. "How dare you touch me? I am the keeper of this gate."

Mari repeated her question. "Who's in charge?"

"Here on Realm, Argen, maybe. Read the proclamation." Librisald pointed to a parchment posted on the wall of the castle.

"All right. All right. Where's Argen?" asked Mari, in a more respectful manner. No sense in alienating the old duffer any further. Returning to gatekeeping part-time had affected Librisald's former helpful personality.

"Argen's in my library, for all the good it will do you." Librisald stalked off, leaving the gate temporarily unattended.

Mari thought for a minute. She hadn't visited Ebony's dusty tome-laden cavern often enough to teleport into the library on her own. She snapped her fingers. "I remember. A large mirror hangs on the wall in the foyer." She wrinkled her nose in disgust. "I hate passing through glass," she muttered, disappearing.

The silver of the mirror formed a mist, letting her enter the room. Through the large archway, she saw Argen in the main chamber, fast asleep at a nearby table, snoring. Mari grabbed a book and slammed it on the table next to his face.

Argen disappeared. His voice rang out from somewhere. "What do you want?"

"I want to see your father, Jarl. So far, I'm getting the runaround."

"Jarl and Mirza took a vacation." An outline of Argen shimmered into existence at the table. "Why take out your temper on an innocent book?"

"Because I've got a problem I don't know how to handle. I'd set my mind on dumping it on the Dragon's Knight—only to find he's on vacation. So, are you taking his place?"

"Instead of putting me in charge, Jarl left this proclamation." Argen handed Mari a copy of the parchment that she had ignored on the castle wall. "I'm good for emptying waste baskets. Otherwise you'll have to see my brother Seren." Argen's pout would have supported a whiskey glass.

"Okay, where's Seren?" Feeling some empathy for Argen and his injured feelings at not having any authority, Mari let her temper cool.

"On Earth, learning to be a military genius." Argen eyed Mari's now tapping foot and crossed arms with concern. "Don't get mad all over again. I'll send Rory to Seren's apartment to fetch him. I can assemble Prince Rand, the dragon Fafnoddle, and other advisors if you explain the problem," offered Argen.

"My consort is your errand boy? How can you find Rory when nobody else can?" Mari queried with interest.

Argen's smile resembled a smirk. "You know Rory and gold. I control the gold."

Mari frowned and launched into an explanation of the situation with the Sidhe.

* * * *

Rory landed on the seat of his pants in Seren's strange apartment. He picked himself up, his dignity wounded. "Blasted Argen is no better than the Fire Wizards for world travel," he grumbled, looking around. He hadn't visited Earth in years.

Where was Seren? The efficiency apartment looked neat and orderly—much too organized to suit Rory. He kicked over a footstool with satisfaction.

"Seren must keep some spirits round here for medicinal purposes," Rory muttered before he set to work locating liquid refreshment in the kitchen, leaving wooden cabinet doors open and items scattered on the countertop as he searched. Finally, he found some Irish whiskey, but no, there weren't any leprechaun-sized glasses in the now-cluttered kitchen. Rory gave a nod of satisfaction. So much for Seren's preference for military spit and polish! Waving his hand, Rory materialized a glass into midair. He grabbed it cheerfully and started on his refreshment. When the once-full bottle was almost empty, he grinned.

"That'll teach him to be home when I call," he said, quite coherently for a drunken leprechaun. He nodded off to sleep stretched out on top of a counter, dreaming of his pot of gold back on Realm. His foot rested against the open whiskey bottle as reassurance that it was there.

The once shipshape kitchen looked as if a tornado had made a pit stop. The shambles, typical of Rory's unannounced visits, awaited the unsuspecting Seren.

CHAPTER TWO

On Widdershins, the slumbering bear uncharacteristically lay on his back, one hind paw trailing in the creek. A large pile of fish bones hemmed his other side. A drumming sound caused the bear, the shapeshifter Rand, to open his eyes. He saw a little boy in a velvet outfit stamping his foot, hands on hips in perfect imitation of his mother.

Seeing the bear was awake, Drak made his pronouncement. "Mother says you have an urgent message from Uncle Argen. Came through the gate it did. Fialla sent the message to the castle by dragon."

Rand rolled and lurched to his feet without falling in the creek or disturbing the bones. He started digging a hole, sending a big clod right into his son's midsection, knocking him down. As Rand swept the bones into the hole, he woofed in amusement when the boy tried to brush himself clean. Good old creek mud. Brushing would never get that outfit clean.

"Mother says you're to come home right away."

* * * *

Filling the hole with dirt, Rand shook his ursine head. Drak had mimicked his mother's voice perfectly. "All right. Lead the way." Rand gestured for his son to go ahead.

Drak marched into the woods, his velvet outfit collecting seeds and briars.

"Your mother teleported you here, huh?" Rand asked.

The little boy stopped and gave his father an exasperated look as if saying, of course, stupid.

"Why don't you climb on my back? We'll make better time. You said speed was important," Rand urged.

"Mother says I get dirty when I ride on your back."

"You're already dirty." Rand could see Drak thinking about riding.

"Mother says you smell. She says I smell after riding you, and she makes me take a bath."

"So, what's the trouble, the smell or the bath?

"The bath," Drak responded quickly.

"What if we go right to the pool when we get home?"

That did it. Drak pulled himself up on his father's back. Once there, he made another pronouncement. "Mother says swimming is not a replacement for a bath."

Rand didn't bother to answer. He broke into a rapid lope.

Drak shrieked with joy. "Faster," he yelled, kicking his father's sides with abandon, hanging onto his father's fur with strength little short of pulling it out by the roots.

Rand complied. Arriving home, they raced right by the castle, headed for the pool behind the horse barns. *Take off your boots and that silly jacket*, Rand instructed his son. The bear and rider never slowed, but plowed into the pool. Two yells of joy penetrated the castle grounds.

When Rand surfaced, he was in the form of a man. He helped pull the rest of his son's clothes off, balling them up and heaving them on the bank. A water fight promptly ensued.

* * * *

When they exited the water, Drak started again. "Mother doesn't like you running around naked. All the maids shriek and cover their eyes."

"Sure, with their fingers spread open," quipped Rand. He stopped by an outdoor cabinet to pull on a robe. He grabbed his moving son around the middle. "Whoa. You've got the same equipment." He tied a towel around the boy. He could see his son deep in thought.

"Would they shriek at me?"

"Some day," Rand assured him.

Laughing, they entered the palace hand in hand.

* * * *

"How could you?" Lealor frowned. "We can only find one boot. Drak's suit is ruined. What were you thinking?"

"Send the boy out with one of the dogs. It'll be an adventure," replied Rand, busy reading Argen's scroll that had required his presence.

"A future king can't run around outside with a pack of dogs, searching for boots," protested Lealor, tapping her foot in disgust.

"He's a little boy. If you're not careful, he'll become a pain in the—"

Lealor interrupted. "When I agreed to be regent, I thought you'd at least help with Drak. You spend all your time with the weren running an invisible kingdom. You're never home."

"Shapeshifters have special needs. Be honest, Lealor. You never allow Drak to go with me. Me and mine aren't kingly enough. Besides, you like being regent. The power, the problems, and the challenges excite you. You're good at ruling. Better than I would be." Watching

Lealor blush with pride, Rand took the opportunity to change the subject. "Which dragon brought Argen's message to the palace?"

"Fafleen," she said.

Lealor wasn't ready to give up. "You could tutor Drak on some of his future duties like your father taught you."

Rand brushed off his wife's last suggestion. "Fafleen can send Argen's message to her consort Flame. Since all the young dragons follow him, he should be at Realm tomorrow, too."

"I wish you wouldn't use that nickname," protested Lealor. "His real name is Flare."

Rand roared with laughter until he noticed Lealor's face. He was in trouble again. "Even Fafleen calls him Flame now. His unstable temper got him dubbed Flame—not me." Rand shook Argen's scroll at Lealor. "Did you read this? Killing a Sidhe, that's serious. Now if I knew where Miklos was—after all, he's a Sidhe and Berdularion's war chief. I'd take him with me."

"That's easy. Try the nearest pub," snapped Lealor. Pausing, she continued, "I thought Arthurian banished his brother, Miklos, from the fairy kingdom forever."

Rand snorted. The faint outline of a bear shimmered around him. "That's like trying to say a purebred weren can't be a shapeshifter. How can Arthurian control Miklos? Remember the Sidhe are guests on Eyre."

"You're willing to run off to Realm on Sidhe business, but not help me manage your son's kingdom?" She pouted, observing Rand's frown. "Yes, yes. I know Argen wouldn't send for help if it wasn't crucial for Widdershins, too," Lealor conceded.

Rand rose and took Lealor in his arms. He knew how to distract her from imagined injustices.

"That's not going to…" she started before relaxing against him.

* * * *

On the top of the volcano, Flare von Berdularion snuggled deeper into the running lava. He used his powerful-taloned hind feet to send weakened rock and cooling lava skyward. If Flare had his way, there'd be a depression wide enough to be a pool here someday. He was always cold lately, which made him cross and irritable. The younger dragons had started calling him Flame. He liked the nickname. He was now Flame. Jarl had told him a flare only burned brightly for a short time. A flame always burned fiercely. At least Fire Mountain was good for something. The lava was warming. Flame snuggled lower into the heat.

An offending rock rolled down into his zone of comfort. Flame scowled and looked up at the young dragon standing nervously on the ledge above.

"Rand requests your presence at Realmgate today," said the little dragon Sparrow.

Flame belched fire at the messenger, who fled. Realm, he thought, home of his mate's family, including his terror of a dragon-in-law, Ebony. Reportedly, there were hot sulphur pools down south where the wyvern ruled. He'd get his other dragon-in-law, Fafnoddle, to help find the pools this trip. He was a good sort. Reluctantly, Flame pulled himself free from the lava stream and vanished.

* * * *

Rand edged into the rural pub and stood inside next to the doorframe while his eyes adjusted. The smell was enough to give one a cheap drunk. Finally, he spotted Miklos in a dark corner alcove. Walking closer, he spotted Berdu hiding still farther in the shadows.

"Are you sober?" Rand asked.

Miklos laughed. "Always. A Sidhe processes alcohol instantly into water, although to amuse myself I sometimes put on an act for the patrons."

"Why come here then?"

"To people watch. I always learn something."

* * * *

Rand held up his hands, stopping the approaching buxom serving girl. "I suppose that's one of the people you watch?"

Miklos snorted. "Not when you're married to a warrior queen—if you want to live. Actually, my little daughter, Killeen, would give me more trouble over watching the serving maid. Of course, she'd have to take her head out of the latest war strategy book long enough to notice."

Rand pointed at the hidden Berdu. "What about him?"

Miklos chuckled. "Even in that form, he dumps bushels of steakfruit down his gullet. A little mead won't affect a dragon with a full stomach."

"Argen needs us on Realm," said Rand, taking a noggin of ale off a passing serving wench's tray.

"Let's go." Miklos and Rand disappeared.

Berdu looked around frantically, and then vanished back to the cottage of Fialla, the gate keeper.

CHAPTER THREE

With a flourish, Seren expertly swung the red, two-seated T-Bird into a parking place in front of his apartment. He preferred his living quarters here on Earth to his suite in the castle on Realm. Climbing out, he pulled a white handkerchief from his uniform pocket and polished a dull spot on the car's finish. As he put his face closer to see himself in the mirror-like metal, he could smell the paste wax. Seren patted his car. He liked the two-door hardtop with its round windows better than a convertible. Someday this sports car will be a classic, he thought.

Seren felt ecstatic. His course at the War College was completed. He had orders to Fort Bragg to head a Special Forces unit. He had been promoted to Lieutenant Colonel after standing second in his class. Best of all, tonight he had finally won a date with Megan, the general's daughter.

Seren stood, remembering the first time he had seen Megan at the officers' club. Her beauty had struck him speechless right in the middle of a conversation. After giving him some good-natured ribbing, his friends had joyfully entered into the quest to determine who she was.

Shaking his head, he started for the door. He had been dismayed to find out she was the daughter of the War College's commanding general. Then he became optimistic when further research revealed she had no steady date. The next step was bribing the program director to schedule dances where the dancers switched partners or allowed cuts.

Seren remembered the closeness they'd shared together in those few dances. Tonight, finally, he wouldn't have to cut in to steal a few moments with her.

The instant Seren opened his apartment door and spotted the knocked-over footstool he knew something wasn't right. He couldn't find anything else amiss in the living room, but when he went to the kitchen, he found trouble asleep on the countertop. Trouble spelled R-O-R-Y. Not tonight, he thought. I waited so long for this evening. He mind-probed the leprechaun gently. Out like a light. Seren grinned, waving his hand, mentally programming the result. A little sleep spell ought to finish this. It was difficult to use magic on Earth, but this was a simple spell. It would keep Rory quiet for a long time.

Seren went to his bedroom, which connected with the bathroom. To guarantee noise suppression, he conjured a silence spell for the two rooms. "I haven't used this much magic in years," he grumbled. He had twinges of conscience. Rory wouldn't be here if there wasn't a problem. Visions of Megan overrode his concern. Quickly he dressed and left the apartment.

* * * *

"I don't know why Seren's not here," Argen answered. "Rory didn't come back either. Let's get together again tomorrow."

Flame blew a small puff of smoke into the air as he addressed Fafnoddle. "Can you take me to the wyverns' hot sulfur pools?"

Fafnoddle looked perplexed. "The wyverns don't like strangers, especially males."

"Yes, yes. You've told me about them before. You know their leaders. You have been in their healing pool. I don't want a healing pool, only a hot one," wheedled Flame.

Fafnoddle made his eyes spin, the dragon equivalent of laughter. "I'll take you to their queendom, but I offer no guarantee of success."

The two dragons shuffled outside and sprang into the air. After a short time Flame asked, *What's that structure to the right?*

"That's Fellkeep, the Shadowlord's old castle. That's odd. The last time I was here, it was nothing but ruins," the puzzled Fafnoddle replied.

"*Looks pretty imposing now. Let's go down there.*" Flame veered off and dropped like a stone.

"Be careful. There's a protective ward in place," warned Faf.

"*Not anymore,*" stated Flame with a wicked chuckle as he landed in the courtyard.

Faf followed him down. He landed with his mouth agape at the improvements to the impressive structure.

"Meddlesome dragons. I must improve my wards," said a black and silver figure from a covered walkway.

"Lo—Lor?" Fafnoddle stammered.

"Don't call me that! I'm the Shadowlord," replied the partially hidden speaker.

"What happened? I thought Oron was going to train you to be a Bright One," Fafnoddle protested.

"Oron and Cronal disappeared—too busy to train a renegade. Baloo is back asleep in Achaeasun. I returned here. As I built things, I became stronger. I'm about ready to make a gate," bragged the Shadowlord.

* * * *

"Don't do that," Fafnoddle warned. "Come to Realmgate tomorrow. We have a situation evolving where I think a new gate on a different world will be required."

* * * *

The evening went better than Seren had expected. Surprisingly, Megan acted as if she might have come home with him, but he had no way to explain Rory. Introducing her to the outspoken leprechaun would spell disaster, probably with a section eight discharge. When they tried her apartment, Megan's roommate was already there with company. He took Megan to a girlfriend's place to stay overnight. He made another date with Megan for the weekend when Rory wouldn't be present to complicate his life. Entering his apartment, Seren slammed the front door and yelled, "Rory, wake up!"

Startled, Rory tried to sit, hitting his head on an open cabinet door. Now besides being drunk, he had an additional reason for his double vision. "Oooh," he moaned, holding his head with both hands. Rory blinked and all the cabinet doors slammed shut. That was a mistake. The noise sounded like the cannon fire portion of *The 1812 Overture*. Rory groaned and peered at the fuzzy human in the doorway. "A little quieter you might be," he whispered.

Seren laughed. Some of his anger at Rory's intrusion disappeared. "Okay, why are you here?"

"Don't shout." The leprechaun had now assumed a new position: head down on the countertop with his rear in the air as if putting his head through Formica would stop the pain.

Seren had seen enough. "I'll get ready for bed. When you sober up, come talk to me." He left the kitchen, chuckling. He undressed, remembering Megan might have been here. Some of his anger at being invaded returned, spoiling his amusement.

* * * *

Rory staggered into the bedroom and flopped on the floor. "Argen sent me. Claimed it was urgent for you to come home, he did. Me headache magic doesn't work on this forsaken world." Rory disappeared.

"My night ruined for that!" Seren exploded. "Well, Argen can wait until tomorrow." Mentally, he started planning his trip to Realm. Seren had military leave until his Fort Bragg assignment. He'd have to hitch a ride on some government flight going in the direction of the hidden gate at his boyhood home. At least that was one of the perks of rank. He settled down and tried to sleep. Every time he started having a dream starring Megan, an image of Rory or Argen interrupted. By morning, Seren's frustration had escalated into a foul mood.

He had to rent a garage for his treasured sports car. The taxi arrived late. The airbase security made entrance slow. Catching a plane ride had been easy. Seren was able to do it in civvies. He took a bus as close as possible, but the rural Midwest location of the gate was still remote.

Thumbing a ride hadn't gone so well. Finally, a woman driving a pickup truck full of kids stopped. Seren would have gladly ridden in the back, but no, she wanted someone to talk to while kids hung on his ears. When he got out, he fell to the ground. Seren heard boyish laughter as the pickup drove away. He never did figure out how they had tied his shoelaces together.

When Seren got to the old subdivision, a farmer worked the fields near where the gate was hidden. Only a handful of people on Earth knew gates to Realm existed. A skilled gatekeeper, who he wasn't, could use them to travel to worlds besides Realm. He was glad his mother, Mirza, the head gatekeeper of the known worlds, had set all Earth gates to default home to Realm.

Seren couldn't help feeling sad at the demise of his old neighborhood. Before all the ammunition plants shut down, this had been a thriving community. Then people started moving away. Whole houses had been jacked up, put on flatbeds and taken to new locations. Now only three houses remained. One was the home he had grown up in.

"You got business here?"

Seren jumped. He had been so engrossed in the past he hadn't heard the farmer's approach. "Yes, I own the house close to the woods. Own the woods, too," he added. "Thought I'd check the place over."

The farmer grunted. City folk, he thought. "You be careful around that old house. I don't have time to bail you out of trouble." The farmer stalked back to his tractor.

Seren was amused. He noted that while the streets were intact, someone had bulldozed the garage paving and old house foundations into a pile. The homesteads were being farmed, no matter who owned them.

Seren approached his house with wariness. He knew Mirza had warded it well so only family could enter. The front porch seemed structurally sound, and as he put his hand on the doorknob he could feel the spell. The door opened easily to his touch. Inside nothing had changed.

This place is like Fialla's cottage on Widdershins, he thought. It's protected and ready for occupancy at a moment's notice. He opened the door to the refrigerator. Mirza had advanced her grandmother Cibby's provider bag magic one better. The refrigerator functioned the same way. He took out steakfruit and a bottle of cold water. As Seren settled in a recliner for a nap, he instructed the house to tell him when the farmer left.

His dreams, full of boyhood memories, started well, but changed into turmoil with the current situation. Rory and Argen opposed his life with Megan. When the chair vibrated, he awoke in a foul mood again. His subconscious warned him about Megan, but Seren blamed his problems on the summons from Argen.

Seren quickly secured the house and headed into the woods surrounding the gate. The passage through the woods at dusk was tricky even for an army ranger.

* * * *

When Seren came through Realmgate, Librisald saw the look of lingering anger on Seren's face and fled. Seren thought for a minute. When they were kids, he could always teleport to his brother Argen's location. He discovered he was out of practice when he landed on top of the table where his brother worked.

Papers, books and an ashtray full of smoking butts scattered everywhere. Seren jumped down and started stamping out the butts.

"What are you doing? They're still good," Argen shrieked, his glasses hanging from one ear as he tried to pick up the papers.

"You shouldn't be smoking anyway. It wasn't long ago when dragon smoke nauseated you. Besides, these things cause cancer." Seren pushed the smoking embers together with his foot.

"There's no cancer here." Argen frantically shoved Seren aside as he jammed salvaged butts back in the ashtray. "My habit is different from the foul odor of dragon smoke."

Seren picked the pack off the floor and waved it at Argen. "These were made on Earth, not Realm, so they aren't good for you." Both brothers sank into chairs and glared at each other.

"Why isn't the gate in the University any more?" demanded Seren.

"Mom moved it. The university shut down for lack of students. Population cycles, I guess," replied Argen as he shrugged.

"Why was Librisald acting as gatekeeper?" asked Seren "Is there something wrong with Mom? Why did you summon me instead of Dad?"

"You're full of questions, out of touch and a day late. Mirza and Jarl went on vacation. Not even the dragons know where. Here, this explains part of it." Argen threw a roll of parchment at Seren. Argen continued picking up the papers and books he could reach from his chair. "Rory couldn't have made this big a mess."

Seren read the proclamation putting him in charge. He laughed. "This is easy. I hereby delegate all authority to you."

"Oh, no, you don't. Something killed a Sidhe."

Seren raised his eyebrows. "That would be quite a trick. I wouldn't want to try murdering a powerful Irish fairy lord. Whoever accomplished that feat would be beyond our present abilities to contain."

"My point exactly. All we need is a war for revenge instigated by the Sidhe." Argen snorted. "I gathered some advisors to discuss this situation yesterday. Most are still waiting to help." Argen's crossed arms indicated his temper hadn't cooled.

Seren, on the other hand, had calmed down since there appeared to be a real problem. "You called me here to have a meeting? I have enough of them on Earth."

Argen nodded, amused that having a meeting had upset Seren.

"I must return there this weekend," Seren emphasized, thinking of his date with Megan. He smiled, picturing her in his mind. "Because of the time differential problems, I'll need your help to make connections."

Seren frowned. "Who has gathered to talk this thing to death? Don't think you're escaping the meeting you planned, either."

"I don't shirk my responsibilities," Argen snapped. "I'll be there to support you although you have brought all this chaos from Earth with you." He indicated the disarray in the room.

"Mari—you do remember she is queen of the leprechauns?—is crucial because she referred the problem here. Prince Rand, his companion Miklos, and the dragon Flame came from Widdershins. Fafnoddle, Dad's dragon companion, was here, but he had a botanical emergency and returned to his flowers when you didn't show up yesterday."

Seren felt regret that Fafnoddle had left. He still remembered riding his father's friend everywhere. He sneezed from the lingering cigarette smoke. "Talking about chaos, you're not giving Rory enough credit. You should see what he accomplished on Earth." Seren's face clouded, remembering how Rory's presence had interrupted his intended seduction of Megan.

Argen laughed as Seren recounted Rory's visit to Earth.

"That leprechaun..." Seren complained.

"...can't resist Irish whiskey." concluded Argen. He put his hand over his mouth as Seren glared at him. It had been years since Argen had last finished a sentence his brother had started.

Seren said, "Okay, let's go."

The brothers clasped hands and reappeared in a large room.

CHAPTER FOUR

Seren recognized the huge chamber. The whole east wall opened up, which allowed dragons access. Mirza conducted all world business here because dragons needed plenty of space. The sand floor assured minimum damage. No drapes or tapestries that might catch fire covered the rock walls. The large table was ornate.

Prince Rand stood as Seren entered. The man was huge, resembling the bear he shapeshifted into. Seren grimaced as his brother-in-law hugged him, almost breaking his ribs. Rand was levelheaded, an island of calm sanity in the sea of disasters Seren's other wacky relatives were constantly creating.

"Since I've been gone for so many years, will you handle the introductions, Argen?" Seren asked, trying to stay in the background as much as possible.

A red dragon erupted into the room with a cloud of smoke. Argen started to cough, fanning the smoke away with his hand. Seren's grin clearly said I-told-you-so.

"Please be seated," Argen requested, ignoring his brother. Only his raised eyebrows showed his surprise at Flame's sudden entrance. Argen gestured to include everyone. "On your left is Mari, Queen of Eyre. I don't remember if you've met. You already know Flame, leader of the Widdershin's dragons and the son of the Dragon King, Berdularion. Next is Miklos, or Mike, Berdularion's war leader."

Flame sniffed with disdain at the mention of his father. A wisp of smoke escaped his snout. The dragon flexed one talon in acknowledgement. More smoke escaped his nostrils. He generated the attitude that his father was unimportant.

A small girl raced into the room, hugged Miklos and ran over to sit in the curl of Flame's tail, giving the dragon a loving pat. "Did I miss anything?" she asked breathlessly.

Miklos smiled down at the little girl. "My daughter Killeen is equal in tactics to many commanders, so I brought her along today. Please call me Mike."

"Welcome, Killeen," said Seren. He had learned military brilliance came from unusual sources. If Prince Rand had allowed her to come, he agreed with her father. The child beamed a smile at him, revealing a missing a tooth.

"I'm surprised Lealor isn't here," Seren said, not seeing his sister.

"She's got her hands full with our son, Drak," Rand explained. "I hate court and its ceremony, so I set the regency up with my father. When Dad retired, my son Drak became King of Widdershins. Since he's a minor, Lealor will be both regent and queen for a while. This allows me the freedom I want, which also means I'm available to help you. Logistics and planning are still my specialties."

Argen pointed to the remaining dark figure. "You remember our old adversary, the Shadowlord."

The Shadowlord? Thank goodness Lealor wasn't here. Seren sensed other conflicts in the relationships. He felt tension existed between Rand and Lealor. If he remembered correctly, the weren were loyal only to Rand.

Flame appeared to be at odds with his father, a possible split between the dragons based on age. Seren remembered that Miklos was estranged from Arthurian, his brother. Seren put the Sidhe ahead of the dragon, Flame, because of experience.

Mari didn't seem happy with Arthurian. A lot of undercurrents eddied here. Now wasn't the right time to pursue the issues. Seren decided to pass and do more research. He had been away too long. "Please continue," he requested, looking at Argen.

"Actually, Mari should pick up the tale," Argen answered. "She has the only firsthand information."

"I don't know much," Mari said. "I got dragged out of bed early yesterday morning. An injured Sidhe had somehow teleported home. He died shortly thereafter. I saw the body. Deep scratches, large bite marks—it was not a pretty sight. All we know is that he was injured beyond the dense asteroid belt."

"Whatever from?" Seren looked puzzled. "What's out there?"

"He hunted gems," Argen said, "but not like Rory hunts gold. Uniqueness is more important than quantity to the Sidhe, and they aren't bothered by the vacuum of space."

"We can sssurvive in ssspace—for a while," Flame hissed with typical dragon pride, refusing to admit any creature might be better at anything than a dragon.

"How do we investigate? There's no way to go into that part of space for reconnaissance. There isn't any gate," Seren protested. "Dragons don't go beyond the last world by choice."

"Mike and the Shadowlord can investigate the asteroid belt together. If we can provide security, the Shadowlord will make a mini-gate," Rand explained.

Lost in concentration, Mike floated in the air. "We need to do more. We must probe beyond where the Sidhe was killed."

"Typical male," Mari quipped. "They must put a stick in a hornet's nest."

Mike frowned. "The hornet has already struck. We must find the nest. Yesterday, we came up with a plan. Argen thinks he has a way to provide the dragons with a temporary shelter complete with breathable air. Flame has six dragon volunteers ready to go with him to act as sentinels in the area where the Sidhe was reported to have gone while we figure out how to go farther into space."

Aha, the leader of the Widdershin's dragons, thought Seren. I was right. Flame controls the dragons, but he's not partnered with Rand. That means the shapeshifters and humans from Widdershins follow Mike.

Seren leaned back in his chair and looked at Argen. "I'm glad you have a plan. I wouldn't know where to start in space. All my experience is on world surfaces."

Argen picked up the story. "On Earth, they have abandoned blimp bases from their Second World War. I've already arranged to buy the old airship frames, which are all that's left. I propose splitting the frames and covering them with new skin, using solar panels to power air compressors and lights—presto, dragon shelters."

"Dead worlds and suns exist beside the asteroid belt." Rand thought a moment. "We could set up there. The Shadowlord needs to make a large gate on one of them."

"That's the rub," Mike told him. "If we use a gate to get there, whatever is in the area could use the gate to return here."

"We ought to be able to safeguard the gate with spells." Seren rubbed his forehead to dispel the headache that was ready to pounce on him with this deep-space dilemma. He looked at the Shadowlord. "I don't see how you plan to build the gate."

"A mini-gate is easy. We should restrict where it goes," the Shadowlord replied. "Now, a large gate requires energy to start."

"The Shadowlord and Baloo together," Argen said.

Seren remembered that the Shadowlord, a mage discovered to be an energy-being called a Bright One, delighted in making gates. Baloo, being a young Bright One, had tremendous bursts of energy from the nearest sun at his command. Seren didn't doubt their proficiency.

"Mom can enhance the gate when she returns," Argen said.

Seren hid a smile at his brother's gaffe. Mirza would tear a strip off him if she heard him refer to her as Mom at a gathering like this. Argen evidently had doubts about how well the Shadowlord's gate would function.

"The Shadowlord is obsessed with making gates. All you have to do is give the go-ahead." Argen stood with his hands on his hips, peering down at Seren in expectation.

With a sigh, Seren accepted the responsibility. "Consider it granted. What's next? All we have is dragons standing watch and a possible gate at an unknown location. We still don't have any method for deep space reconnaissance."

Argen shook his head. "Maybe we do. The Soviet Union is trying to sell their old diesel submarines to Cuba. Cuba has no funds available. Russia wouldn't sell them to us. We provide Cuba the money, plus have them buy a large number of Soviet rocket boosters.

"We hijack the submarines and boosters from the Cubans and take them through the underwater gate at Atlantis to the new gate we proposed. There we get rid of the diesel engines, weld on the rockets"—Argen made a grandiose gesture—"spaceships. Or at least dragon boosters." His grin wasn't at all modest.

"That's the wildest idea I've ever heard. Have you been sampling Rory's whiskey?" Seren asked.

"We think it might work," Rand said. "There's no other way to obtain spaceships. Nobody has the capability to build them. At the rate of technical progress, maybe someday Earth can do it. That's too late for us. At this point in time, earthmen are still orbiting in capsules. Try putting a dragon in a capsule."

"Fortunately, the Russians have created big, solid-propellant boosters," Argen continued. "The Soviets always need cash. There are elements in that government that would sell their own grandmothers, if the price was right."

"We'll get the rocket engines one way or another," Mari looked determined.

"There is some danger for you," Argen told Seren.

"For what? Taking responsibility to put these crazy plans into motion?" Seren scoffed. "All this will take months. Jarl will stop this operation when he returns."

"Not exactly." Argen sighed. "The United States will go ballistic over the Cubans having Soviet subs. I'll use a Swiss company when I make these financial transactions, but the Americans will trace them to me. They know we're brothers. It may affect your military career."

"So what? To paraphrase, damn the rocket boosters. Full speed ahead. All I want is to return to Earth and Megan by this weekend." Seren laughed. "Jarl will never write a proclamation putting me in charge again."

A jet of fire signaled Flame's agreement.

CHAPTER FIVE

Argen held out an arm, stopping Seren before he entered Realmgate. "Have you kept up your commercial flying skills?"

The question puzzled Seren. "Of course. When I hitch a ride with the Air Force, I always try to log more flying hours. The pilots are usually happy to grab flying relief after they review my logbook. Why?"

"I've already hired Cuban refugees from Miami to replace the real forces being sent by Cuba to Russia for training. They'll handle the submarine's return. Hijacking the Cubans' plane en route to the Soviet Union will be easy, but I'm unsure of my mercenary pilots. If you're still on leave, I'd like you on board in case they prove unreliable," Argen explained.

"Schedule your hijacking mission to switch crews within the next thirty days. I'll be there." Seren's attention was divided as he stepped into the gate. His thoughts of Megan were driving his brother's schemes out.

Argen managed the time change well. When Seren returned to the Midwest gate, he went to the Chicago airport. He got back to his apartment in Georgetown by Saturday afternoon. The quiet, tree-lined street with the old brick buildings made Realm seem unreal. Seren managed to shower, shave and dress in time for his date with Megan that night.

"I almost gave up on you," Megan complained later, pointing to her watch. Evidently, he was supposed to come early.

After dinner at an exclusive restaurant, Seren escorted the breathtakingly beautiful Megan to the opera. Waiting for the curtains to open, he couldn't remember what they talked about at dinner or what he'd eaten.

By the middle of the opera, even with sidelong glances, none of her glamour had worn off. Seren tried to concentrate on the presentation. A few singers reminded him of dragons. They were certainly big enough and made as much noise.

As they were leaving, Seren suggested dancing, giving his date a choice of nightclubs.

Megan interrupted. "We need to get to know each other better. Let's go to your apartment and talk."

Megan stayed the night.

In the morning as the light streamed into the bedroom, Seren opened a nightstand drawer and took out a velvet box. He gently shook Megan. "Wake up, sleepy head. I've got a surprise for you."

Megan opened one eye, only to be blinded by the sunlight glittering off a diamond. Still groggy, she sat up to inspect the ring. "Are you trying to make an honest woman out of me after only one night?" She slipped the ring on her finger and smiled at Seren. "I'm confused. Were you that sure you'd get me in bed, or do you keep this around for anyone you sleep with?"

"It's yours," Seren assured her. "I had planned to give it to you in a more romantic place. I want you to be my wife."

"I'll accept this ring as an engagement present, if you agree to my conditions. First, no marriage for a while." Megan stretched and the sheet fell to the floor. She saw Seren's eyes glaze over. Megan reached out, covering herself, and shook him. "Later! Listen to me. I'm serious." She gathered the sheet around her. "You know I'm an Army brat. I've watched my dad go on long assignments—some dangerous. When he's home, the military takes up all his time. So he got to be a general—big deal."

Agitated, Megan rose and started pacing, holding the sheet tightly. "Look at my mother, stuck in military housing, in places she didn't want to be, with people she didn't like and alone too often. I won't let that happen to me. I'm staying right here in Washington where I have interests and friends, a career and a lifestyle I like. I'll move in with you here, and I'll join you for career enhancement engagements that require a simpering woman's attendance—but I'm living in D.C." She moved back to sit on the bed. "When you're duty-free, you can hitch flights back for weekends and days off. Those are my conditions. Do you want to try it out for a while?"

"Won't your father disapprove of you shacking up instead of getting married?" Seren asked, too hurt and disappointed to choose his words carefully.

Megan laughed. "Typical man's trick, asking a question when you want to buy time to think. I doubt you really care about his feelings. I'll make it clear to him we're living under my conditions. I'll handle him. You haven't agreed. What's your answer? Do you accept the conditions?"

"I accept, but I always felt it was unfair to the woman. Living together without marriage shows a man's lack of commitment," Seren explained. "Also, I had a special place to take you."

"I know it's selfish, but it's my approach to the stress of being a career military wife. I made up my mind about not following my husband to military bases long before I met you. I'll marry you after trying this out for a year, if you still want to—but the conditions are for life." Megan let the sheet drop. "Now that's settled, let's start the morning off right." Megan grabbed Seren and shoved him flat. He didn't resist.

After Megan left, Seren worried. He wouldn't have dated her while attending the War College because her father was the commanding general. He didn't want the relationship interfering with his career and future assignments. Was that any different from her conditions? She was right. They would probably be separated more than together for the next few years. Still, her conditions were unexpected and troubling. He doubted that she'd follow him to Realm.

The phone rang. It was Megan. "It's all set. We're having dinner this evening at Mother's. Could you rent a panel truck or van and come by my apartment to pick up a bunch of things now? Wear moving clothes, but bring your good clothes. You can dress here. No uniform."

"It's Sunday. Where can I rent a panel truck?" protested Seren. "Maybe I could try renting a large car at the airport."

"Yes, and what were you doing this morning instead of going to church?" Megan gave a wicked laugh. "A big car will do—but hurry. Get here as soon as you can. Love you." Megan hung up.

Well, he'd asked for this, Seren thought as he gathered together a reasonable outfit for dinner. He stuffed dress-up clothes into the T-Bird's back seat, locked the apartment and roared off to the airport.

Traffic was terrible. It would help when they got the Dulles Airport construction finished, even if it was out in the country. Renting a big car didn't prove that easy. The only thing he could get was a four-door sedan. When he got to Megan's apartment, he was greeted by a bunch of grinning women. They didn't stand still long enough to be counted. Soon they had stuffed the trunk and back seat with more junk than he thought his apartment could hold. It was like a yard sale going the wrong way.

"Don't worry, I'll find movers tomorrow for the big stuff," said Megan with a fetching grin. "Now, hurry. Get dressed for dinner, or we'll be late."

Seren changed clothes in a non-locking bathroom hardly big enough to be a closet. Two or three strange woman barged in, assuring him that he had nothing they hadn't seen before. If true, why couldn't they stay out until he got dressed? He put his clothes on in the shower stall.

Megan was subdued during their trip to her parents, who lived on a secluded military base with rigid gate guards. The general had sent one of his aides, who didn't help with the guards. A rented car, with a stuffed back seat, screamed danger to the paranoid military police. Seren's army ID card also proved useless. Everything had to be unpacked and inspected.

The gate ritual made them late. The general was more amused than angry over their tardiness. Dinner was cordial and polite, while Megan and her mother carried on most of the conversation. To Seren's horror, they discussed which creature comfort items Megan could take from the general's home. The space in Seren's apartment was shrinking at a rapid rate.

After dinner, the General and Seren excused themselves and walked onto a screened porch. It was sticky outside in more ways than one.

"Well, Colonel, I never suspected you of stealing my daughter."

"Actually, sir, this happened a lot faster than I planned," Seren answered.

"You'll get used to that with Megan. I've been told to keep my mouth shut until she and I have had a discussion tomorrow about 'conditions'. I've had senior commanders that weren't that forceful. I guess you two will live in sin. Until tomorrow, anyway." Megan's father held up his hand to stop Seren's reply. "I saw the size of that rock, so you probably had more in mind than shacking up. Never could have afforded that on military pay. Are you rich like your brother?"

"I'm not into the markets like Argen, but our family is comfortable," Seren replied.

"Never could understand why Argen would give up his citizenship, even to become Swiss. He is the only black mark on your record," the general grumbled.

Seren was startled. "Argen's choice was motivated by taxes and unregulated financial opportunities. I'm surprised that my brother is part of my record—or that you would have it."

The General snorted. "The only thing I could do after Megan's orders, was pull rank and demand your file. While I had met you at War College and heard good reports—you weren't in line to be my son-in-law. There are interesting time gaps in that file. I don't understand why they have been left uninvestigated. Otherwise your record is just short of brilliant. In fact, it appears to me that you've been hiding your talents." The General stood. "Don't look so flabbergasted, son. Time to go back inside before we get indicted for being out here alone."

Seren wondered what his prospective father-in-law would do if he knew Seren's talents included being a mage, and his circle of friends included dragons and a leprechaun who dropped in to drink whiskey. For his part, Seren was concerned that the women had this much control over the general. What did that promise for his future? He wanted a marriage partnership, not a female dictatorship.

Megan greeted Seren with two piles of items that had to be added to the load in the car. After polite goodbyes, the aide was summoned to help them unpack everything again and clear each piece at the guard shack. This time the guards were sure military property was being stolen. Afterwards, Megan and Seren headed to the airport to retrieve his car. Megan would drive the T-Bird home.

"You have driven a stick shift before?" Seren asked as he opened the door of his sports car.

"No, but how hard can it be?" Megan answered, while she bounced a couple of times on the seat. She started the T-Bird and revved the engine. The car jumped forward, stalling.

Absolute terror feathered down Seren's back. He shuddered as Megan restarted the car and lurched off into traffic without looking back.

Or left. Or right.

CHAPTER SIX

Seren paced the sidewalk in front of his apartment looking at each approaching car for his T-bird. Megan was late. Everything from the unpacked rental car was strewn all over the apartment. His usual parking space for the T-bird had been taken long ago. He worried. Where was she? Could she have been in an accident? Traveling at five miles an hour, she should have arrived forty minutes earlier.

Finally he saw his car coming down the street. A bright yellow Corvette followed it. What was going on here? Megan sat in the T-bird's passenger seat. The man driving the T-bird stopped right in front of the apartment and both got out.

"How can I ever repay you for your help?" she asked, at the same time giving the stranger one of those smiles Seren had thought were reserved for him alone.

Seren looked with horror as the man swept Megan into his arms and kissed her soundly. The man grinned, got into the passenger seat of the Corvette, and sped away. Meanwhile the red T-bird sat idle in the middle of the street with both doors open.

Seren steamed as he worked magic. The Corvette's driver ran two stop signs before the spell wore off and he could get his foot off the gas pedal. Seren would have been happier if he could have seen the police car with its blinking light behind the Corvette.

Seren felt exhausted with the worry, his anger, and finally, the strain of doing magic. He had used more magic in the last week than in his previous ten years on Earth. Anger evidently increased his power.

Megan seemed dizzy from the kiss. She wobbled up the steps past Seren and into the apartment without a word.

Seren got into the T-Bird, found a parking place and returned to the apartment. "Well?" he asked, still angry, watching as Megan hurriedly put things away.

"I got stuck at a light on a hill. How do you keep your foot on the clutch, the other one on the brake and use the accelerator, too? I sort of slid back into that nice man's car. When I explained my problem, he offered to drive me home in your car. So, here I am."

Seren wondered what bothered him most, the stranger kissing Megan or the possibility that she might have damaged his car.

Megan, as if sensing his mood, had moved closer and cuddled up with a contrite expression on her face. "Why don't you sit down and let me finish putting these things away? I'll fix dinner and then we can go to bed." Megan walked down the hall, swinging her hips to emphasize what was to follow.

Seren sat and continued to struggle with his emotions. Usually, he was slow to anger, but Rory and Megan's lack of commitment had both managed to trigger his temper. Seren watched as she returned from the kitchen and quickly restored his apartment to military standards. Dinner was excellent, as was what followed.

The next morning the phone rang at five. It took two swipes for Seren to grab it.

Argen's voice boomed from the headpiece. "You must get to the National Airport by ten this morning. I arranged a ticket in your name on the commuter flight to New York, as well as a seat on the plane from there to the Azores. There you will meet my charter flight number six. You're listed as the engineer on that aircraft to Lisbon, Madrid, Algiers, Tripoli, Cairo, Ankara, Simferopol and finally to Athens. I've booked you passage to England and back to the States from there."

Seren's head pounded. "That trip will take more than a week."

"Right. It's important you make your ten o'clock commuter flight. Don't worry. The tickets are all there. Paid for, too."

Seren frowned. Generosity with his millions was not a usual trait of his brother—unless he had schemes that he needed Seren's help to pull off. "Simferopol is on the Black Sea. The Turks will never let you bring the subs through the Straits of Bosporus," Seren objected.

"That's not your problem. I've already contributed to several Turkish relief agencies. This phone is probably tapped. To paraphrase the famous World War II saying, 'loose lips sink subs'. Stop objecting and get a move on." Argen hung up, and the dial tone buzzed like an alarm clock.

Seren grumbled as he dressed. Megan turned over with a snort that sounded to him like 'I told you so.' Luckily, he kept a suitcase ready for unscheduled trips. She woke completely when he took it from the closet.

"You're leaving me?"

Seren could tell from the volume and tone of Megan's voice that she was not happy with him. "Sorry, darling, but a little family business problem has come up and I have to take a trip. Now!"

Seren thought the astonished face she wore looked cute. Her words, however, were not.

"Where do you think you're going, mister? You can't run out on me. I've planned your entire leave. I left no time for business."

Seren didn't enjoy leaving Megan when she was angry with him, but he had no choice if he was to make the flight Argen had arranged. Knowing it was a mistake, he said, "Be a love and return the sedan to the airport for me, please. You can have one of your friends pick you up from there. I'll call you soon."

Grabbing his suitcase, he leaned over to kiss Megan, but she turned away. Wow! She was in a royal snit. Hopefully flowers, candy, and tickets to something really expensive would get him back in her good graces. Eating crow was not one of his favorite occupations. He quietly closed the door on her howl of outrage. As he got into the T-Bird, he saw her head stick out of his apartment window.

"Don't you dare leave now, you—"

Seren slammed the car door and zoomed out of the parking lot. His T-bird was safer in the airport lot than having Megan drive it. Darn Argen anyway. He'd never have agreed to this trip earlier if he'd known Megan would move in with him.

Argen had warned him that this charter flight to Russia was important. He remembered something about switching Cubans. A little judicious magic produced green lights all the way to the airport. Seren smiled. No sense in being magically inclined if you never used the skill, was there? He was more than a little surprised how well it worked here on Earth lately. Maybe Argen had augmented his strength.

Seren accidentally pushed a startled passenger out of the way in his dash to a window seat. The commuter didn't have assigned seating. He spotted his apartment from the air. After all that effort, nothing was moving. He couldn't even sense Megan by using magic.

The rest of the trip to New York was uneventful. Seren had no problem getting through customs on his civilian passport. He'd have to report this trip to the military later. He ran into a problem with his carry-on luggage.

"I'm sorry sir, it's a sixteenth of an inch over size. You'll have to have it checked into the hold," said the officious clerk with a sneer.

"Please summon your supervisor," Seren requested.

The baggage clerk soon returned with another man. "What seems to be your problem? Our carry-on baggage limit isn't different from any other airline's."

Seren flashed his military ID. "I'm late to an assignment and need to carry this with me. Surely you could overlook a sixteenth of an inch."

"Of course, Colonel. For our military officers, we'll make an exception."

Seren ran to the plane. This time he had been assigned a window seat with nothing but water to look at. The stewardess gave him a pillow and twitched her hips as she walked down the aisle. He felt ashamed. Here he was, practically engaged, and now he was ogling another woman. Maybe those 'conditions' and Megan's temper were having more than one kind of negative effect.

The stewardess sat beside him for part of the trip, talking about the layover the crew was taking in the Azores. Seren could sense a veiled invitation there. After she left, another lovely lady moved over to sit beside him, chatting the rest of the way. What was it? He wasn't even in uniform. Did getting involved with a woman automatically create competition? They could call it Seren's Law, he thought.

As soon as the plane touched down, he asked for directions to the chartered aircraft. The pretty stewardess arranged for a driver to take him to that part of the airport. This way he avoided the terminal and customs. Seren had no trouble locating the chartered plane, but was surprised to find it was a DC3.

"Hurry up. Get aboard. I'm Bud, the pilot. Over my shoulder is Alex. I want as much daylight as possible getting into Lisbon."

"Does this thing have enough fuel to take us there?" Seren asked. The pilots gave him some static because he was listed as the engineer, before good naturedly showing him where the extra fuel tanks were.

Everything stayed normal until they approached Libya. Seren had logged plenty of flying hours. Both pilots were glad to escape the monotony of flying over so much water. Off duty, Seren had made friends with some of the Cubans aboard. Military types recognized each other the world over. When Alex, the copilot, pushed a chart with a new heading in his face, Seren objected. "That's not the right bearing for Tripoli."

"I know, but this sealed envelope calls for us to land at a deserted World War II airbase. According to this, you're supposed to verify the instructions."

Seren looked at the paper, recognizing Argen's writing. "Don't look at me. I didn't know anything about it—I do know the writing. Consider them verified. You and the pilot better take over. Lord knows what kind of runway we'll find."

"That's what's wrong with your logbook," Alex replied.

"What are you talking about?" Seren asked.

Alex had taken over the controls. Bud slid into the seat Seren had vacated. There was hardly any room in the cockpit. It had been upgraded with the latest instruments, but not very artistically, and comfort had been sacrificed. "Not enough takeoffs and landings," Bud explained. "I can understand missing this touchdown, but you should do the takeoff and handle the rest of the airports on the trip. They have long runways built for bombers so they're easy."

"You'll never fly a better plane," Alex added. "This is a neat little smuggler's ship."

'Smuggler's ship?' Yes, it sounded like Argen was doing everything possible to avoid taxation. Seren didn't understand why. Argen made money hand over fist. It must be for the game alone. Argen was certainly devious. He had been asked to leave Merrill Lynch for trying to get a lower commission schedule. Seren's laugh at how put out Argen had been startled the pilots.

Although it was a dirt runway, the touchdown proved easy. The desert had left it in excellent condition, and the facilities, obviously abandoned, were huge. The Cubans left the ship. Seren started to go with them. Alex stopped him.

"Remember our instructions—stay with the ship. No passports required, no customs inspection or trouble that way."

Seren, looking outside, noticed the group of nomads serving the ship. "They're refueling from barrels by hand. We're going to be here a while. That's a slow process."

Alex laughed. "As I told you, a smuggler's operation."

Like all military-trained personnel, all three had learned to sleep anywhere. Before dropping off, Seren put a magic ward around the cockpit. He awoke to the sound of gunfire. Men were running toward the plane.

Seren was surprised when Miklos was the first person up the ladder. He put a finger in front of his lips. "Remember my name is Mike. Quick! Get the plane airborne." An entirely different group of people had piled on. Mike made a fast count before closing the door. The pilots started the engines and taxied to the end of the runway. Without any wasted time they were in the air headed for Cairo.

Seren went back to talk to Mike. "What happened? Why are you here?"

"We are replacing the Cubans sent by their government. These Cubans are refugees living in Miami. About half of this group came from Widdershins. Shapeshifting is not limited to animal forms. In the last week, we've gradually changed to look like the leaders of the other group you had aboard. We all speak Russian, even the Cubans. Their English isn't that good."

"What happened inside the airport?" Seren asked.

"First, we captured your former passengers. We got their documents and removed any weapons. We fed them and were trying to work out the terms of their release with the nomads. Someone tried to buy his release with gold he had hidden in his boot. At the word 'gold' everything went crazy. These guys make Rory look like a sissy. The nomads started shooting the prisoners and stripping them in a frenzy. I got our people onto the plane, and you helped to get us off the ground." Mike shook his head. "That group we left is as dangerous as what we're facing in space. I'm glad I don't live on this world."

Seren did the landings at Cairo, Ankara and Simferopol. Refueling had all been arranged beforehand. Mike was the only one that left the plane, returning each time with new provisions until the plane reached Simferopol. Fifteen minutes after discharging their passengers, Alex and Bud were winging their way towards Athens. While only the three of them were left, Seren wasn't sure they had taken time to top off the tanks. The mercenaries had no desire to stay longer on Russian soil. Also, his lessons were over. Things had changed. The pilots were only interested in winding up this business and disappearing.

Seren deplaned and passed through customs with no problems. He tried calling Megan at every plane change, but couldn't get any answer. True to Argen's promise, all the tickets to get him from Greece to England and home were waiting.

By the time he reached Washington, Seren was worried. At least his car was okay. He roared off to his apartment. Several notes waited inside, telling Seren where to find Megan. It was evident she hadn't stayed here. Her latest note indicated he had time to meet her at a luncheon. Seren hurried to get ready and rushed out of the house.

When Megan saw Seren coming in the door, her face lit up. She ran across the room, throwing her arms around him, oblivious of the smiles on various faces.

"I have been so worried," Seren started. "I couldn't reach you on the phone. It doesn't look like you stayed at our place."

Megan put a finger across his lips. "Hush, we're together now. We'll talk tonight."

This was the start of a two-week whirlwind for Seren and Megan. They went every place Megan wanted to go to make up for his absence the week before. Megan seemed to enjoy herself. Seren didn't. He found himself secretly looking forward to active duty. The last night before he left was stormy, with wild lovemaking, tears, rage and accusations that left Seren drained.

Seren enjoyed the drive from Washington to Fort Bragg. He wheeled into the parking lot at base headquarters with high expectations. There was a bounce to his step as he entered. After the duty officer exchanged salutes, he took Seren's duty orders.

"Follow me, Colonel. You've been expected," the lieutenant said. He led Seren to a small conference room.

There, sitting alone at the table was Megan's father.

CHAPTER SEVEN

The Shadowlord was angry. Instead of Miklos, Flame was making the search into space as his partner. The dragon was slow and required teleportation back to Realm to recharge. The only good thing was, once Flame identified a secure world or landmark, he could return them both there instantly.

Finally, after a week, they had reached what must be the asteroid belt. The Shadowlord could see no end to the belt. It was so dense that Flame couldn't fly in it. There were several larger asteroids outside the belt and one dead world. The nearest sun was a red dwarf, which emitted little light. While Flame, in search of heat, examined the sun, the Shadowlord explored the world.

Nobody had ever occupied this world. It had little atmosphere and no surface water. Craters gave evidence of meteor strikes. To set up the mini-gate, the Shadowlord picked a recessed area in a partial valley where rock cliffs both hid and protected the portal. He didn't value the new experience of manual labor. Usually he had minions to do physical work. He couldn't tell which bothered him most, working or the weak red light.

The Shadowlord sent a boulder to Realm as a test of the gate. Argen's dragon shelters and breathing air equipment came back quickly. Six dragons boiled out of the gate in confusion.

Where is Flame? they asked.

By applying mental jolts, the Shadowlord forced the dragons to start putting up the shelters. The first one had barely been erected when a small meteor shower holed the covering. The dragons wailed in terror. *Find caves,* the Shadowlord ordered. Instead, they bolted back to Realm through the mini-gate.

The Shadowlord put a protection spell over the portal and followed his own advice. His search for caves was productive. The place was a cave explorer's best dream, but none could be made airtight. Gaping holes were standard.

A pallet of air tanks popped out of the gate. Rand, complete with spacesuit, followed. "Wow, this place is desolate," blared his radio, inaudible in space.

Use mental communication, the Shadowlord instructed. *I never thought I'd see the day when I was starved for conversation.*

You'll have to help me change air tanks every forty-five minutes, Rand explained. *Where's Flame?*

I have no idea. If he's typical of dragons, I don't understand how your forces ever beat me. They're a flying liability, the Shadowlord retorted.

Rand chuckled. *Dragons and humans work best when they're partnered. Flame is more headstrong than most.* Rand thought he might be guilty of understatement. *Is the whole world like this?*

I need more exploration time, but everything I've seen is like this, the Shadowlord replied.

Poured concrete and block construction is a possible answer on how to survive here, but I'll need time to train dragons in that type of construction, Rand explained.

The Shadowlord shrugged. *I can manage in nearby caves. I'll send back a list of things I require. I want to do subsurface exploration, too. What is that dinging?*

It's air cylinder replacement time. Take one off the pallet and follow the instructions so you can help me. When you're ready to exchange the tank, I'll switch breathing to a new one, added Rand.

More minion work, the Shadowlord complained.

If you can find one airtight cave, I could send you a dragon survey crew. There's one of those already trained, Rand bragged.

I'll search. Not too hard, thought the Shadowlord. *You get Flame back if he ever returns. Come on, I'll show you around.* They had barely started when Rand's air tank alarm sounded.

Rand laughed. I'll go back now. Protect my air tanks. When I return I'll bring a full-time air-cylinder dragon minion.

The Shadowlord shook his head in disgust at himself as he watched Rand disappear in the gate. He already missed Rand's company.

* * * *

On Earth, Seren saluted. "Reporting for duty, sir."

"At ease, Colonel. Officially, I'm not here. Come sit across from me and look at these pictures." The General pushed a group of photos toward Seren to look at.

Seren sat down at the large table and picked them up. The top photo showed him looking over the DC3 prior to takeoff in the Azores.

"That plane captured the government's interest after filing a flight plan for Mexico, because it later turned up in Cuba," explained the General. "No effort was spared in tracking it."

The next pictures were taken in Lisbon, Madrid and Cairo. Seren looked at the General and raised his eyebrows. He hadn't been enthusiastic about using submarines as spaceships. Now the idea looked like a personal disaster.

"The government doesn't have any pictures of you between Madrid and Cairo." The general pushed some additional pictures across the table. "These photos were recently taken in Libya at the abandoned Adam Air Field which hasn't been used since World War II. The corpses have been identified as Cuban military personnel."

Seren shuffled through some gruesome photos. Now he knew why Mike had been in hurry to leave that airbase. "So, what do you want me to say? I never left the plane at any stop." Seren dug in his briefcase, pulled out some folders and furnished the General with the required forms for visiting foreign lands while off-duty.

The General sorted through them methodically. He waved one in the air in anger. "Ah, yes, Simferopol," he sneered. "Some of the Joint Chiefs wanted to shoot you at this point. What were you thinking? To be aboard a plane landing in the Soviet Union is treason in their minds." The General sighed in exasperation. "I warned you about getting involved with your brother. We know he financed the Cuban purchase of those diesel subs. At first, everyone was elated because Russia sold Cuba their junk. The good diesel subs had been sold to governments in the Mideast." The general shook his head in disbelief. "The State Department was sure you would never get them out of the Black Sea. They were shocked when the subs passed into the Mediterranean. The Navy tracked them across the Atlantic. They lost them near Bermuda in what is known as the Devil's Triangle. A few days ago the Navy picked a group of Russians and Cuban refugees from a small island in the same area. They were at each others' throats with no coherent story."

Knowing the general wouldn't understand anything about an underwater gate, Seren decided to try indifference. "An interesting story, General, but all I did was fly in a chartered aircraft as the engineer. You know I have a pilot's rating. That kind of flight allowed me to pick up more flight hours than I usually get in a year. I can submit my logbook as evidence—if you want it." Seren started to pull his logbook from his briefcase.

The general ran his fingers through his hair in disgust. "You don't get it—do you? First, the military has some operation underway with Cuban refugees. I don't even know what it is. There is a big concern this little escapade might have blown it.

"Second, where are the submarines? Lastly, what were they towing?" The general banged his fist down on the table in anger.

"I don't know anything about a Cuban refugee operation. I did talk to several Cubans on the plane, but not about anything military. The only information I got was that their navy consisted of army personnel who had grown up on fishing boats. I guess that's true of those manning patrol boats off Cuba, too. I don't know the location of any missing submarines. I gather that they are not in Cuba, which you said was the main government concern. What's next?" Seren didn't figure the general's temper would improve if he told him the subs were towing rocket boosters.

"Your military career is over! You won't get a job flying commercial aircraft either. I suppose the government can't stop you from piloting charter flights. You're lucky we don't put you in Leavenworth and throw away the key. Filling out those forms won't save you. All they'll do is ruin the officer that approved them. I'll pretend I never saw them," the General replied, flinging the forms in Seren's face.

"So, do you want my resignation now?" Seren carefully gathered up the forms and put them back in his briefcase. Between the General and Megan, Seren had become thoroughly disgusted. He disregarded a warning in the back of his mind that something wasn't right here.

"No, the base commander has a large group of ROTC cadets coming in for six weeks of training. He wants you to figurehead that operation. As usual, a group of sergeants can handle most of the exercise. Leave the resignation with General Danner after you complete this assignment. That saves face for everyone. The military will claim you resigned because of your change in assignments. You'd get nothing but desk jobs from now on. You can use the same reason." The general waved his hand in dismissal.

"All this meeting proves is that you don't have anything to court martial me on. What about Megan?"

The General sighed. "Her mother's breaking the news to her. I expect her to cut bait." He shook his head in exasperation.

"How is the government going to blacklist my commercial flying?" Seren asked, feeling an almost impersonal interest in his destroyed Earth career. The threat from space made all this ridiculous.

"In this case, it'll be the truth. We consider you a security risk. Attenthut!"

Seren jumped to his feet, years of training moving him by instinct.

"Get the rest of your assignment details from the duty officer. To have deliberately self-destructed your future after the promising start you achieved is incredible. Dismissed!" The General pivoted his chair, turning his back on Seren.

As Seren left, he grinned wryly. He'd never been the general's first choice for a son-in-law. Seren should have expected continued disaster after Rory appeared. Considering the way Seren had watched his romance disintegrate, he was secretly glad to be going home to Realm.

Seren wasn't the only one to grin. The general's was more feral. Seren was right, he thought. Not only was there no court martial offense, that trip wouldn't have impacted Seren's career. Knowing of his interest in Seren, his contacts had forwarded the information he needed to manufacture this crisis. No woman was going to dictate to him who his son-in-law would be.

* * * *

Megan was in a snit. She wondered what was so important that her mother had ruined their scheduled activities. Slamming the front door of her parent's house, Megan announced both her presence and mood.

Megan's mother waited for her in the study. She looked at her angry daughter with dismay. "Sit down, dear. I've got some bad news about Seren."

"Is he hurt?" Megan started for the phone.

"Megan, sit down, now! Actually it's worse. He's disgraced. Your father is busy cleaning up the mess right now. If you want to continue your present lifestyle, don't see him again." She glared at her unfazed daughter.

Megan sank into a chair. "There's a problem, Mommy Dearest. With any luck, I'm pregnant."

"What?" Megan's mother shot to her feet. Now she was the angry one. "I trained you better than that!"

"Chill out, Mother. I love Seren, but I love my lifestyle more. What do I do now?"

"We get you married. Your father's retired friend, General Arnold, has always wanted you as his wife. He's independently wealthy and politically powerful enough to protect your reputation. You can carry on with your current social life. In fact, you'll be in position to increase your power."

Megan jumped to her feet to confront her mother face to face. "Mother, he's over sixty! I overheard daddy say he can't have children."

"He's not even fifty-five. General Arnold's retirement was from a disability, not age. He was a war hero.

"He'll take care of the child problem. We know the general well enough to know he'll be tickled to raise your child. I'll start setting up this farce. You stay away from Seren. Don't even talk to him on the phone—no contact. This is all his fault, anyway." She marched out the room, ignoring her daughter, who burst into tears.

CHAPTER EIGHT

"What do you mean I have to keep the subs at the Atlantis gate?" Argen shrieked.

"It's going to take time to get a large gate working at that dead world," Rand explained patiently. "Send the rocket motors to Realmgate, but leave the subs where they are."

"Chill out, Argen. Nobody's electronics works right in that area. The navy will never find the subs. I'll take that dragon survey crew and join the Shadowlord," Miklos added. "Maybe I can speed things up."

"I envy your being able to function out there without a space suit. Is there any way we can adapt to be like your race?" Rand asked.

"Arthurian could make the modifications, but you might not like the cost," Miklos warned.

"What kind of body changes would be required?" Rand asked.

Miklos laughed. "Not body changes. He'll want you to join the gene pool."

Rand looked shocked. He visualized Lealor's reaction and shook his head. "Not me then. Body changes would be safer." He pointed at Argen. "You and Seren are going to have to pursue this path!"

* * * *

On Earth, Seren got his orders, BOQ assignment and met most of his staff. He was determined to leave the army with an outstanding performance. Seren had one lieutenant and six sergeants assigned to him. Sergeant Major O'Roark was a prize. He had been assigned to this detail for the last six years. Seren sat down with the sergeants and went over the TOE and SOP for the last several years. He didn't see anything that needed changing. "Where is Lieutenant Rivers?" Seren asked.

"In the base hospital with a broken ankle from his last jump, Sir," O'Roark replied.

"Drop the sir when we're alone, Sarge. I guess any boring paperwork can be routed to the Lieutenant."

O'Roark's face lit up with a grin like a Christmas tree light.

"Let's see. My first official act is Officer's Call Friday night. Will any of the officers coming from the colleges outrank me?" Seren asked.

"There's a Lieutenant Colonel from Ohio State. I'll get his date of rank. The rest are all Majors or below. A lot of the enlisted specialists, now E8's, used to be full birds. They would outrank all of you," O'Roark replied.

"It must be hard to be reduced in rank to enlisted status to finish out the years needed for retirement even if they do revert to their highest rank," Seren observed.

"The good ones add to our military knowledge. They're worth listening to. I'd get them involved if were you, Colonel."

"Set me up a separate mess with only them Saturday morning. If some of their officers want to horn in, let them, but I'd rather have the ex-colonels alone.

"On a different subject, I'm out of date on my last jump. Is there a way I could get current before Friday?"

"There's a three-day exercise starting Tuesday. I happen to know it's short of observers. The cadre would snap you up, if you're volunteering. The referees and observers normally don't jump. It would impress the men if you did, sir."

Seren ignored the 'sir.' "Can you arrange it, Sarge? I need to warn you I'm so far in the doghouse they're piping in air."

"The base commander would never stand in the way of a jump. Consider it done," O'Roark replied.

Tuesday morning, Seren was pleased to find he was jumping with a Special Forces unit. Rather than pull his ripcord right away, Seren floated in the air. He experimented with several body positions, finding the one that slowed his fall the most. Finally he was forced to open his chute.

Like everyone else, he had packed his own chute. Unlike them, his chute had several panels missing. This made his chute more maneuverable. He landed on his feet, not needing to roll with the shock. Unknown to him, he had been photographed several times.

Seren was pleased to see the Special Forces lived up to their reputation as he scored the three-day exercise a win for their side. He was surprised when one the sergeants approached him at the end of the exercise.

"Begging your pardon, Sir. Could you brief the noncoms on the techniques you used in your jump? This exercise was photographed, and we have your jump on film."

"If you can work it out with Sergeant O'Roark, I will. I would like to see the film first," Seren replied. That evening at the officer's club, a messenger brought Seren a notice of his briefing the next morning, Friday at 0900 hours. Sergeant O'Roark had also enclosed an envelope full of photos.

* * * *

The next morning the sergeant drove him to an auditorium where two hundred men had gathered.

"Attenthut!" sounded in the room.

"At ease. Seats," Seren commanded. "Good Lord, where did all these troops come from? Are there any officers present?" he asked O'Roark.

"One, sir. He may choose not to identify himself. They're here because they want to know how you did the jump."

Seren started the briefing. He was glad to see many enlargements of the pictures on easels on the stage. "First, I did this because I didn't want the jump to end. Second, it's not an original idea. I've seen others do this better. There are military advantages and dangers if you try this." Seren moved over to one of the enlargements on the wall. "This picture shows the best position I found to slow my fall. If you try this, set your chute with a timer that opens it automatically. You can get hypnotized and lose track of your altitude. Set the timer for fifteen seconds and then add more time as you get used to the sensation." Seren moved to another photo. "Notice when I pull my arms to my side and close my legs, I drop like a stone. That's why this photo is out of focus. This position provides a good fright." Seren moved again. "I have torn several panels out of my chute. This makes it easier to maneuver, but you drop faster. Someday they will design a chute that is more like a rectangle which will allow more maneuverability." Seren pointed to the photo of him landing on his feet. "This is grandstanding. Don't do it. Any questions?" Seren almost felt like a fraud. With his magic, he probably didn't even need a chute. It was easy to take chances with that protection behind him.

Several hands shot up. The first question was, "How many jumps like this have you done?"

"I think this is about the tenth one. I still don't have a perfect position yet to maximize slowing the fall. This is the only time I've been caught on film. I'm going to study the photos myself to see where I might make changes."

"Why did you start jumping this way?"

"The joy was over too fast. Floating down after the rush of free fall is boring. I was looking for a way to extend the feeling. The military advantage is you're not a good target in free fall. Remember, this is not original. I saw other special forces troopers doing it first."

"How did you configure the missing panels?"

"By accident, I had a panel rip out one day and discovered I could direct the chute easier. Don't take out two panels side by side. I know I'm wasting my breath, but don't try the standup landing until you're satisfied with your chute design."

"Attenthut!" The men jumped to their feet.

"Stand at ease," a voice came from the back of the room.

Seren was shocked to see the base commander coming down the aisle.

"I'm officially classifying this meeting 'Secret.' I don't want you trying freefall on your own. I'll put a group together to develop these tactics. If you want to be part of the group, notify your commanding officer, code name 'DROP.' Dismissed."

As the troops filed out, General Danner mounted the stage and approached Seren. "Ride back to headquarters with me, Colonel."

"I suppose I should order more air pipe," Seren mused as they walked to the jeep.

The general chuckled. "No, those techniques can save lives. Assuming that free fall position in case of main chute failure alone is worthwhile. Most fatalities are caused by panic and not pulling the second rip cord. The whole philosophy of enjoying the fall is great."

They had climbed into the jeep and started back. "Now, between the two of us, what were those subs pulling?"

"Rocket motors, no warheads. You'd better tell the powers that be to check what those Russian supply ships to Cuba are carrying. You'll find they're carrying the same thing with warheads." Seren spoke calmly.

"I can see why the Joint Chiefs don't like you—a free thinker. I scare them too, but they need me for now. Do you know where the subs and rockets are?"

"I think so, but there is no danger to the United States."

"I'm not going to ask. This conversation never happened. I can't help you. If you'd been under my command when you pulled that stunt, I would have taken a strip off your hide, but protected you. Between assignments, you're out in 'never-never land.' Do your training assignment well and I'll add a good endorsement to your file. The stuffed shirts won't like it, but they can't remove it. If you ever feel free to tell me the rest, I'll try to be objective. I'll expect your resignation on my desk twenty-four hours after the ROTC cadets leave."

Seren nodded. The rest of the ride was taken in silence.

Seren had waited to call Megan until after the jump. It didn't surprise him that there was no answer at his apartment. After the charter flight debacle he had gotten the phone number of one her friends. "Hello, Anne. This is Seren. Have you seen Megan? I can't get an answer at home."

"Hi, Seren. No I haven't, which is funny. If you leave your number, I'll make sure she gets it. How do like being back on active duty?"

"It's keeping me jumping, thanks." Seren gave her his number at the BOQ and hung up. His expectations of a return call were low.

The next day Seren picked up a rumor of a group of sergeants caught stealing equipment for their units. "What's going on, Sarge?"

"A green lieutenant reported his sergeant when the unit inventoried out with extra equipment," O'Roark spat. "Now, I won't be the only sergeant retiring when you do."

"I don't understand. Why are you leaving?" Seren inquired.

"I can't jump anymore. Bad knees. You don't survive on this base without jumping," the sergeant major grumbled. "I don't feel like starting over. There's nothing out there for me. No family, no job."

Had any of Seren's friends or relatives been present, they would have noticed the look on his face that usually appeared when he was planning something.

* * * *

On the dead world, the Shadowlord was impressed. Miklos had Flame running a surveillance pattern in space. Buildings were springing up and gas powered compressors were producing breathable air. Small bulldozers were clearing a space for the large gate. "You've done wonders," he told Miklos.

"Had lots of help. Mostly it's a matter of attitude. I think Seren has that skill. We'd be further behind if that dragon hadn't invented the pressurized gas to mechanical conversion unit. That's saleable somewhere. That news will make Argen happy. Remind me to tell him." He glanced out into the velvet blackness and said, "We're ready to bring the subs."

* * * *

That Friday night on earth, officer's call went off without a hitch. Seren listened to their complaints about past years and solicited suggestions. The meeting the next morning with the E-8 specialists was formal until sergeants assigned to Seren's staff joined them. The ex-officers weren't used to anyone valuing their opinions. Seren again solicited their 'horror' stories of past training and suggestions. That afternoon Seren met with his sergeants and reviewed what changes they should incorporate based on the feedback they'd received.

* * * *

Monday started without any hitches. The ROTC cadets were put into companies with four platoons. Each platoon had a resident 82nd airborne sergeant as a combination DI and mother. The company officers were cadets with regular army officers from the universities as advisers. The cadet officers were changed weekly.

At daybreak the morning started with the mile run to the PT area for an hour workout followed by the run back to breakfast. The rest of the day the cadets went to field courses taught by the 82nd cadre. The officers from the universities and the E8s assisted where they had expertise. The cadets were getting the equivalent of basic training and OCS combined.

Seren visited as many platoons as possible, starting with PT, until evening mess, adding the burden of his presence for the cadet officers. The highlight for Seren was watching the field courses. Everything went off without a hitch. Tuesday afternoon Seren sat down with Sergeant O'Roark. "I know we haven't had any snafus. What about unusual incidents?"

"One of the cadet platoons stole a floor buffer from the area dispensary so they wouldn't have to do so much work by hand. The regular army lieutenant from their school assigned to another platoon demanded that they share it or he'd report them. They sent the buffer to him in pieces. He went ballistic. Senior officers of the school cooled him off." O'Roark grinned because the kids had showed initiative. "Our sergeants have a betting pool on what happens to the buffer. We've had the usual fights. The first inspection Saturday ought to be interesting," replied O'Roark.

"Let's up the intensity. Give each company's winning platoon the weekend off while increasing the misery for the losers. Also, can we get enough 82nd airborne officers to run the inspection instead of using the officers from the universities for this first one?"

"No problem, sir. They'd love socking it to these kids, especially making those officers assigned to cushy university ROTC programs look bad. The DI's will go all-out not to look bad to their regular officers. That's a good idea," O'Roark replied with a wicked chuckle. "I'll leak the plan immediately."

"Good. I'm going over to the base hospital and visit Lieutenant Rivers. Do we have any cadets there?"

"Not yet," O'Roark answered as Seren left the room.

Getting past the head nurse proved to be challenging. Seren ignored her tirade about normal visiting hours. He found the lieutenant working on forms. Stacks of paper filled the room. "At ease, Lieutenant. I'm Colonel Koenig, your new commanding officer." Seren picked up some forms and raised his eyebrows. These had nothing to do with his command. O'Roark was still collecting favors.

"I never knew the army had so many chicken shit forms," Rivers complained. "Sorry, sir."

"I think Sergeant O'Roark has outdone himself for you, Lieutenant."

"Actually, sir, I don't mind. Television reruns and girly magazines get old fast. I had to give up playing chess. I got bawled out for beating senior officers. Can you believe that? The doctors said I was upsetting them. I'm not even a very good player. The only acceptable game is bridge." Rivers had run down.

Seren smiled at his exasperation. "When do you get out of here?"

"The day after tomorrow. I go on medical leave for two months, then I'll be reassigned."

"Why will you be reassigned?"

"I'll walk all right, but I can't jump. If you don't jump, you can't stay here. They say the General makes his wife jump every week at the parachute club in Fayetteville."

Seren laughed. He could imagine Megan being required to jump out of an airplane. That made him laugh so hard tears came to his eyes. "Sorry, Lieutenant, I was imagining my last girlfriend being forced to jump."

Rivers smiled. "My wife wouldn't think much of the idea, either."

"I'll get Sergeant O'Roark to take this stuff out of here. Good luck, Lieutenant."

When Seren returned to his office, he was surprised to find O'Roark waiting for him. "I had a good look at that paperwork you gave Rivers."

"Well, that's the second 'Oh shit' for the day. Here's the first one."

O'Roark handed Seren a DC society newspaper clipping.

CHAPTER NINE

The Shadowlord looked in horror at Miklos sitting in his chair doubled over in laughter. The dragon taking up most of the space in the single-room building squatted with what Miklos had assured the Shadowlord was a smile.

"What's going on?" the Shadowlord demanded.

Miklos sat up with tears running down his face. "There's a dragon stuck in the sub's conning tower. This I've got to see." Miklos started to laugh again.

"I don't understand. I thought every dragon working inside the sub had been given a rigid series of measurements to prevent this sort of thing." The Shadowlord saw the incident as a system failure.

"Iss also who it iss," the dragon hissed. "The one Miklos calls Junior Flame. He got sstucked in by what you call a wager."

"Sucked," Miklos corrected.

"What are you going to do about it?" the Shadowlord asked.

"Cut off the conning tower," Miklos replied, starting to laugh again at the look on the Shadowlord's face. "Relax. I planned to cut it off anyway. I may leave that troublemaker stuck for a little while as an object lesson while removing it. Argen's come up with a new low profile prism system to see with."

The Shadowlord shook his head in disgust. Every time he thought he understood this crazy group, some incident put him back to square one. Instead of fighting dragons for the last several years, he should have hired them. That way, they would have self-destructed.

* * * *

Seren had been in a blue funk ever since reading about Megan's wedding. The next four weeks on base sped by with problems the sergeants could handle. His army assignment, the last reason for being on Earth, was rushing to a close. Seren was looking at the latest weather bulletin. "How many training companies are still doing field exercises?"

"There's only two left out there," Sergeant Major O'Roark replied.

"I don't like what I see on this weather map. Round up the necessary trucks and we'll go get them."

O'Roark rushed out the door.

Seren instructed another sergeant to alert the other training companies of possible inclement weather.

Sergeant O'Roark appeared a short time later with one truck and two ambulances. "That's it," he explained. "Evidently you're not the only clairvoyant officer. There's also a major exercise going on. These vehicles were in maintenance. The drivers are mechanics because they might still have problems."

"We're going out there. Get some tarps and rope. Lots of heavy rope," insisted Seren. "Also fill the truck with rations. Pick something you can eat in the rain."

A short time later the small convoy was ready to roll. "Sergeant Major, find something to get those troops out. Anything with wheels, my responsibility, and use your favors owed. Remember, we both leave shortly." Seren got his jeep and motioned the driver forward.

* * * *

Two hours later they had found one ROTC company. It took another half hour to find the other. Neither was in its assigned area. They found two aggressor units complete with small tracked vehicles called scorpions and three tanks working with the training companies. Each group also had food trucks manned by regular army cooks.

Seren got all the regular army troops together. It made an odd group, formed by colonels and majors from the universities, sergeants, who commanded the aggressor forces, mess and the tank units, the older E8's also from the colleges and the lesser ratings troops. "I believe a major storm will be on top of us in less than four hours. You're looking at the available transport. We are going to march out starting now. Strip the mess trucks. I've brought tarps so you can protect and bury equipment. I need the trucks. Get any injured and those you have doubts about being physically strong enough loaded. We'll send them out with what we have. The tanks can take the cooks. Those of you not under my command need to get back to your units."

"No, Sir," the sergeant in charge of the cooks protested. "We're airborne. We'll march with the kids. I know why you've brought the rope. We can all help."

"The kids will think it's a lark riding the tanks," the tank commander agreed. "Limit six to a tank if it's going to be messy. We'll take some of that rope to increase hand holds and tie them on if we have to."

"We're staying and marching too, Sir," said the aggressor leader. As marchers come up injured, they can ride the scorpions. When one fills up, we'll send it home. There's no way I'm going to miss this."

"I suggest you keep one ambulance," Specialist Kruger, one of the E8's, recommended "Carry as much rope as possible in that and then unload for injured."

Seren grinned. "I'll take 'No Sir' to mean 'I volunteer'. Any of you not stationed here, feel free to ride out. It won't do us any good to have leaders collapse along the way. Besides, I need command presence with the leaving group and someone must organize our return."

The tanks were the first off. The cadets chosen to ride were elated, not knowing they were judged weakest. The other youngsters were envious. The convoy got off next. Seren was glad that most of the university officers and E8's were going.

Major Ramsey, a university assigned officer, saluted. "We got rid of about three platoons and some brass."

Seren was amused. The major had grown a walrus mustache while stationed at Bragg and was very popular with all the cadets. He and the ex-aggressor Sergeant Jones had become Seren's staff leaders.

"Form them into one company with regular army officers. Put cadets in charge of platoons and squads. Do we have enough airborne troops for each squad?" Seren asked.

"Yes Sir," Sergeant Jones responded. "Some of those southern cadets don't like my black soldiers."

Seren snorted. Sergeant Jones was least six foot six and black as midnight. "Put them together with a black ranger-paratrooper. I'll understand any bruises came from tripping over tree roots. Major, as soon as you get the first platoon organized, lead 'em out. Every step we take puts us on more accessible, if not safer, ground."

"Uh, Colonel, I've got some black football players who would like to be part of the southern squads. No sense the airborne having all the fun," the Major suggested.

"Okay, but don't slow us down," Seren said. "Start with forty-five minutes marching, fifteen rest. Carry on."

Ten minutes later Major Ramsey led the first platoon out, followed by three more platoons in good order. The last platoon took another fifteen minutes after the previous unit had marched away to shake out. Typically this was the misfit unit. Seren seethed. His order, "Double time, Sergeant Jones," was greeted with a big grin.

After ten minutes, Seren relented and ordered standard marching. An airborne squad, less blouses, with ropes coiled over their tee shirts, double-timed past with the usual airborne cadence.

"I give up. Why the ropes?" asked a university-assigned captain who was marching with Seren.

One the few E8's remaining, Specialist Kruger, laughed. "Runs, draws, creek beds can be a raging torrent in an instant. If it has flowing water, the Colonel is going have ropes installed. One side to assist, one side to net."

Specialist Kruger continued. "Colonel, you should send Major Ramsey back here. Then we'd have the carrot and the stick. You and Sergeant Jones are too much alike."

Seren laughed and started forward. He stopped at each platoon and marched with the cadet leader and regular army advisor, getting their thoughts, answering questions, seeing what they would brag about. It took two hours to reach the head of the column.

"Major Ramsey, Specialist Kruger requests your presence with the last platoon," Seren said with a chuckle after the exchange of salutes.

"It's a conspiracy to get me to come in last," the major complained.

"Actually, I heard the reference to you becoming a carrot. Kruger seems to be handling the march well."

"Don't ever let Kruger lead PT," Major Ramsey warned Seren. "That old devil beats most of our school's cross country team to the finish line. At least, I have it easy. They have to come to me."

"Take some time to walk with each of the cadet leaders," requested Seren as the lead group left the major behind.

An hour later the rain started. "Don't wear your poncho unless you're cold," the airborne troops warned. 'You'll be soaked from sweat if you do," they explained. The rain intensity increased with darkness. So far all the streambeds had remained dry.

Seren saw headlights bouncing towards him. Master Sergeant O'Roark stopped his jeep on the side of the road with a big grin.

"I've got you a ride at the next crossroads about mile down the road. We had to use the crossroads to turn around in. One of the rangers out on point, checking water crossings, told me where to find you."

At the end of a wet mile, Seren discovered Fayetteville school buses. Not asking any questions, they got the lead platoon loaded and off.

"You only required wheels," the sergeant volunteered.

"I'm not sure I want any details, but I'm glad to see them," Seren answered. The second platoon was appearing in the driving rain. The loading process was repeated and another loaded school bus disappeared. As expected, the fifth platoon was late. Seren was getting extremely nervous when Sergeant Jones appeared out of the storm.

"They're fifteen minutes behind me," he announced with a big grin. He gave O'Roark a whack on the shoulder, almost knocking him down. "What took you so long?"

"Will this road base hold up?" Seren asked both sergeants. To Seren, this last fifteen minutes had seemed like hours.

"Should," assured Sergeant Jones. "It usually takes a day of this crap to turn to mud. We don't want to get on a shoulder though."

At last the final platoon marched into view with Kruger and Ramsey out front, singing a marching song.

* * * *

The last day of Seren's army career arrived. He'd already sent his resignation to General Danner. Sergeant Major O'Roark had signed a personal service contract with Seren. The sergeant didn't know it, but he was going to Realm.

All the ROTC cadets had remaining was an award ceremony and their parade. Seren had let the university officers select the cadets for awards. He'd had Sergeant O'Roark invite the bus drivers. It sounded like the mayor, the school superintendent, most teachers, maybe the whole town, was coming.

As Seren approached the reviewing stand, he waved to the packed bleachers. He noticed Sergeant O'Roark pacing. "What's wrong, sergeant?"

"The stupid band is late," the sergeant complained.

Seren observed the ROTC companies lined up ready and sighed. "We have the music on tape. Use that." A sound of bagpipes and drums intruded. "Bagpipes, Sergeant Major?"

"That's the drill team band," the puzzled sergeant said as he watched the band, the drill team performing as they marched, and a large body of soldiers march to the center of the parade ground and stop in front of the ROTC companies.

A jeep roared up and a collection of colonels and majors got out. More drums were heard along with marching men shouting airborne cadence. "That's the base VIP show band," gasped the confused sergeant as he rushed to make introductions.

The officers weren't waiting. "I'm Major Reynolds, the cooks were from my unit. My unit is first behind the VIP band."

"I'm Colonel Scott. No salute. A handshake is fine. Sergeant Jones belongs to me. My unit is next in line."

"I'm Colonel Nelson, but I didn't bring my tanks," he said with a laugh. "They'd chew this surface to bits."

As the officers climbed up into the reviewing box, Seren noticed the VIP band had marched across the front of the formation, so they were now the lead unit. The airborne units had positioned themselves in line with the ROTC companies. Seren quickly introduced his guests to the

Lieutenant Colonel stationed at Ohio State who then started announcing the cadet awards. Other officers on the parade field gave the actual award as the cadet stepped forward. The crowd clapped enthusiastically each time. Thirty minutes later, the colonel stepped back, awards finished.

Colonel Scott stepped forward. "Sergeant Major O'Roark, will you present yourself in front of the reviewing box? I know Colonel Koenig presented you with your new service stripes this morning, but I have several awards."

The unit beside the drill team now marched behind the sergeant.

"Every Master Sergeant on the base," Colonel Nelson whispered in Seren's ear. "Even the ones supposed to be in those airborne units."

Seren watched in a daze as both real and silly awards were presented.

Colonel Scott finally concluded. "All right, Sergeant Major, get your butt here in the box along side your colonel."

"Colonel Koenig?"

Seren quickly gave the order, "Pass In Review."

The band led, the cadet companies marched with "Eyes right" from each unit filling the air, followed by the airborne units. The marching sergeants were last. The drill team performed, and the crowd cheered each unit. It approached being a circus, but Seren felt elated.

* * * *

Seren started to pick up his last piece of luggage, when a captain interrupted.

"General Danner would like to see you, sir. Please follow me."

"I'm not in uniform, Captain."

"Neither is he, sir."

Seren shrugged and followed.

"Come in, Colonel. I changed your resignation. You no longer have a regular army commission, but I gave you a reserve commission as a full colonel and assigned you to the standby reserve.

"I made the last order stand-alone. Nobody will ever put the two together. Regular army and reserve snobbery, you know. The assignment will last until you're sixty-five. You can join the active reserve any time you want to. You're too good to lose, and the reserve is going to be more important in the future. Good luck. Dismissed."

Seren joined O'Roark, waiting at the T-Bird. Seren felt shocked and flabbergasted as they drove away towards the Midwest gate.

Tom O'Roark, sensing Seren's confusion, asked, "What?"

"I saw a general disobey orders like a sergeant," was all Seren would say.

CHAPTER TEN

When Seren drove past the mothballed ammunition plant, he pointed it out to ex-sergeant O'Roark. "They made the first automated loading-line there. The product was 76 mm tank rounds, which were already obsolete. I don't know if they ever made a production run."

O'Roark shook his head in disgust. He was no stranger to procurement miscues.

"That's funny. This road to nowhere has been made into a three lane highway," Seren continued. He came around a curve to find, not his home and acres of corn, but a large, fenced-in warehouse. Seren could see his house, still standing inside the fence. As Seren drove up to the gate, he read: 'Procurement Associates.'

The guard came out of his shack. "Move on, buddy. This is private property."

"My name is Seren Koenig. That's my house over there, inside your fence," Seren replied.

The guard pulled the holster flap loose on his sidearm. "Not any more. The state condemned this land. Like I told you, move on."

Seren was getting angry. He cast his mind at the house and felt an answering surge of power. No, wait. The power came from below the house. Seren didn't care where. He grabbed hold. "You have three choices. Open this gate, call someone in higher authority, or run!" he told the guard.

"Run?"

"Okay, if that's what you want." Seren blew the gate to smithereens. The blast knocked over the guardhouse. Seren carefully drove around the litter and went straight to his house.

"That's odd," he told O'Roark. "The drive's been improved and the porch and steps are new." He parked his car, opened the door, and bounded up the steps. Carefully he let his hand rest on the house doorknob until it recognized him, then he entered.

O'Roark took the time to retrieve one of his travel bags. Looking around, he didn't see any activity coming this way. Pickups with flashing lights and wailing sirens littered the gate location. Shaking his head, he mounted the steps and walked through the open door, closing it behind him.

"Name your favorite drink and food," Seren said from the open refrigerator. After hearing the request, Seren tossed O'Roark his brew. "You'll have to cook your own steak. I don't do short orders." He threw a steakfruit at his friend. "Try this."

O'Roark had dropped into a recliner. He put his bag nearby, opened his beer, took a large swig, then sighed. "I'll cook us both one of my special steak dinners after I unwind. This chair is a hundred percent better than that bucket seat." Cautiously he took a bite of the steakfruit. "This isn't bad, but my steaks are better."

A knock came from the door. As Seren went to answer, O'Roark pulled a pistol from his travel bag.

"Vigan!" Seren yelled with joy as he hugged the keeper. "What are you doing here?"

"Argen's got me running this gate. I told them it must be you. So like your father. A little trouble and things blow up. Very Jarlish." Vigan stopped, noticing another recliner and the steakfruit on the arm of O'Roark's chair. "More Andronan chairs and steakfruit as well."

"Andronan chairs?" the perplexed O'Roark asked.

"Andronan is an ancient mage who is a relative on my mother's side. My dad took him a recliner, and he lives in the chair," Seren told him.

Vigan had settled into a recliner. He pointed at the steakfruit. "If you don't want that-"

O'Roark flipped him the fruit while easing his gun back into his pack.

"Vigan, you might introduce us," came from the doorway.

Seren saw a young lady and frowned. He had no interest in any female since Megan left him.

O'Roark saw a girl in the shortest mini skirt he'd ever seen. His eyes narrowed at the sidearm she wore.

"That's Debbie," Vigan said between bites. "She's—" Another bite. "—head of security."

"I'm Seren Koenig. How's the guard?"

"Nothing but cuts and bruises. I sent him to the mental hospital," she replied.

"I'm Sergeant O'Roark. Why the mental hospital?"

Seren laughed. "An old military trick. Nothing gets into the paper and probably the police aren't even notified."

"Right," she agreed. "The police do get some kind of report from the hospital, but they seldom read it. I'm sorry this happened. All the guards had standing orders to call me if a red T-Bird or anyone called Seren showed up at the gate. This is your brother's company."

"Figures," Seren muttered his reply.

"If you'll give me your car keys, I'll secure it for you. We have transport and baggage carts outside that go right through the gate," Debbie continued.

Seren flipped his keys to O'Roark. Seren had no intention of trusting his beloved car to another woman. He dropped into still another recliner.

O'Roark couldn't take his eyes off Debbie's shapely form. He wondered why this situation had not happened in his younger days when he could do more than bark. Even the steps went the wrong way. As O'Roark stumbled to his feet and went out the door, he saw two hardcases standing beside an airport luggage tractor and two trailers, one with seats. He unlocked the trunk and watched them sweat.

When everything was out of the car, he and Debbie traded keys.

She got into the T-Bird and roared away.

The muscle walked back to the warehouse.

O'Roark barely restrained his laughter as he went inside. Seren's car was going to get a workout.

* * * *

The vibrating chair made Seren open his eyes. O'Roark had been true to his word and made a steak dinner that tasted out of this world. His only problem was that everything he needed had to come from the refrigerator.

Vigan stood, patting the recliner. "I don't suppose—?"

"Yes, you can take the chair with you." Seren laughed. He came over and showed Vigan how the back came off, then watched Vigan cart the pieces outside.

"What shall I do with the garbage? Put it back in the refrigerator?" O'Roark asked, only partly in jest.

"Put it in a plastic bag and take it along. There's bound to be a waste bin somewhere." Seren waited while O'Roark took the bag to the trailer. He watched O'Roark pull Vigan's cork by trying to put the bag on his prize chair.

When O'Roark returned to get his last bag, he stopped dead in his tracks. There were still three recliners in the house. "I know the refrigerator was shut tight," he muttered.

Seren laughed. "Things are only going to get worse," he assured the ex-sergeant.

When they got to the portal, first, they had to set up Vigan's chair. Then Debbie wanted to attach twenty carts. Seren was skeptical although Vigan assured him everything would be fine.

"The tractor will shut down automatically when the last cart clears the gate," Vigan promised.

This from the man who couldn't even put his chair back together, thought Seren. "If the gate passage doesn't work, I'll haunt you!"

Vigan pulled back in horror. Debbie spoiled the effect by giggling. O'Roark closed his eyes as Seren drove the tractor onto the portal.

Coming out, Seren saw half the circle was gone, replaced by a gravel road. Two castle walls had been torn down to extend the road. True to Vigan's promise, the tractor shut down when the last cart exited the portal. Seren stamped back to where his brother was waiting.

"Mother is not going to like what you've done to her gate. Why didn't you—"?

"—move it back to the university?" finished Argen. He quickly put his hand over his mouth, knowing he'd completed Seren's sentence again. He had gotten into the habit when they were children, and he knew how much it irritated his brother when he did it.

"Well?" Seren demanded.

"I don't know how," Argen explained. "I thought about asking the Shadowlord, but figured Mother would be upset with him messing with her special gate, so I'll take my lumps. I need to transport large amounts of material through this gate."

* * * *

"Meet Sergeant Major O'Roark," Seren said. "My first contribution to the war effort."

Argen stuck out his hand and shook the sergeant's hand heartily. "Too bad you couldn't have cloned him."

"Why?" Seren and O'Roark asked simultaneously.

"Both Rand and Leon want their armies trained."

"Henning," O'Roark said. "The sergeant that was court- martialed over having excess equipment. He has no place to go. Let me get his file from my pack. It will have information on where he might be."

Seren protested. "I can't have you running back to find him. What all have you got in that backpack anyway? First a forty-five, now personnel files."

"I'll write a note of explanation. Send Debbie to find him. That boy's a real skirt chaser. Chances are, he'll never read the note," O'Roark said.

"Debbie?" Argen looked puzzled.

A disgusted Seren said, "Don't you notice the people you hire?"

The next morning Argen helped Seren into his space suit while O'Roark tried to be helpful to Rand. O'Roark didn't know anything about space suits. When Rand had shown up the previous night, Argen had introduced him as Prince Rand. Taken together, the sergeant was being very careful.

Rand needed little help, but he worked his way through the procedure so O'Roark could help Seren in the future. Rand laughed at O'Roark's skittishness. Rand teased, "Next time we'll suit you up."

"Yes, Sir!" the horrified O'Roark replied.

"Stop scaring the help," Seren commanded with a chuckle.

****

"Only if I don't come back," Seren assured O'Roark. He watched the sergeant major fidget, trying to figure out if his superiors were serious.

Together Rand and Seren clanked through the gate like knights of old.

"It's always like that when those two are together," explained Argen. "This time they focused on you. Usually I get to be the object of their gallows humor. What would you like to do now?"

"Last night they said I'd be training the weren. Tell me about them," O'Roark requested.

Argen reached out and grabbed O'Roark's hand. At his touch, both men vanished.

O'Roark slowly opened his eyes. He stood in a small sitting room. Argen had already flopped into an overstuffed chair. O'Roark looked around and frowned.

"What's the matter? This is a lot more comfortable than standing in that gate breezeway," Argen commented.

"I was looking for one of those Andronan chairs," O'Roark explained.

"Andronan chairs?" For a moment, Argen looked puzzled. "Oh, I get it. You want a recliner." Argen snapped his fingers and a straight-back chair reconfigured itself into a padded recliner.

"Ah," O'Roark sighed as he settled into the chair. He had always prided himself on his ability to stay calm in any situation. "Now what about the weren?"

****

Seren could hardly see. Looking up, he saw camouflaged netting. *How long until daylight?*

This is it, Rand answered. *Look up at three o'clock. That red dwarf is the only sun. This is all the light we get, and it's always the same.*

Seren could barely make out a red spot in the sky. Hearing a noise behind, he whirled, going into a defensive position.

* * * *

Rand chuckled. Paranoid, are we? This place will do that to you. Here comes your air-bottle changer.

Seren saw a small dragon carrying a rack of breathing air-bottles, one cylinder in his talons—ready.

Follow me, Rand instructed as he started for a concrete block barracks. Inside, dragons were sleeping, some squatting, others on their sides and one on his back with wings partly extended. Rand's helmet light went on as the door to the pitch-black room closed. *Notice the walls are covered with the material Argen originally meant to use as outside skin. It keeps in heat and helps make the room airtight. Stop! Don't disconnect your air. This place is airtight for dragons only.* Rand motioned Seren outside as his alarm went off.

Seren switched bottles as his dragon changer was already detaching the old cylinder. With surprising ease, the dragon replaced his bottle. He sprayed the old container with a blast of red paint and stood ready.

If you had looked up when you were inside, you would have seen that the blimp steel was used to form the barracks roof, Rand explained. We left the steel forms and plywood in place when we poured concrete. Argen's happy we used all his material—not as he planned, however. Come on. We're going on a dragon patrol.

Seren found it harder to get mounted in the space suit, but grinned with pleasure as his dragon sprang into the air. How he had missed dragon riding! Looking behind, he had a good view of the dead world. Seren marked the deep fissures in the surface for later. He also observed his bottle dragon flying behind them.

The world disappeared quickly. Seren searched for some new landmark.

Then his air alarm flashed.

CHAPTER ELEVEN

"Weren are shapeshifters," Argen explained. "Most of them live on Widdershins, so I better tell you about that world. There used to be two major kingdoms of humans, Mancy and Fire Mountain. Now, there is only one, with my sister as Regent.

"Mancy fell under the spell of some wicked priests, who persecuted the weren. Most fled to Fire Mountain. A minority stuck it out, believing in their ability to stay hidden."

O'Roark listened, wondering why someone wasn't chasing Argen with a butterfly net. On the other hand, his brother Seren, the sergeant's superior, had mentally blown up a parking lot gate, had a refrigerator that never ran out of anything, and had dragged him through some kind of portal with a caravan of trailers. Who said the military didn't prepare you for anything? Maybe the guy with a net should be chasing him.

Argen continued. "You know how ordinary humans act. Some protected the weren, others turned the shapeshifters into witchfinders. My sister, Lealor, was a captive of the priests for a while. This persecution caused a lack of trust between the weren and humans. Add to that, a weren must spend a year in an alternate shape to be considered adult. Lealor, though not a weren, can shapeshift. There's no way she's going to spend a year in another form, so the weren don't accept her as queen. They consider her husband, Rand, to be king and only obey Lealor because he orders them to. The humans of both kingdoms accept Lealor."

"What other magic can the weren do?" O'Roark asked.

"None that I know of. Rand is a half-weren and does magic because of his mother's blood. One other thing. The weren have lodges. Rand likes to shift into a bear, so he belongs to the bear lodge. I don't know what other lodges exist, but I'll bet there is some rivalry."

"What happened to the priests?"

"The Dragon's Knight destroyed the temple and all the priests in a flash of green fire. The king of Mancy was always nervous after that. He could hardly wait to abdicate in favor of Lealor." Argen shook his head. "Actually, Lealor is regent for her son, Drak."

"I think I'd be nervous, too," O'Roark said. "The Dragon's Knight is your and Seren's father? Can the two of you do things like that magic fire?"

"No, only Lealor has unlimited magical power. Seren and I got short-changed. Our father, Jarl, is more like a channel. You're right. He's the Dragon's Knight and has learned to perform some magic. Mirza, our mother, is the mage. She thinks that Seren and I will be able do more things like father as we use magic."

O'Roark continued his questions, delighted to have someone explaining things to him. He'd accept Argen's information as true until proven wrong. "So, the old gate area by the river where I'm to train weren is on Widdershins?"

"Is that where they plan to play soldier? I'll send you to Fialla. She's the gatekeeper on Widdershins and can show you the area. Fialla is good example of acquired magical skill. For years she was only an herbwoman. Then Mirza trained her to be a gatekeeper. Now Fialla is better at magic than I am."

Argen waved his hand, causing O'Roark and all his belongings to disappear. Maybe I'd better send along some bargaining chips, thought Argen. A large box filled with steakfruit appeared at the gate and then vanished, following O'Roark's trail.

* * * *

The dragon Seren was riding spread his wings and glided. Dragon magic, Seren thought. There was no air in space to allow dragon wings to work. Seren felt the dragon with the bottles land behind him. Looking up, he saw that dragon also had his wings spread. As a pilot and paratrooper, Seren was impressed. Seren's air cylinder replaced, the little dragon sprang away.

Seren asked Rand, Why have I had to change air canisters twice and you haven't changed once?

You're hyperventilating. Take deeper breaths and slow your frequency down. Everybody does this at first, but over time you start to breathe naturally.

Seren concentrated on deep breaths at a slower rate. He noticed a beacon directly ahead. His dragon veered to the left. Looking back, Seren could no longer see the light. It must be shielded. He could still make out the box the beacon was mounted on.

Was that beacon mounted on a submarine battery? Seren asked.

Sure was, Rand replied. *The beacon drifts a little, but so far the dragon flying patrol has always found it. The dragons also record the beacon's position each time by some method only they understand.*

Several hours later, which seemed like days to Seren, they approached another beacon. Again his dragon turned left. This time Seren saw another dragon approaching, now turning left, taking up their original course. He watched Rand's air cylinder replacement in flight.

We're cutting short the patrol, Rand explained. *I wanted you to get a feel for what I'm going to be talking about later.*

When the dragon landed, Seren was exhausted. He staggered after dismounting only to be steadied by the small dragon. Seren went up to his mount and placed his hand on the dragon's neck. *Thanks!*

You're welcome, floated back as the dragon rose from the ground.

Rand beckoned. *Follow me. We're going to join the Shadowlord and Miklos in an airtight cave.*

* * * *

O'Roark looked around. So this was Widdershins. He saw a cottage right out of a picture book. The circle he was standing in was a beautiful piece of stonework. All of his duffle bags and his footlocker were accounted for. An arriving box almost knocked him down. That Argen! If he was shortchanged with magic, then O'Roark figured he didn't want to meet the other magi.

He saw a lady about his age approaching. Two other figures farther off were running toward the gate.

"I'm Fialla, the gatekeeper," the woman told him, putting her hand out to shake.

"I'm Sergeant Major O'Roark, Ma'am."

Fialla smiled. "I don't see any uniform, Sergeant Major. What's your first name?"

"Thomas. I mean, Tom. I haven't used that name in thirty years," O'Roark muttered.

By now, a small girl slid to a stop outside the circle. The second figure was a little old man. O'Roark couldn't figure out how the old man kept from tripping over his long white beard. He walked inside the circle and started sniffing the large box.

* * * *

"Tom, this is Killeen." The little girl curtsied. "The old duffer over there is Berdu. Killeen, you're barefoot again," Fialla scolded.

O'Roark smiled at the little girl's missing tooth. He noticed Berdu was also barefoot. There was something strange about his feet. They appeared blurry to O'Roark's eyes.

"Berdu, you go to Riverville and tell Aldon to bring a horse and cart here before you open that box," Fialla instructed.

"No! Box is Berdu's. Not following any witches' orders. Mine. All mine."

"Berdu, you know Fialla isn't a witch." Killeen stood, arms akimbo.

Fialla's eyes twinkled. "This is Dame Smith's pie-baking day. I'm sure she'd share one with a messenger."

Berdu appeared to be thinking. "Pie? For messenger?" He vanished.

O'Roark picked up his footlocker while Fialla grabbed a duffle bag. Killeen tried the smaller bags until she found one she could drag. They started toward the cottage.

"I knew someone was coming when the cottage grew a room yesterday," Fialla said.

"Grew a room?" O'Roark was skeptical.

"Actually, it's always there. It sinks into the ground when no one needs it. Less cleaning that way." Fialla dropped the bag she was carrying on the floor. "You're going to have to repair the roof. Also, there's no door. You'll have to live with a curtain for privacy."

"I'll help." Killeen tripped over the bag she was dragging. "With the roof," she explained, picking herself up.

The room inside the cottage was ideal, although O'Roark could see sky through the roof. It contained a bed, a chest with plenty of room for his belongings and a straight-back wooden chair. He closed his eyes and commanded the latter mentally, 'Turn into an Andronan chair'. When he opened his eyes, nothing had happened.

* * * *

Fialla smiled gently. "If you show me a mental picture, maybe I can help."

O'Roark closed his eyes and pictured the recliner. When he opened eyes again, it stood there in his quarters. Pleased, he gave Fialla a hug.

Startled, she stepped back. "My, My. You'll have to drag that out into the main room part of the time."

"Sorry, Fialla. That chair makes this room perfect."

It was evident that Fialla had let her feelings for O'Roark get away from her. She patted his arm gently. "I understand. It's quite all right." She straightened her shoulders and got back to business. They started towards the gate for the rest of O'Roark's belongings.

"Killeen, go and get your shoes, then meet us at the gate," ordered Fialla.

For a minute, Killeen's expression looked like Berdu's. She lowered her eyes and replied, "Yes'um." Quickly, she skipped away.

"She and Berdu have a half-hectare war box. When she plays inside that, it's impossible to keep shoes on her."

O'Roark nodded, as if he knew what a half-hectare and war box were.

Killeen and Berdu beat them to the portal. Killeen was carrying her shoes. "You said get, not wear," she said, responding to Fialla's glare.

Berdu's beard was now stained red around his mouth. "Aldon will be here after his morning hunt." A large talon sprang from Berdu's finger. With it he easily opened the box.

"Ten percent keeper's fee," Fialla intoned. "No eating that here. I had enough of your belches the last time."

"He passed wind, too," Killeen added, lowering her head at Fialla's look.

O'Roark, seeing the finger talon, knew what he could barely see on Berdu's feet. Talons were there, also.

"Highwitch robbery," Berdu mumbled. He took out four steakfruit and laid them on the ground. Picking up the box, he raised it over his head as he ran down a nearby path, vanishing into thin air.

* * * *

On Dead World Seren stopped to watch a half-track with a cement-mixer pouring a roof. *That's a novel idea.*

Argen claims the army is making mobile coffins called armored personnel carriers, so half-tracks are really cheap. He has them modified on Realm and then gate-shipped here, Rand said.

Rand, I don't know what's wrong, but I'm exhausted. Do you have jeeps? Walking across this rocky surface, even if the gravity is lower, is wearing me out.

At a nod from Rand, the bottle dragons picked them both up, grasping them under the spacesuit arms, and transported them to an open cave.

Seren was pleased to find lights on inside. He was tired of the dim red glow. However, they walked for what he thought must have been miles. No dragon lift would work here. Finally, they stopped. Part of the wall slid back from the rock, like a pocket door. They entered the conference room.

You can take off your helmet in here. The dragons will remove your air supply, Miklos announced.

The dragons soon had both Rand and Seren stripped of helmets and air bottles. Seren felt much better as he grasped Miklos' hand. "You show up in the darnedest places," he told Miklos.

"If there is an air alarm, use the bag in the orange box. It connects to the hose you see in the orange panels. Be careful. That's highly oxygenated air, so no sparks," Miklos explained. "Come down front. The whole wall is a view screen. Sit down. You'll feel better."

Rand explained to Seren why he felt so tired. "It's the combination of the space suit, breathing air and that dim light. You'll adapt in time."

"I'd rather be like Miklos and be able to survive without these restrictions." Seren noticed both bottle dragons had squatted down and were sound asleep.

"There may be a way." Miklos stood with an intense look on his face as he considered. "Arthurian could change your body to be more like a Sidhe, but he'll want you to contribute to his gene pool. You could be modified, too, Rand."

"If I understand your meaning, not if I am to stay happily married to Lealor. It would be the same as suicide."

"Modification sounds good to me," Seren said. "What do I have to do? I'll take Argen along."

"Go to Eyre. I'll get Mari to prepare a contract and set up the meeting. Don't get tangled in a long-term agreement." Miklos snickered.

"Take Prince Leon, too. He'll be eager," Rand urged.

"Are we through populating the worlds?" The Shadowlord unfolded himself from a corner chair. "After you're modified, press Arthurian about who else can make the same changes. Using you as a model, of course."

"I'm surprised you're still putting up with this situation," Seren said, noticing the Shadowlord appeared to be younger.

"What else is there? Baloo the Bright One is still asleep. I hope Oron, his mentor, is as far away as the few stars you saw in the void. Sit down. I'll bring you the emptiness, up close and personal."

CHAPTER TWELVE

Rand and Miklos finished their presentation on the void. The Shadowlord remained mostly silent. Now, all three peered at Seren, ready for his assessment. "I think you did an excellent job to put together this skirmish line and mount both search probes and watch patrols under horrendous conditions. I'm somewhat terrified by the size of the void. I have several ideas."

"Shoot," Rand encouraged.

"We need to add more items to this skirmish line. It's obvious the objects aren't coming from the void. Can we move small, unoccupied worlds or asteroids from our known space here?"

"That sounds like an interesting assignment," the Shadowlord said. "Let me play with the concept."

"We need to improve living conditions," Seren emphasized. "I'd like to explore building structures in the fissures. How good is our engineering?"

"We don't have any," Rand replied. "I do have two excellent dragon survey parties. I'll start mapping the surface."

"Miklos, you have to run things here, at least until I can get Arthurian's fix. If you have to build any new structures, do it in caves like this one. How is Flame going to react?"

Miklos pointed at the bottle dragons. "They've been transmitting this meeting live to Flame. Since he hasn't stormed in here, we haven't upset him. I let Flame lead the probe phase, and I manage the world. I help Flame whenever he asks and he assists me. We know each other pretty well. After all, I've been around him since he was a dragonet. His mother would never have approved of his current nickname."

Flame is my name, war leader—not a nickname, pounded into their heads.

"Get me suited up and send me home to Realmgate," Seren said. "Rand, follow me as soon as you can. I'll get to work on gap analysis."

* * * *

On the roof of the cottage on Widdershins, O'Roark wiped the sweat from his brow. He didn't like roofing. This world had hammers, but no nails. Every shake had to be fitted and hammered into place. He was glad he didn't have to go up and down the ladder. Killeen made the trips willingly. Right now she was dancing on the ridge row.

O'Roark's knees protested as he got back to work. At least this was a repair job. He was almost finished. He sneezed as Killeen dumped thatch beside him. "What's that for?" he asked.

"It goes over the shakes. I'll show you how," Killeen said, pointing to the adjoining roof. She scampered down the ladder facing outward.

"Fine!" O'Roark snorted, "Even the kids know more about roofing than I do." He finished driving the last shake in place as Killeen appeared with more thatch.

A half-hour later O'Roark eased himself down the ladder. Killeen had done most of the thatching and was now peering down at him with a frown, clearly wondering why he was so slow. As his feet hit the ground, he heard a snicker behind him.

"Have Killeen show you the shower," Fialla instructed. "I'll send you a robe."

Killeen ran down the ladder and took O'Roark by the hand and started pulling him toward a grove of trees.

"You run ahead," O'Roark said, massaging his shoulder. Man, that kid was strong, he thought as he watched her disappear into the grove. Trudging on, he wondered what didn't ache. Roofing was worse than jumping out of airplanes. He stopped, horrified, before entering the grove. On the path lay a little girl's dress. How wild were the woods around him? Could some animal have attacked her? Tired as he was, he broke into a run.

* * * *

"I need to reopen the University here on Realm, Grandfather." An agitated Seren was pacing back and forth in Andronan's study.

Andronan relaxed on his recliner, perplexed by Seren's urgency. "All right, but where are you going to find enough students with keeper's skills?"

"No, No! I need a real university with specialties in engineering and construction, manufacturing, space physics and astronomy. King Caeryl's people are eager to learn. Did you know Argen used them to take cement mixers off trucks and install them on half-tracks? They did this with no technical training. Think what they could do with knowledge."

"Why space physics?" Andronan asked. "You must know dragons warp all the rules of physics."

"When they're not present, time is different between Earth and Realm. I suspect time is slightly different between Realm and Widdershins. If time is not the same, what other differences are we missing?" Seren frowned.

"It will be good to hear voices in the halls again. There is sufficient staff to support about fifty students living close by. I hope any testing will check for gatekeeper skills," Andronan mused. "It would be fun to teach again."

"Why did you allow Argen to move the library to a cave?" Seren asked.

Andronan laughed. "Ebony maneuvered that. She offered Librisald and Argen her library intact if the books remained where they were—in a cave. They also got a bonus of Fafnoddle's collection. You'll find the university still has a fair collection. Librisald left the duplicate copies. I don't think anything in either library fits your new course of study." You'll find the university still has a fair collection."

Seren scratched his head. "Why give their library away?"

"First Egg," Andronan said. "Ebony can hardly keep up with the little dragon monster. Fafnoddle isn't any help. He's only interested in plants. Ebony figured Fafleen would remain on Widdershins, and the only way First Egg pays any attention to *The Dragon Chronicles* is if you're beating him on the head with them, so they decided to let some-one else maintain the library."

"Faf's not little," objected Seren. "What happened to the idea Faf was an adult when he got his first piece of gold?"

"Ebony isn't accepting bribery as finding gold. She is four times as big as First Egg and a very determined dragoness. I know who I'm bet-ting on," Andronan said.

"If I know Faf, he'll disappear." Seren chuckled. "Thanks, Grand-father. Now, I have to convince Argen to honor Mari's contract with Arthurian, and also find instructors."

* * * *

"Hurry up, the water's still warm," Killeen yelled from the shower.

"I don't shower with little girls," a frustrated O'Roark told her. The sounds of Killeen's bath hid his gasps for air. He had been worried some-thing had happened to Killeen. He should have known she was probably friends with every wild creature for miles around.

The shower stopped. A small face peeked out of the branches. "You don't?"

"Right. Do you have a robe?" O'Roark asked, averting his eyes as Killeen emerged.

"What's that?"

"Never mind. Run down and get the one Fialla has for me."

"Okay." A bronze body streaked down the path to the cottage.

O'Roark examined the shower. It was better than some lister bag setups he had used in the Army. Praise be, he thought. The water was still warm.

Later he emerged to find a robe hanging on a bush. He pulled it on and marched to his curtained room. After dressing, he opened the curtains and sank into his recliner.

"So do you shower with big girls?" Fialla asked with a small giggle.

"Don't start," O'Roark warned.

Fialla handed O'Roark a mug of ale before she pulled up a chair. "Wait until tomorrow when she goes swimming with the dragons. I can't make anything that doesn't get ripped. Standing on a dragon's head and diving doesn't do much for homemade swimsuits."

"Dragons? Seren has not said anything about dragons."

"Of course, it isn't much better when she plays with Berdu," continued Fialla, ignoring O'Roark. "She comes home dirty as a pig, but her clothes are spotless."

"Tell me about the dragons!" O'Roark yelled, for once losing his unflappable demeanor.

* * * *

"I won't do it," Argen, shrieked, pounding his fist on Seren's desk. Angry as he was, he made a mental note to find out whether he had an office here at the University.

"He's still a virgin." Prince Leon snickered.

"Is that the problem?" Seren asked. "Relax. Your partner will help you. That's one thing they're good at."

"Mother wouldn't approve," Argen countered, frowning. Something wasn't right with Seren. He radiated hatred of all women. What had happened between Seren and Megan?

"Mother isn't here. Even if she were, she'd probably be in the mess hall waiting for Dad's rescue. I need you to be able to go into the void without a spacesuit. This is a small inconvenience for big gain," Seren insisted.

"Not only a virgin, but afraid," Leon inserted.

"I am not afraid. I'll do it. You—you owe me," sputtered Argen, pointing his finger at Seren.

* * * *

"Now, Tom, don't get riled," Fialla soothed. "Here on Widdershins dragons don't usually bother humans. They like Killeen."

Embarrassed by his outburst, O'Roark asked, "Are you in touch with Argen? I have an idea on where to get a swimsuit for Killeen."

"I can send a message tube through the gate."

"Ask him to get us a competitive swimsuit catalogue from Earth. If he does it quickly, we can order a couple yet today."

Fialla wrote out the request and their need to receive the suits today. She put it in a cardboard tube. "Killeen," she called. When Killeen stuck her head in the door, Fialla asked her to take the tube to the gate and send it to Argen.

"Killeen can operate the gate?" O'Roark didn't try to hide his surprise..

"She pretends she can't." Fialla thought a moment and asked, "Do you know anything about raising wolf cubs?"

O'Roark pulled back in confusion. "They're cute, but dangerous."

Fialla nodded. "That's Killeen. She can do anything she wants to. Magic, use gates, enlist dragons or incinerate you with her eyes. That 'kill' in her name is not an accident. She may be a little girl, but she is one of the most dangerous beings on this world. Ask her to work out with you on martial arts sometime." She settled down in a chair across from O'Roark. "Now, explain about these swimsuits."

"I had to take an officer's kids to a swim meet because a jump was late. Bored, I got suckered into lane timing. Everything was fine until the young lady got out of the water. She was wearing a skin suit made out of a material called Lycra. Nothing was hidden. I got so flustered I zeroed the watch. The other timers were gleeful. I'm glad they weren't military, because that story never made it back to the base.

"I wouldn't recommend the suit if Killeen was fully developed, but at her age the Lycra should stay on and she'll love the patterns. Don't get a solid color."

Killeen burst into the cottage. "The tube is back." She and Fialla removed the catalog. Killeen was enchanted with her choices. She picked two and Fialla worked through the sizes. Only minutes had passed before Killeen raced back to the gate with her order.

"If Argen can only get the suits here in time," Fialla murmured.

＊ ＊ ＊ ＊

On Realm, Argen stood on the platform his mother had built so she could look into the gate. He could see Vigan at the central Earth gate. Argen was nervous. The platform didn't have any handrails around it. He wasn't sure Mirza even used the stairs to get up here. Maybe this was where Seren got his desire to ride dragons and jump out of airplanes.

Vigan cleared his throat, reminding Argen of their conversation.

"Did you get the swimsuits?" Argen wanted to know.

"Yes, Debbie got them. I sent them directly to Fialla," Vigan replied.

Argen held up a bundle of paper so Vigan could see it. "Is this everything you could find on Mrs. Megan Arnold?"

"I didn't send the gossip columns." Vigan tilted his head to show his disdain of rumor in print.

"What do they say?" Argen persisted.

"She's pregnant. It's too early for her to show after their marriage. General Arnold had a vasectomy. Nonsense like that."

Exasperated, Argen pointed his finger at Vigan. "When I say everything in print, that includes gossip. When she has that baby, I want to know about it, and I want a copy of the birth certificate. If I'm an uncle, I want to know it.

"Now, bring me up to date on the list of specialties that Seren requires."

Vigan shrugged. "The only problem is the civil engineer. The best one is married and has a family. His wife is supporting the family by teaching. He's taking care of the children and doing yard work. You need to revise your edict on married personnel. His family isn't going to survive financially on Earth."

"Okay, get everyone together at the gate. I'll come and present the positions and contracts," replied Argen. "Put the family in Seren's house. The rest can stay in the guard's dorm."

"How am I supposed to get in the house?"

"Put your hand on the doorknob and picture a time you were with Mirza. You should hear a click if the house accepts the bond. If that doesn't work, I'll come early. Make sure I have notice of when everyone's going to be there." Argen waved his hand, eliminating his contact with Vigan.

* * * *

Aldon arrived driving a two-wheeled cart. The horse kept looking behind him at the strange plough.

Fialla gave up trying to run down Killeen to put some clothes over her swimsuit. "Aldon, if anything comes through the gate, leave it there. Cover it up to protect it from weather. If someone comes through, direct the visitor to the cottage. Don't go inside the gate. Do you understand?"

"Yes," Aldon replied. "I want to hunt anyway. Can I get out of sight?"

"Don't be away more than two hours." Fialla turned and observed O'Roark squatting down beside Killeen. He was demonstrating what a thorn could do to his shirt.

Killeen ran into the cottage, returning with clothes over her suit. Fialla nodded her head. O'Roark was turning into the perfect grandfather.

O'Roark helped Fialla load the cart. "I'd prefer you drive," he told her.

Fialla smiled in agreement. Killeen and O'Roark climbed in, and with a wave to Aldon, they were off.

Killeen was soon running down the road ahead.

Hearing Killeen shriek, Fialla murmured, "Oh dear." She quickly applied a hummingbird spell on the horse so it would see dragons as birds.

A huge dragon swooped down and carried Killeen into the sky.

CHAPTER THIRTEEN

On Eyre, Seren wandered into Arthurian's throne room and silently asked with an open hand if he could sit on a couch. Receiving a nod, he flopped down. Seren observed Arthurian's frown. "What's wrong?"

"You and Argen fathered girls. Only Prince Leon sired a boy."

"So, what's the problem?"

Argen entered the room and dropped into a chair without permission.

Arthurian's frown deepened. "Prince Leon doesn't have any magical ability. The vacuum breathing spell didn't take. Bright Ones know if the child will have any ability."

"Wait a minute," interrupted Seren. "Does that mean you still owe me a breathing spell conversion?"

"I thought you stole babies. They didn't have any magical ability," inserted Argen.

Rand burst into the room. "Seren, come quick. Flame is preparing to blast into the void. The modified subship is ready for liftoff."

"There!" Seren said. "Spell Rand since you owe me."

"Done!" Arthurian snarled. "The babies we stole had magical abilities," he told Argen.

"Wait a minute. I don't want to get into trouble with Lealor," Rand objected.

"Oh, don't worry. I'll send Prince Leon and his Sidhe Princess to explain the situation to Lealor," Arthurian promised.

"Quick, let's get to the gate," Rand urged.

"You don't have to do that any more," Arthurian told him. "You're like the dragons. Think of where you want to go."

Seren and Rand vanished.

"Maybe some good came out of this liaison," Argen remarked. "Where is Prince Leon anyway?"

"With his princess, Mortal. You can go anytime. I'll get Leon to Widdershins. Your brother tied me up in knots with Mari's contract. Nothing is worse than a leprechaun's contract."

"Why do you and Miklos hate each other?" asked Argen fearlessly.

"Miklos knows the spell that will allow a male Sidhe to be conceived. Not only will he not share the spell, Killeen was supposed to be male. Miklos cheated the nation out of their perfect king. Get gone, before I turn you into a female."

Argen vanished.

Arthurian allowed himself a small smile. *As if I could,* he thought. *I'll fix Argen. If I die without a king for our people, I'll have my will declare him King of the Sidhe. Of all the magi, he is the only one I'd trust to fulfill the obligation.*

* * * *

"Aren't you worried at all about Killeen being with a dragon?" asked O'Roark.

Fialla pointed at two specks in the sky. "Dragons. There go two more to join the fun. I was upset when she dove from the back of a flying dragon into the river. I got her to promise not to do that again. She's with the biggest dragon all the time at home anyway. If Killeen's magic and the dragons can't protect her, nothing can.

"There's a secret ford up the river a mile, Tom. We might as well go there. The river is too deep right across from where the gate used to be. We'd get wet trying to cross here even if the children weren't playing at that spot."

O'Roark enjoyed the ride along the river to the ford. When they crossed the river, the water never reached above the wagon's axle. "What is this? A magic place? I can't see any difference in the width or depth."

"There is an illusion here, Tom. See the two fir trees back fifty chains from the edge of the foliage? They are not normal in this area. Find the two trees and line up for the ford."

Before they got even with the place where Killeen and the dragons were frolicking in the river, the woods gave way to a clearing of about a hundred Earth acres. "This would make a perfect training area." O'Roark was enthusiastic over the site.. He walked over to some stones, noting the area was covered with the debris. "This isn't native rock. What happened here?"

"You're right. All that stone came from buildings of some kind. Between the priests trying to destroy the gate and Mirza moving it, any structure once here got destroyed. Will that hinder your using the area?"

O'Roark had a wicked grin on his face. "No, all this rock will be perfect for building muscles and discipline. I wish I had a sawmill here."

Fialla shook her head. "Even Riverville doesn't have one. I understand Duke Reynal has been trying get rid of a sawmill near his castle. You'll need Queen Lealor's help to get it moved here. Does she know anything about Rand's plan for a weren army?"

"Beats me. I don't mess in the general's business until things don't work. Can we stay the night? I'd like to locate where I'll place the sawmill. We could camp there."

Fialla snorted. "Well, I do interfere when Lealor is being blindsided. When we get home, I'll see if she'll visit us for a mini-vacation. Lealor still loves the cottage."

Fialla frowned, watching O'Roark loosen a stone from the ground and then shot put it like an Olympic field athlete. Showing off with two bad knees, she thought.

"We can spend the night. I don't think Killeen has ever camped out," she continued.

O'Roark was like a schoolboy, walking the river, planning where to put his sawmill and set up camp.

* * * *

Seren really disliked being on the surface of the dead world. Give him a planet lit by a earthlike sun any day. He walked around the subship in disbelief. In addition to the three large rocket motors, three smaller rockets were also attached. "Why the smaller rockets?"

"The German scientist who designed the rocket motors said Russian quality control wasn't good enough to guarantee that the three motors would have equal thrust. We don't want the ship going into the asteroid field. A smaller rocket will fire if the ship goes in the wrong direction. Best case, more boost after the big motors shut down," Rand explained.

"Let me talk to Flame." Seren shook his head. "I'm glad I'm not riding that monster. It looks like something out of a horror movie."

Worker dragons reopened the hatch. Flame's head popped out. "What iss the delay?"

Seren climbed a scaffold to be level with Flame's head.

Seren really disliked being in space on the surface of the dead world with no atmosphere. Give him a planet lit by a earthlike sun any day. He walked around the subship in disbelief. In addition to the three large rocket motors, three smaller rockets were also attached. *Why the smaller rockets?*

The German scientist who designed the rocket motors said Russian quality control wasn't good enough to guarantee that the three motors would have equal thrust. We don't want the ship going into the asteroid field. A smaller rocket will fire if the ship goes in the wrong direction. Best case, more boost after the big motors shut down, Rand explained.

Let me talk to Flame. Seren shook his head. *I'm glad I'm not riding that monster. It looks like something out of a horror movie.*

Worker dragons reopened the hatch. Flame's head popped out. *What iss the delay?*

Seren climbed a scaffold to be level with Flame's head.

You understand you're out there for reconnaissance—not to fight.

Flame cocked his head. *Reconnaisssssance?* he hissed.

Try and get information. Who is the enemy? What do they look like? Where did they come from? How many are there? Try to do this without being seen, Seren explained.

You joke? Flame kill, then there is no enemy.

This unknown antagonist murdered a Sidhe. Even you could be in danger. Besides, we don't want them following you home. Information only. Do you understand?

Yesssss. Flame kill!

No! Flame will only observe or I'll put some other dragon in this ship.

Flame shot a jet of fire at Seren. The fire divided around Seren with no effect. Flame's eyes whirled as he looked at Miklos. Flame knew who protected Seren.

That's right, Flame. You're not leaving the ground unless you agree, confirmed Miklos. *Look at the Shadowlord.*

Flame looked around, puzzled that he couldn't sense the Shadowlord. Finally Flame located him with his cape tightly wrapped around him, sitting on top of a rocket booster.

At a signal from Miklos, the Shadowlord opened his cape, letting silver rays loose. Miklos shielded his eyes, watching an additional lens drop over Flame's eyes for protection. *You didn't notice the Shadowlord. That was an example how reconnaissance should work. That's the way we want you to act.*

Flame let loose a small jet of flame. *Flame understands the concept now. I don't see how the ship can be hidden in the void, but I will observe first.*

Miklos asked Seren. *Is that promise good enough?*

Seren shrugged. *You know Flame better than I do. I sense that's the best we're going to get. I'll delegate the decision to you.*

Snout shut, Flame. Remember you promised all of us to observe only. Miklos turned back to Seren. *You and Rand should command from the cave-conference room. We've set that up to be our mission control.*

* * * *

Seren and Rand had barely made the conference room and removed their helmets when the roar of blast off added vibration to the room. The large screen showed a poor image of the subship leaving. They noticed a small deviation from vertical, but it was not in the direction of the asteroid field. A tracking chart replaced the image. Seren recognized input from the patrol dragon, Miklos and the Shadowlord.

After several hours Miklos alone was sending data. When the Shadowlord entered, Seren asked,"Where is Miklos and how is he getting that flight information?"

The Shadowlord shrugged. "He is out in space following that ship as if he had a long rope attached to it. Who understands what a Sidhe can do?"

* * * *

When Fialla, O'Roark and Killeen returned to the cottage, they were amazed to see two new rooms growing.

"Boy, am I glad to see you," was Aldon's greeting to Fialla. "What's going on with that crazy house?"

"Company coming. Can't tell how soon. Those are brand new rooms," Fialla replied. "One must be for Queen Lealor, although I haven't invited her yet."

Aldon could hardly wait to gather up the horse and cart. Even having been exposed to magic before, a cottage growing rooms was enough to spook him.

"I hope they grow their own roofs," O'Roark grumbled.

Only Killeen was overjoyed. She sat singing in the middle of a growing room.

"I'd better send my invitation to Queen Lealor." Fialla hurried into the cottage to find writing materials. A short time later she came out carrying a message tube. "Killeen, please summon one of your dragon friends."

O'Roark shuddered. So far he had kept the dragons at a distance. That was about to change.

CHAPTER FOURTEEN

"Anything new?" Seren asked as Rand entered the conference room.

"Flame acknowledged that the rocket motors had shut down. They kept ninety percent of their speed. Nothing's in sight, not even an asteroid. Miklos is still trailing behind," Rand replied.

"What about the Shadowlord's project to move objects here?"

"He claims without Baloo, it's hopeless. He wants to try a rocket motor. I told him go ahead, but figure out how to stop anything he gets moving." Rand sent Seren a mental picture of dragons snagging moons with nets. Both doubled up in glee.

We are not amused, crashed into their minds, a Shadowlord reminder that he listened in.

* * * *

Outside the cottage on Widdershins, O'Roark very carefully assisted Queen Lealor as she dismounted from Fafleen. He remained nervous. First royalty, now a dragon's head lying on the ground with a whirling eye larger than his height.

"Hi, Lealor," Killeen yelled as she ran by. She quickly scampered up Fafleen's back. She settled her sled and roared down to the dragon's neck. "Faffie, you need to raise your hind end so I can go faster," Killeen complained.

"I do envy her energy," Lealor said, taking O'Roark's arm as they walked towards the cottage. She stopped abruptly, observing the cottage. "My goodness! It's as big as a manor."

"We don't know who else is coming," Fialla added, giving Lealor a hug as O'Roark disengaged himself. "It doesn't matter. They will have to eat stew," Fialla said with a smile.

Lealor laughed. "As I remember, your stew is better than some banquets I've endured."

The gate shimmered as Prince Leon and a beautiful woman appeared.

"Oh, dear," Lealor said. "I bet King Caeryl doesn't know a thing about this."

Killeen had left Fafleen to run to where the newcomers were.

Fafleen didn't wait to make good her escape. She leaped into the air. *Call me when you're ready to return to the palace*, she sent to anyone who could hear.

The woman knelt before Killeen. "I'm your cousin Arafel."

"Cousin?" It was obvious Killeen didn't know the term.

"Yes. My grandfather is your father's brother. Therefore his queen is your aunt. My mother is your cousin. I'm a second cousin."

"Your grandfather doesn't like us," Killeen told her with a pout.

"True, Arthurian and Miklos are feuding, but even Grandfather has said that you are the best Sidhe living."

"How can that be?" Lealor asked. "Killeen is only half-Sidhe."

"Not so," Arafel told her. "Her mother, in addition to being a Celtic warrior queen, is three-quarters Sidhe." Arafel giggled. "Poor grandfather. Killeen was scheduled to be a boy, but her parents wanted a girl. Grandfather's greatest weakness is that he doesn't value females properly."

"Well, I value you," interrupted Prince Leon, hugging Arafel. He turned toward Lealor. "We're married. Do you think father will be mad?"

"As a father, probably not, but as a King—oh, yes. You were a pawn to be married off to secure the kingdom. What possessed you?" Lealor felt sympathy for King Caeryl.

"That's why I'm here, to explain the situation," Prince Leon confessed.

"It will have to wait until after supper." Fialla hoped to have the little girl with big ears trundled off to bed before confession time.

* * * *

On the dead world control room, Rand punched his fist into what would have been air on an ordinary planet. "They have spotted something," Rand reported excitedly.

"What's Flame doing? Seren tried seeing into the darkness, wishing he had Sidhe vision.

"According to Miklos, he fired the small rockets."

"To brake the ship, I guess." Seren agreed with the action.

"Uh, no. Towards the objects."

"Blast! He's going to get in trouble."

* * * *

Back at the cottage Killeen was regaling the adults with her latest swimming episode. "I have this new suit which stays on. I wanted to take it off to save it." Pointing at O'Roark, she continued, "he wouldn't let me. I must wear a robe." She thought for a minute and then added her largest complaint. "He won't shower with girls."

Prince Leon started to laugh, only to get an elbow in the stomach from Arafel.

Queen Lealor had a hand partially over her face to hide a smile.

O'Roark sighed, while gazing the ceiling to hide his embarrassment.

"That's nice, dear, but it's time to retire for the night," Fialla instructed. "Distribute your hugs and off to the loft with you."

Killeen put up a perfunctory argument for staying up, but seeing the look on Lealor's face, left.

Lealor instructed Prince Leon to begin his tale. "Quietly," she warned.

"Seren's been struggling with breathing air out in the void. Miklos had Mari draw up a contract with Arthurian to modify Seren and several others to be like the Sidhe in space. Seren, Argen and I went to Eyre to be modified."

"The price?" prodded Lealor. She understood that the Sidhe did nothing without some bargain being struck, usually much to their advantage.

Prince Leon blushed. "We had to add to the gene pool. Rand wouldn't go. He said you'd kill him."

"He's right." Lealor shook her head. "I can't imagine Argen being involved."

"We forced him. Seren claimed duty. I'm guilty of using ridicule. This started out as a big lark to me—like raiding the serving maid's quarters."

"Which you won't be doing anymore." Arafel smiled sweetly to mask the iron in her voice.

"Things didn't go as planned. I—I fell in love and the spell wouldn't work on me. When Rand showed up because of Flame, Seren demanded that Arthurian spell Rand since I had already paid the price."

"Grandfather sent me along because he didn't know if you'd believe Prince Leon. I swear Rand was adapted without engaging in any nighttime activities." Arafel spoke earnestly. "Also, I wanted to be with my husband. While the spell didn't work, he's gained some magic abilities. I may be able enlarge his new talent. Child raising on Eyre is not rewarding."

"What possessed Seren? I thought he was engaged. Mother will take a strip off him. Forcing Argen is really vile." Lealor looked as if she wanted to hit someone.

"Megan threw Seren over for a general," O'Roark said. "Though my commander indicated her father was dishonest about Seren's off-duty activities, so she may have been tricked. Right now, Seren probably lines up with the way Arthurian thinks—at least about women."

"I would have believed you on your own, Leon, but I appreciate it that Arafel was willing to back you," Lealor said. "I'll write a note that you can give to your father telling him my kingdom supports this marriage. This isn't appeasement, either. I do support both of you. If things work out badly, you can come to Widdershins and rule Mancy for me."

Prince Leon and Arafel excused themselves from the table. Princess Arafel gave Lealor a hug. With tears in her eyes she whispered, "Thank you."

"Next," said Lealor, looking at Fialla and O'Roark. She could sense some sort of bond had formed between them.

* * * *

"What's happening?" demanded Seren. Human vision was worthless on the dead world. He felt as if he was trying to read a newspaper in a closet with the door shut.

"Miklos is having trouble seeing. He has to look through both Flame's eyes and the prism periscope," Rand squinted. "Whatever it is looks big and it's moving. Of course, there is no communication from Flame."

"Order them to abort. Leave the subship. Relocate back here now."

Rand shook his head. "Flame refuses. Miklos says he has to obey a geas to protect Flame."

Seren threw up his hands in anger. "What good is being in command when you're ignored?"

"Miklos is reporting that something has broken away from the unknown mass and is heading for the subship."

Seren waited, grinding his teeth in the literal and figurative dark.

* * * *

In the comfort of the cottage, O'Roark was bringing Lealor up to date. "Seren and Rand want me to train a weren army. I'd like to use the old gate site. I want to move a sawmill in from somebody called Duke Reynal and build a camp," O'Roark explained.

Fialla snorted. "I bet you didn't know anything about the project."

Spots of anger showed on Lealor's face. "You're right. Rand needs to spend some time at home. I don't care about the weren army. I've got about twenty weren in my jails you can have immediately."

"Hard cases?" O'Roark asked.

"Maybe one or two. The others are disorderly. The site is acceptable. Have Fialla check it periodically in case you disturb something magic mother missed. You'll have to help Reynal dismantle the sawmill. Getting it up the river will be hard. I'll have Reynal notify you when the convicts get to his castle. No magic. Make them work."

"Do you still do any healing?" Fialla asked.

"I haven't in years. Why?" Lealor was surprised by the question.

"Tom has bad knees and I hope…,"

"Tom, is it?" Lealor smiled. "Sit over here in front of me, sergeant." Lealor put a hand on each knee and closed her eyes. A green glow appeared over her hands and O'Roark's knees. When the glow faded, Lealor opened her eyes. "Well?"

"They don't hurt," said the surprised O'Roark. "How do I ever repay you?"

"I'll think of something. Get off of them for the time being to let the magic continue." Lealor smiled as O'Roark hurried to his recliner.

"Tom, is it?" Lealor repeated in a whisper to Fialla. "Does he have any idea how old you really are?"

"No! We aren't telling him either," Fialla sputtered.

Early the next morning Lealor was surprised when she received a kick. Peering under the covers, she discovered that sometime during the night Killeen had crawled into bed with her. Fialla would have a fit. Touched by Killeen's trust, Lealor gathered the little girl into her arms and fell back to sleep. When she awoke the second time, Killeen stood at the foot of her bed.

"Berdu is outside."

Lealor groaned as she dragged herself out of bed. It was still too early to be up. She wrapped a blanket around her nightclothes and staggered outside. The sun was not even above the treetops. Killeen skipped by. Lealor could see O'Roark splitting firewood.

"Hello, witch."

Lealor jumped. "Berdu, you know my name. I am not a witch. We settled that a long time ago."

"Berdu remembers when you first came and made promises. You always were a pretty witch."

CRY HAVOC seared across Lealor's mind.

Berdu changed into a mighty dragon and thundered into the sky. The force of his exit knocked both Lealor and Killeen to the ground.

O'Roark ran across the clearing and helped the dazed Lealor to her feet. "My Lord, is that what Fialla meant by 'She's with the biggest dragon all the time at home anyway'?"

Killeen remained huddled on the ground. She sobbed loudly between agonizing words.

Lealor barely understood what sounded like "Father's in trouble." She observed Fafleen barreling in for a landing. Lealor sent, *What's going on?*

Older dragons are lifting all over Widdershins. You aren't going to believe this, but many have Sidhe riders. Berdularion's army is taking wing.

"I'd better get back to Fire Mountain Island," Lealor started.

No! Something tells me we must wait here, disagreed Fafleen.

* * * *

Berdularion swooped under Miklos, allowing him to get seated as the rest of the dragon's wing caught up. Berdularion could see the broken subship and two dead dragons. His son was still fighting. *Attack on our right flank. We must turn them.*

The battle was joined.

The enemy was fighting one another over the remains of the ship. They treated the ship as if it was dessert. Others were devouring the dead dragons. Berdularion flamed both the enemy and the carcasses. Then he was attacked on every side. *Turn them. Turn them,* he kept sending. It was working. The enemy was now directed back toward empty space.

The cost was half the wing destroyed.

Flame was no longer fighting.

Berdularion felt Miklos being ripped from his back by two different sets of pinchers. He used his eyes as lasers to do surgical strikes on his opponents as he sent Miklos to the Widdershin's gate.

He scooped up what was left of Flame in his talons, belching fire on the enemy about him while observing he and Flame were the last living dragons. Everyone else had died in the fierce fight.

Ignoring his sorrow, he sent a message to Realm and vanished.

CHAPTER FIFTEEN

On Realm, Fafnoddle dropped the second tray of seedlings as Berdularion's message seared into his head. He had lost the first tray when *Cry Havoc* had intruded into his mind. Faf had not understood the phrase, but the force of it had completely upset his coordination—now this. He rushed to the cave entrance and sprang into the air, forgetting his apron, which was shredded by the wind. Faf knew the wyvern queen moved around in the marsh so he couldn't teleport directly. He would save time by teleporting to Fellkeep, then flying a search pattern south.

When Faf appeared over Fellkeep, he was surprised to see how large the castle had grown. Leaving the edge of Fell Forest behind, he soon flew over marshland. As he neared the seacoast, Faf sensed the caverns hidden by mist. He sent a message for help.

Fafnoddle von Fafnir requests that Queen Lythyr designate a landing area.

A hole in the mist appeared over an island. Faf sank wearily to the ground. He recognized the wyvern standing at the edge. "Hi, Seabreeze," he said.

"Queen Seabreeze," a second wyvern hissed.

"Mother's retired," Seabreeze explained, shushing her guard. "What problem brings you here?"

"My king's son is sorely wounded. Berdularion seeks help from your valued healing mud. Can you show me a large pool so Berdularion can find the place and drop his son into it?

"A large one is a little way off. I've never tried this," she said, climbing on Faf's back to the horror of her guards. "Send the males and a healer to Big Muddy," she ordered. "Now, Faf, take me airborne and I'll show the location from the sky, so your king can get the landmarks from your mind."

Faf and Seabreeze didn't have to wait long after she pointed out the pool through the mist. An exhausted Berdularion appeared over the pool and literally dumped Flame into it. "Iss there a landing site near by?" requested Berdularion.

"We need a flotation device," a male wyvern yelled. "He has a big head."

You can say that again, thought Faf and then gulped at the insult. Berdularion had probably heard.

More mist cleared and the dragons landed. Berdularion showed both exhaustion and battle damage.

"Maybe I'd better find a pool for your king," said Seabreeze, climbing down from Faf. Her guards rushed up to inspect her to assure themselves that dragon flight hadn't damaged her.

"Not necessary," assured Berdularion. "Besides, your homeland must be unbalanced by having three male dragons here. I hope you can save my son."

"The healing mud is powerful, but I've never seen holes in a dragon like that before." Seabreeze was concerned. "You're right. It would be best if you and Faf left. Send his mate here to help. A female will help counterbalance his force, even if is feeble."

Both dragons lifted rapidly.

Thank you, Berdularion sent.

You're welcome. Faf, I'd like a longer dragonride when Flame is healed, Seabreeze added.

At your pleasure, Your Majesty, returned an amused Fafnoddle.

We can return to my cave. Ebony has salve she can treat those injuries with, he told Berdularion.

No time. I will join Seren to take Flame's place, and you must go to Achaea.

Whatever for? Fafnoddle objected. The crisis seemed to be over and he wanted to return to his garden.

Miklos needs to go there. The main gate is still unstable. Besides, it's on the wrong Achaea continent. The portal is on the land Zeus gave to the Celtic and Norse gods. There's a hidden gate where Miklos' wife, Branwyn, rules. Zeus would be the best keeper to reopen it without waking Baloo who is sleeping in Achaeasun. You can get there without using a gate, but Zeus is not going to like the fact that a gate was hidden from him.

Thanks a lot, grumbled Fafnoddle to empty air.

Berdularion had vanished.

* * * *

As Fafnoddle appeared in Zeus's throne room, he was dismayed to find it empty. Maybe not, he thought, hearing something buzz by. Also, a speck of light glinted that was not in direct line with the sun's rays from the windows.

Fafnoddle sniffed. Nothing. Then he heard the buzz again. Ah ha! The light speck had moved. He closed his saucer eyes. When Faf heard the buzz again he swatted, guided by only his hearing.

Impact. Opening his eyes, Fafnoddle saw someone's head. Their legs were flat against the wall.

"Apollo! Apollo!" screamed the immortal.

Sounds like a wounded human yelling, 'medic,' thought Faf.

Apollo appeared in the throne room. Ignoring Fafnoddle, Apollo rushed to the crumpled figure. He stooped and then stood upright. "Hermes, you're not hurt. Stop play-acting and get up. What's going on in here anyway?"

"I'm looking for Zeus. Miklos, Queen Branwyn's consort, is badly hurt, and I need Zeus to open a hidden gate on her continent," Faf explained. "I don't have time to play silly games."

"I'll wager—" Hermes began.

"Hush!" Apollo ordered. "I'll take you to Branwyn's fortress. Zeus and the healer Aesculapius will meet us there."

When the three appeared on a hill overlooking a large wooden stockade, Zeus was already present. "I can't sense any gate," he complained. Horses wandered everywhere.

"There aren't any caves," Fafnoddle observed. "It must be underground."

"I'll get Hades to sniff it out," promised Zeus as Aesculapius joined them.

"Meddler!" Hades roared as his head appeared above ground near a grove of oaks. "You know the Celts always put things in groves." Hades disappeared.

Fafnoddle sprang into the air and glided down to the grove. "Something is buried here."

Zeus made the ground shake while Faf started digging. Soon the surface of a rose-colored granite circle appeared.

"It's sleeping. How do you wake up a gate?" the perplexed Fafnoddle asked.

"I'll send Hermes through it," Zeus explained.

"Wait—" Hermes yelped as his head disappeared into the granite. His legs windmilled wildly before they completely disappeared.

"The gate's awake now," Zeus said with a chuckle.

"Uh, oh," Faf did not like what he saw coming toward them.

Carrying a golden spear, a woman riding a white horse led a mass of mounted warriors toward the gate.

* * * *

The Widdershin's gate shimmered as the crumpled body of Miklos appeared. "Father!" yelled Killeen, starting for the gate.

Quick as a flash, Lealor grabbed her arm. "Wait! He must be healed and I'm going to need your help." Lealor approached the portal and shook her head in dismay. "Here, Killeen, face me. Wrap your arms around me and transfer as much life energy as you can."

Lealor raised her hands toward the body and green light shot out, encircling Miklos. "Faffie, I don't have enough strength yet. Can you help?"

The dragoness positioned herself so a talon extended between Killeen and Lealor. The green glow now covered Killeen, Lealor and the talon. *Run human*, Fafleen ordered O'Roark. *Get Fialla and Arafel.*

The blazing mental command shook O'Roark out of shock. As he raced towards the cottage, he passed Fialla.

"I heard," she explained.

Inside the cottage, O'Roark hammered on the doorframe of Prince Leon's quarters. "Arafel, help," he yelled. O'Roark averted his eyes as she came out wearing less than Killeen did at night. "The—the gate," he stammered. She immediately dashed past him and out the door, her night shift flowing behind her.

O'Roark observed Prince Leon still sleeping. He picked up a discarded blanket and followed Arafel. What was it with the females of this world? They didn't act as if clothes were necessary.

Approaching the gate, O'Roark dropped the blanket over the now-glowing Arafel. "It's cold in the morning," he offered. He saw Arafel smile slightly.

"Don't stand there gawking, Tom. Get some hot water and bed sheets we can use as bandages." Fialla never looked up.

"O'Roark noticed she was separated from what he thought of as the glow group working at cutting away clothing. He nodded, started for the cottage and almost got knocked down by a brown dragon sliding to a landing stop. Another talon joined the group.

"Thanks, Sparrow," he heard Killeen say between sobs.

"He's stabilized enough to move him off the gate. Everyone keep your connection tight," Lealor ordered.

Fialla took Arafel's blanket and spread it on the ground. Miklos' body floated to its new position. Poor Tom. His attempt at modesty is undone, Fialla thought.

As if to prove Lealor right, Hermes burst through the gate. "Help comes," he announced. "I'm sure not going back that way." Hermes vanished.

The gate glowed and both Aesculapius and Fafnoddle appeared.

"Father, I didn't know you ever used gates," observed the surprised Fafleen.

"Time constraints," Fafnoddle told her. "First time, though."

Aesculapius examined Miklos. "Stay connected," he warned. "Excellent work. There's still some internal bleeding. Let me direct you mentally." He put his hand on Lealor's shoulder, but otherwise was not included in the glow.

"There. Now we can transport him home. I need two of you to go along to help keep him stabilized," instructed Aesculapius.

"Are Killeen and Sparrow adequate?" asked the exhausted Lealor.

Aesculapius touched both. "Yes. Good choices. Both are young and have more reserves left. Put Miklos back on the gate by physically carrying him. Now, those not going disconnect and quickly leave the portal."

The gate started to shimmer and those in the center disappeared as Lealor, Fialla and Arafel exited.

"Don't worry. Apollo is at the other end," Fafnoddle assured Lealor.

"Flare?" asked Fafleen.

"Flame—the name he prefers—is in a wyvern's mud pool on Realm," Fafnoddle told her. "Seabreeze is the new queen, and she asked if you would come to help stabilize him.

"I'll take Lealor home. Get the position from my mind. When you are close, ask for directions. Teleport to Fellkeep first."

Fafleen vanished.

"What about Rand?" Lealor inquired. She now looked both apprehensive and exhausted.

"Not even close to the battle, like me," Fafnoddle reassured. "Can you mount all right?"

"Probably, with O'Roark to boost me."

O'Roark looked around wildly, holding his unneeded hot water and sheets. Boost a queen? Never, he thought.

"Here, I'll do it," said Fialla, giving Lealor a leg up. With Lealor safely secured, Fafnoddle sprang into the air and beat his way north.

They had barely disappeared from sight when Prince Leon sauntered up. "Did I miss something?"

"You can carry me back to bed, to sleep," ordered Arafel, who was so exhausted she looked almost transparent.

O'Roark gave Fialla a look out of the corner of his eye. He certainly wouldn't attempt carrying her to the cottage, even with his newly repaired knees.

CHAPTER SIXTEEN

Rand could hardly wait to unload the information he had gathered. "Guess who's training the dragons."

Seren looked up in irritation from the diagram he was toiling over. He hadn't been sleeping well since the space battle, and it showed. By military standards, he was unkempt. Dark circles gathered below his eyes. "The Shadowlord, probably."

"No, No! Berdularion himself, the dragon king." Rand stopped to observe Seren's response. There wasn't any. "You don't seem very impressed."

"Why should I be? He recently sacrificed a whole dragon wing, which I didn't know existed, to save Flame. Miklos, my right arm, is gone. Worse, I don't know any more about what we're facing out there than I did before the defeat."

"That's not fair. The enemy turned away during the confrontation. Berdularion bought you time," Rand protested. "Besides, I received word from Fialla. Miklos lives."

"That's good news." Seren gave Rand the first smile of the week. "When's Miklos coming back?"

"Not right away. Lealor was there at the Widdershins gate. Fialla said she could only stabilize him. They sent him home to Branwyn on Achaea."

"So I'm no better off than when I thought he was dead," grumbled Seren. "I suppose I better debrief Berdularion."

"He's already on his way. Your Sergeant O'Roark was also at the Widdershins gate. I better return home and face Lealor," Rand observed in a pensive mood.

"Well, where is Berdularion?"

"Already in the tunnel. He's walking here."

"Walking?" Seren couldn't believe what Rand had told him. Berdularion almost never walked anywhere.

"Berdularion didn't trust the bottle dragon's focus enough to teleport directly."

Seren snorted like his dragon friends. "I don't blame him, but walking? It'll take him all day to get here."

"I know. That's why I'd like to go to Widdershins and explain things to Lealor," Rand agreed.

Tight lipped, Seren glared at his friend. He knew how little Rand liked explaining anything to Lealor. Evidently, that was preferable to being part of the meeting with Berdularion. Rand wouldn't be back today either. He always celebrated disagreements by taking Lealor to bed. Seren could understand Rand, but what possessed his sister to fall for the ruse every time?

"All right. Take care of your business with Lealor. I'll leave Berdularion in charge here and pay a visit to my brother, Argen. This submarine fiasco belongs to him. I intend to emphasize the items I need to defend this place, which I expect him to provide."

Relieved to have permission to escape, Rand leaped to Argen's defense. "It's not fair to blame everything on Argen. Some of his ideas have worked well, like that prototype gas turbine that produces electricity and steam, for example. That's so much better than getting light from submarine batteries, even if the dragon's gas-mechanical converter allowed us to charge them easily.

"What are you going to do with the second subship?" Rand asked.

"Fill it with explosives and put it out in the void for bait, if I can ever figure out where. Go on! Beat it!"

Relieved, Rand didn't waste any time getting to the gate.

* * * *

When Rand stepped off the gate surface at Widdershins, Fialla's glare almost made him reexamine his plan. "What's wrong?"

"Everybody's gone. Tom is taking apart a sawmill at Duke Reynal's castle. Killeen is on Achaea. I don't know where Berdu is. I haven't seen a dragon since Lealor left, and I don't have any news from anyone."

"Tom?" Rand inquired.

Fialla blushed faintly. "Sergeant Major O'Roark to you."

Rand chuckled. "Berdu has shifted back to being Berdularion and he's out with Seren taking Flame's place. How am I going to get to the palace at Fire Mountain Island?"

"Sparrow will take you part of the way," came from the gate.

Both Fialla and Rand whirled to face the portal. In the center of the gate stood Killeen and Sparrow, the brown dragon.

Fialla was shocked by the way Killeen was dressed. She wore pants, boots and a chain mail shirt. She carried a short sword.

Killeen announced, "I'm going to join O'Roark at Reynal's castle. I'm taking O'Roark's training, before I report to Seren to take my dad's place. I've already studied with Berdularion and worked problems in the war box. You can have Sparrow take you to the palace from Reynal's."

Killeen mounted Sparrow and they flew away.

Rand shook his head. Seren's problems were multiplying. "I don't suppose you have a horse?"

Fialla shook her head no. "I thought you were Sidhe-enhanced. Why don't you teleport home?"

"I don't have any focal points at Riverville or Duke Reynal's castle. I'm not certain of my range. The palace seems too far. I'll go to Riverville as a bear. I can get a horse and directions from there."

Fialla turned her back on Rand. "I'll put your clothes in a bag you can carry. Remember to take a bath in the river. No horse will allow you to ride it smelling like a bear." The stink told Fialla it was safe to turn.

"Pook, get down," ordered Fialla as she gathered up his clothes, watching the bear drop to all fours. After putting his outfit into a bag she tied it to a stick, which she stuck into his mouth. "I know you're Rand, but in that form you'll always be Pook to me. Tell Tom that his room is sinking. I've saved his chair. Be gone with you!"

Pook lumbered toward Riverville, leaving Fialla alone again.

* * * *

Berdularion barely scraped through the opening to Seren's office on the dead world. Patches of scales showed concrete residue, but the door still worked enough to slide closed. "I understand you are not pleased."

Seren shook his head, "Let's not go there. Describe what the creatures we're facing look like."

Berdularion hunkered down. "They are about the size of Ssparrow but black instead of brown." He cocked his head observing Seren's lack of reaction. "You don't know Ssparrow?"

Seren shook his head. "No, try again." He noticed Berdularion was still upset from the way he was hissing his esses.

Berdularion scratched his snout with a talon, thinking. He closed his eyes for a few seconds, then they snapped open. "First Egg, when he visited you on Earth, that size.

"The enemy warriors have a tail, otherwise they are like a giant beetle. I'd say ant, but they can't bend in the middle. Their jaws crush metal or rock. The holes in Flame came from breaking free of their jaws. Their pincers can cut a human in two. In a fight their tail delivers a massive blow. Dragons have the advantage if we get beside them, then our talons do a lot of damage. The best approach is to stand back and flame." Berdularion's talons clenched and unclenched in remembrance.

"Do they communicate in any way?"

"They must, because they work together as a group instantly. I feel a sshrill vibration sometimes, as if their communication may be mental, above our threshold."

"How fast do they maneuver?"

"In sspace, nothing is sslow. They form units faster then dragons can, all bent on eating. If they were animals, I say they were sstarved. Look what they did to that metal contraption Flame came in. They fought each other over who got feeding rights."

Seren sighed. "With the subship gone we don't have a marker to know where the battle took place in the void."

"Not true. They didn't eat everything. I took this material from your remaining vehicle." Berdularion scratched a scale and then pushed a talon towards Seren with material covering the point.

Seren tugged the material off Berdularion's talon. He rubbed it between his first finger and thumb. "Plastic? I need to build plastic spaceships? No way."

"Whatever you call that sstuff, there's enough out there for me to return to the battle ssite anytime. Of course, everything drifts."

"What about bodies?" Seren demanded.

"They ate them, even their own. Don't you have a word for that?"

"Yeah, cannibals. Okay, the big question. Where did they go?"

Berdularion's eyes spun backwards, the human equivalent of a shrug. "I don't know. Their force was massive. Once it gets in motion, it sstays that way. That's why we worked to turn them. It proved effective once before."

"What?" shrieked Seren, losing his composure. "You've fought these things before?"

"Yesss! Eons ago. I don't remember when. It was harder turning them then. We killed thousands. Eventually they traveled in another direction. They never returned until now. My dragon wing were winners that first time."

Seren shuddered. "Did they create the void by eating everything?"

Berdularion's tail lashed. "I don't know. I don't understand why they don't eat the asteroids. I want to return to train a new dragon wing."

Seren nodded agreement. "Good! I'm going to be gone a while. Take command of the whole base. Please guard the portal and destroy it if you're being overwhelmed. I'll return soon."

"I'll serve until Flame returns. I owe you that. I don't want responsibility for more war—that's why I take the silly Berdu shape." Berdularion vanished.

Things not firmly fixed to the walls or floor moved from Berdularion's disappearance, which was different.

Space, or dragon agitation? Seren wondered.

Two questions loomed. What were their enemies? How could he stop them?

He needed to confer with Argen.

* * * *

At his palace on Widdershins, Rand was explaining his plan to his wife.

"I don't mind you forming a weren army, but what good does it do?" Lealor asked. "They have to use air cylinders or be underground out there with Seren."

"I don't have foresight, but I do have this feeling that problem will resolve itself."

Lealor snorted like her brother. Both had been around too many dragons. "For someone with few magical abilities, you certainly are a mystic."

Rand wasn't about to tell her about the increase of his ability since Arthurian's spell. Time to change the subject. "Seren is going to have his hands full with Killeen."

"Is that a sexist remark?"

"No, no! O'Roark told me she arrived at Fialla's gate in pants, a mailed shirt and sword, ready to take Miklos' place."

Lealor frowned. She certainly didn't like the idea of the young girl leading in battles against the unknown enemy. "Mari started this mess. According to your father's stories, years ago she was a real nasty warrior. Why doesn't Mari take Miklos' place? If Killeen shows up, make her Mari's aide."

"Killeen will show up, all right. Both the dragons and weren love her. Worse, she has been well-trained as a war leader—but she's a kid." Rand scratched his head, deep in thought. "I never would have considered Mari. Then you can't always believe my dad's tales. King Erik didn't meddle that much outside Widdershins."

Lealor sat up. "I'll make you one of your famous *deals*. I won't harass you about your palace responsibilities, and you'll sponsor Mari's military leadership to Seren. Maybe that will give her something to do besides making Sidhe mating contracts. When Mother gets home, she is going to hear about Seren's behavior."

"Deal," agreed Rand, pulling his wife back under the covers.

What was he missing? This seemed too easy.

CHAPTER SEVENTEEN

Rand opened the door to his father's study, and paused to take in all the bookcases. Free wall space was nonexistent. Maybe reading became your life when you got older, he thought. Then Rand remembered Argen, who managed a library to hide his collection. Even the dragons were readers.

"Well, are you in or out, Unking?"

Rand closed the door behind him. "That's unfair, Dad. You've already agreed Lealor is a better ruler. If you want to participate, why don't you spend some time with Drak?"

"I'm afraid to. Look how you turned out."

"I didn't come here for insults." Rand growled, his bear aura partly visible. He restrained himself from shifting to ursine shape as a courtesy to his father. "You told Lealor that Mari was a warrior. Care to explain?"

Rand's father shrugged. "Dragon hearsay. Before that world was called Eyre, Mari's father was king. Reportedly goblins, brownies and fairies lived with the leprechauns. A goblin killed Mari's father. I've forgotten why. After she avenged her father, no goblins were left alive, and the brownies had moved deep in the forest. No one mentions what happened to the fairies. The rumor is that guilt is one reason Mari let the Sidhe relocate to Eyre."

"That's hard to believe. I've met Mari. She claims to be an empath."

"A leprechaun empath?" Rand's father, King Erik, looked doubtful and changed the subject. "Which dragon is in charge out in space now that Flame is hurt?"

"Berdularion showed up in full dragon form to take charge."

"There now. Ask him," the old, retired king retorted. "That means Berdu is no longer running loose on Widdershins. Think about it. Berdu is not what he seems. He eats like a messy dragon. His pronouncements never match up with that shy-scared act. Both Berdu and Mari are not what they seem. Berdularion can set you straight on Mari."

Rand tried to spend some social time with his father, but the grudge Erik held over Rand's not wanting to be king after him was too large an obstacle. Rand fled back to Lealor.

"That was quick," Lealor remarked as Rand entered their quarters.

"I feel as if I'm chasing my tail."

"Oh?" Lealor moved so she was behind him. "I don't see any."

"Don't be a pain in the posterior. I must return to that dust bowl in space and interview Berdularion to confirm my father's story. Then I'm off to Eyre. Maybe the Shadowlord will be at space headquarters and will accompany me.

"Speaking of the Shadowlord, he thinks you can observe the changes in me and cast the same spell, eliminating Arthurian's bargain with Seren when we need to convert someone to operate in the void without a space-suit."

"I never scanned you before Arthurian changed you," protested Lealor. "How would I know what has been modified?"

"Wait right here. I'll be back with two cousins. One a weren, and the other a standard human."

True to his word, Rand returned shortly with two young men in tow.

Lealor scanned all three. A green glow surrounded each man as she did her scan. The two cousins escaped as soon as she finished, not waiting to hear Rand's thanks.

"Well?"

"I don't know, Rand. I never had any training on being an x-ray machine."

"X-ray?"

"Earth has a machine that does what I've been trying. I can see differences. Your lungs, for example, but the biggest change is in your brain. See, now I've admitted you have one."

"Lealor, cut the comedy! This is serious."

"I know, but I'm afraid to try a spell. Bring me the next poor person before Arthurian changes him. Then perhaps I can get a better handle on things."

Rand sighed.

"Good grief, I'll be supporting Arthurian's population policy. I could sure use Mother's help on both subjects." Lealor looked chagrined.

Disappointed, Rand prepared to return to the gate at Fialla's cottage. He had noted details of places along the way and was prepared to test his new teleportation ability.

* * * *

O'Roark scowled down at Killeen. He had listened to her oration on why she was prepared to join his training group. "You can't use that sword on anybody—that's rule one. This is a rough group and they won't treat any female kindly, let alone a young girl. I hope Fialla is right, and you can take care of yourself in hand-to-hand combat. Rule two—don't break any weren's bones. The last rule—come to me for help before you get in over your head."

Killeen gave O'Roark an impish little smile, turned and marched into the saloon where her future classmates were relaxing with liquid refreshment after their meal.

Mort, both the biggest and nastiest, thought of himself as the true leader of the group. He rose to his feet and came around the table. "Come here, little girly, you can sit on Uncle Mort's lap while you eat." He reached for Killeen and found himself face down on the floor.

Killeen marched over his body as if it were a rug.

Mort snarled, and half upright, grabbed for Killeen. He ended up sideways against the wall. Several of his buddies started out of their chairs.

"Gentlemen! This is my aide, Killeen," announced O'Roark from the doorway.

There was a crash and a large brown dragon's head poked through the wall.

O'Roark sighed. "Rule four, Killeen. Your pets may not eat the troops."

"Gentlemen," announced Killeen. "Empty that swill in your cups on the floor." As the men complied, she conjured good Irish whiskey per Rory's training. "A toast to the Sergeant-Major."

The next morning, the bleary-eyed weren rose, moaning over their headaches, hearing shrieks of joy as Killeen cavorted with the dragon, Sparrow, in the river. By the time they marched out, she was dressed and waiting with a grin on her face.

Mort pointed at the barges loaded with the sawmill. "The stupid Irishman still hasn't figured out the river's running the wrong way."

O'Roark strutted down to the barge and started uncoiling a large rope. "Four of you will each grab hold one of these ropes and start pulling the barge toward Riverside.

"Killeen, there is a rope on the other side of the barge. Will you and Sparrow take the end over to the other side of the river, please?

"Mort, take two of your buddies and join Killeen on the other side. The good news is that where the river is wide, you won't have to do much. Please try to work hard enough to please Killeen. Medical treatment for injured weren is nonexistent."

Growling like the beasts of burden they were, the weren uncoiled the ropes and started trudging toward Riverside, inventing new swear words as names for O'Roark and his aide.

For his part, O'Roark was riding a horse, singing songs about the Erie Canal. Killeen joined him in a duet after she quickly learned the words.

* * * *

Seren stood behind his brother's chair, jabbing his finger on the diagram on the table. "See, this is the first place to put a barrier to stop anyone. The dead world ties in well defensively with the asteroid belt. Then things fall apart. Neither the Shadowlord nor the dragons have been able to move much to extend the existing line. It's a skirmish line at best. There is no depth. I need space mines."

"Lots of luck," replied Argen. "All mines are becoming politically incorrect because of the problems with clearing them. Earth is only doing orbital missions, and you want to mine space? Nobody's working on inventing space mines."

"Get old sea mines then. We'll try to cable them together and rig manual triggers if they won't work in space. I want land mines, too. How are you doing on getting staff for the university?"

Argen groaned. "I've got everyone coming to a meeting at the warehouse next to our old house on Earth. The problem is, the only civil engineer that fits your requirements is married and has children. The others are all single."

"Start him working on Earth with photographs. An underground bunker design using the fault crevices is as important as mines."

"You want more than I can do by myself," protested Argen. "Why don't you come to Earth with me and help? You could explain what you want in bunker design better than I can. I don't suppose you want to forget this list of other weapons to try out in space?"

"Of course not," Seren snarled in disgust. "I have to try everything. Only the mortars work the same so far." Seren tugged his ear as if that would change what he was hearing. Argen hadn't a clue how frustrated Seren was, trying to make weapons function in space. "All right, I'll join you. I can't do anything here now anyway."

"Good. You can attend the meeting with the academics and help size them up. I got a tremendous response by offering assumption of all their loans if they showed up at the meeting with no other commitments."

"Where are you getting all the money for this stupid agreement and buying weapons, too?" Seren asked.

"Most comes from investing in Earth's financial markets. If I get into trouble I look ahead in the future to know what the next day will be like. I don't do that very often. It takes the fun out the game."

Seren groaned, wishing he had never asked.

"Also, I've a got a good supply of jewels from our worlds to sell. The Sidhe are real finicky about what they want in jewels. Try getting gold off a world with both dragons and leprechauns looking over your shoulder. Every time I tried, Rory showed up complaining how poor he was."

* * * *

On entering Arthurian's throne room, Mari was surprised to find both Rand and the Shadowlord present. She knew there was trouble because a throne stood waiting for her next to Arthurian. This had never happened before. He had always practiced one-upmanship by putting her chair lower than his throne.

"What's this summons for?" Mari sat.

"Have you heard about the space battle where Flame and Miklos got hurt?" Rand inquired.

"Yes. Berdularion arrived with a dragon wing and Sidhe riders." Mari looked at Arthurian for an explanation of where the riders came from.

Rand continued, "Seren isn't happy. It's true Berdularion saved Flame and Miklos, but the wing was destroyed. Both Flame and Miklos are on other worlds being treated for their injuries. I don't think Miklos will return to battle."

"Where did the wing come from?" There, thought Mari, so much for being discreet. *Answer that, Arthurian, you old fraud. No male Sidhe, indeed.* She knew he heard her thoughts.

Rand and the Shadowlord heard her demand also. Ignoring Arthurian, Rand continued. "They were hidden on Widdershins. No one but Miklos and Berdularion knew they existed."

"Why am I here?" Mari stood as if she planned to leave immediately.

"Killeen is on Widdershins taking O'Roark's training. She intends to replace Miklos," added Rand.

"She's a kid," protested Mari. Then light dawned. "Oh no you don't. I'm not taking Miklos' place. I'm an empath."

"Not a very good one, or you'd have figured out this mission earlier," Arthurian said with a smirk. "What you are is a warrior, and a good one. You only have to do the job until Killeen is old enough. I agree with Rand. Miklos is not coming back." He leaned forward, projecting an air of confidence.

"I'll resort to bribery. You do this task and not only are we even, I'll leave your world when you find a suitable replacement," Arthurian continued.

"I suppose you're running Eyre while I'm gone?" Mari thought it was really a good deal to be rid of the Sidhe. "Killeen isn't going to like this."

"Seren will bring Killeen around. Right now Berdularion is in command. We need you there to lead the weren. Seren keeps me running errands," Rand explained.

"Which is what you prefer." Mari frowned. "You never accept responsibility."

"You and my father would get along well." Rand's bear aura formed around him. a sign he wasn't happy with the criticism. "I'm good at what I do, and smart enough to know my limitations."

"Does all this blather mean you've accepted?" the Shadowlord demanded, startling Mari. As usual, he had stood back from the others, watching and remembering everything.

"Yes, but I decide when Killeen's ready to take my place—no one else," insisted Mari. She looked hard at Arthurian. "I thought you hated Miklos and Killeen."

"Killeen is the Sidhe's future, even if she is female. The same as Flame is part of the dragons' future. Which is why his father sacrificed the dragon wing," Arthurian said. "Rand, see me before you leave the palace. Mari, stay a while."

Recognizing dismissal, the Shadowlord dissolved into a million silvery sparkles. Rand closed the door softly on the way out.

"I'm not airing my dirty linen for your enjoyment, but I didn't know about the Sidhe on Widdershins," Arthurian said. "I know how Seren feels. They're all dead now—for what? Killeen becomes even more important. That's why I offered the bribe. To survive out there in the void, you need dragon shape. Close your eyes and open the channels to your mind. This spell will allow you to change to dragon form anytime. In that shape you're as invincible as I can make you." He could see Mari was preparing to refuse. "In addition, you can breathe better in the void with the dragon shape."

Mari scowled, but nodded her agreement.

Later Arthurian greeted Rand by saying, "I'm surprised you gave away the leadership of your weren to Mari so easily. No wonder you drive your father crazy."

"It isn't important that I lead the weren. What's important is that they be led well. I'm good at making things happen, a catalyst. That's how Seren uses me. In between I function well as a gofer. I hope you didn't call me back here for 'the duties of command' lecture."

"No. I gave Mari a spell that will allow her to shapeshift into a dragon. I have a spell for you that will allow your race to add the dragon form to the shapes you use now. It is important that your weren greet Mari as dragons. The result will change the future."

Rand found himself back on the dead world with Berdularion. He had a tremendous headache that only got better when he taught his subjects the spell for dragon shape. Bright Ones in a bucket, Arthurian must have laid a compulsion on him.

CHAPTER EIGHTEEN

Observing the grin on his brother's face, Seren frowned. "Why are you so happy?" He was content to be back on Earth although his return was temporary.

"You can't believe how far the United States has come in developing space vehicles. First there was a one-manned orbiter, then a two-seater. Now they're working on three-man crew ships."

Seren nodded. "When I left Earth the last time, mankind was sending small satellites into orbit. Besides pride, why the grin?"

Argen strutted across the room. "I bought four shells for obsolete orbiters, two single-man and two double-man ships. They had already been paid for once, so I got a bargain. The fabricators think I'm going to use them under water, because I didn't want the instrumentation or a heat shield."

"Could they handle the design for an external oxygen booster tank?"

"No problem. I emphasized the orbiters must have both a vacuum and undersea rating." Argen pouted. "The government had some finished models, but they wouldn't sell to me—no trust. Probably wind up as museum mockups."

Seren laughed. "After the fuss over the obsolete submarines disappearing, I'm surprised you're not in jail. Did the government know about buying the frames?"

"Probably, but there are no internals for them to worry about. How did you make out on getting space mines designed?"

"As you predicted. The subject is politically incorrect. Actually, I did get to talk to the head engineer. The design problem is how to trigger them. The current proximity sensors are unreliable. We're back to buying all the existing mines we can. I'll stop on Widdershins and talk to O'Roark about getting some help on rigging firing-nets." He pushed the refrigerator door shut with his elbow, having both hands full of goodies.

"When do we talk to your university professor candidates? I need to get started on the underground design."

"That's who we're waiting for," replied Argen. "He and his family should be here shortly."

"Family? Why are they coming here?"

"They're going to be staying here overnight," answered Argen.

"Here? This is my house." Seren exploded in anger.

"Cool it, brother. I didn't have any other secure family quarters. You and I can stay with the other candidates over at the bachelor quarters we built in the warehouse."

Seren wasn't happy. He really needed the civil engineer—but this was too much. "You'd better have an Andronan chair there, or start conjuring one PDQ."

A knock at the door produced Debbie and the houseguests. "This is Mr. and Mrs. John Knoxx with the children, Andy and Sally."

"Welcome to my house, John and...." started Seren with hand outstretched.

"Jack," said the man, shaking hands. "Call me Jack."

"Nell," added the woman, offering her hand. "Thank you for the hospitality of opening your house for our use."

"Gentlemen, you need to get over to the warehouse for the meeting," interrupted Debbie as she left.

"My, she looks good in that mini skirt. Jack, you keep your mind on business," Nell instructed.

Argen grinned as the three men hurried out the door.

* * * *

On Widdershins after a rough piece of river where even Sparrow had pulled on ropes by grabbing them in his mouth, O'Roark pushed his way across. "Mort, do you and your squad want to switch sides of the river for relief?"

"No! We're staying with Killeen. What you asking me for? She's in charge," snarled Mort in reply. He walked away in obvious disgust.

"Okay. How did you pull that off?" O'Roark asked Killeen.

"I have one of Cibby's provider bags. It predates Seren's refrigerator, and I reward good performance." Killeen grinned.

"Ah, through the stomach," observed O'Roark with a smile. "The legend begins." As O'Roark went back across the river, the smile changed to a chuckle.

* * * *

On Earth, Argen banged on the speaker's podium for quiet. "You were invited here because each of you has been a college professor who got fired and blackballed for being honest. The agreement was that attendance alone guaranteed payment of all outstanding debts. Please review the folders you have. If the financial statements are not correct, get with Debbie for revision." He extended his hand in Debbie's direction.

The audience all clapped. Argen frowned. His reading of the audience registered more appreciation for Debbie's figure than the debt reduction. "I have an offer for you to consider: a full professorship position at a university where you will have some research assignments and enough time for your own investigative interests. There are two major catches. First, your students will not have any prerequisite courses. You and the rest of the staff will have to get together and figure who teaches those subjects. You will be able to tap outstanding students for research and future teaching assignments.

"Second, the assignment is not on Earth. The university is on the world of Realm and you will never return here." Argen paused to allow the message to sink in. He read skepticism and disbelief. "I should add that not all your students will be human. For example—"

Rory, complete with backpack, appeared on the stage. A small pick-axe was in one hand. "Blast ye, Argen, I'd found a good vein. Slavery, that's what dealing with you wizards is. What'd you want now?"

The force of the audience's stares penetrated Rory's senses. He turned to face the audience and vanished.

"If you don't want this kind of challenge in your life, you can turn down this chance of a lifetime. You'll have twenty-four hours to decide. My brother Seren, Keeper Vigan and I will be available to answer questions."

Both Seren and Vigan had stood at the mention of their names.

Seren leaned over and told Jack, "Because of your family, the rules are different for you. I'll explain in a few minutes."

Argen continued. "There are interview rooms outside along the hall. Sign up on the sheet posted on the door. There are individual guest rooms for tonight. Meals and snacks will be served in the cafeteria. Feel free to consult or compare answers among yourselves. Debbie will remain here to assist with details." Argen left the stage.

The room was abuzz with the voices of men who were trying to reconcile what their eyes had seen with their scientific knowledge.

* * * *

As Jack entered one of the conference rooms, Seren rose to greet him. "Because of the children, they and your wife would be able to return to Earth several times a year," Seren started. "I need your expertise so badly; I am willing to set you up as a consultant here while the family decides."

"What if we chose not to go?"

"First, the debt elimination agreement is still good. I would ask you to find a protégée who would go to Realm. I could only fund your consultant business for the period for which I need your design work."

"Tell me about the work," Jack urged.

Seren pulled some large photographs from an oversized envelope. "I want to build rooms and passageways in the fissures you see here. By the way, this is not Realm. The clear ceilings have to be seventy-five feet above the floor."

Jack was puzzled. "Isn't there danger that the fissures will try to close?

"Not so far. We've had strain gages on the edges. Nothing. There's no moon, seas or molten core on this world. The center seems to be filled with a fuel gas.

"That's part of the problem. The ceiling and floor will have to be designed to stop any closure attempts. I must have the clear space, so I envisioned pre-stressed concrete beams like engineers are starting to use on bridges. I'm going to fill the remainder of the fissure with rock and gravel. I want the areas to be airtight and able to withstand a nuclear bomb."

Jack shook his head. "You're right. This floor can't be the standard CRSI slab on the ground, but you've given me no basis for design."

"Guess, and write the design like a code using the stated safety factors. If we ever have a failure, we'll change the code. I thought you might get some data from Earth's tectonic shifts and develop forces as a starting point, although it's not the same."

Jack laughed. "No real consulting group would touch this. What liabilities would I have?"

"If you come to Realm, you might be out there someday. If you never leave Earth—none. You have the reputation of being one of the best concrete slab designers prior to your arguing that the existing building code slab design was unsafe. I need structures now, and I'm willing to trust your instincts."

"The job is crazy, but better than what I'm doing now—nothing. I'll talk it over with my wife. She's going to want to know all about Realm where we'll live. She'd be great for teaching some of those prerequisite courses."

Seren smiled. "Tell her Realm is both rustic and magical. The inside of the house you're staying in is very similar to what she'd be living in except without electricity. The strange thing is that I have electricity on the dead world because of the fuel gas. My brother had some kind of turbo-generator installed. If you're into solar power, you could have electricity on Realm."

"Would you visit your own house about nine tonight to answer Nell's questions? If we're lucky, the kids will be asleep."

"Sure. If Argen's not tied up with candidates, I'll bring him along."

* * * *

"How many are going to accept?" asked Seren.

"Every candidate has chosen to join my team," Argen announced as he paraded across the room. "What about your civil engineer?"

* * * *

Seren was torn between amusement and anger. The need and idea to reopen the university had been his. Now his brother claimed the cadre. "He's going to remain on Earth for a while. I need you to set him up in the consulting business. His wife's a teacher, and she wants to finish the semester. She also wants a tour of Realm during the first student holiday."

"Debbie can set up his business. She gets away with more and manages quicker than I can."

"If she's dealing with men, I can see why. Which relative was it that claimed men could see better than they think?"

"One of Mother's smart old aunts, I guess. Debbie handles women equally well," Argen continued. "Then it's, 'my boss requires me to dress this way, and I'm so embarrassed. Can we do this quickly so I won't feel ashamed?'"

Seren laughed. "That works?"

"You should see the letters I get from businesswomen demanding *I* reform. I give the letters to Debbie and she puts them on the wall. That woman is so smart, she's dangerous."

"Speaking of smart, dangerous women, you'd better get Realmgate cleaned up before Mother returns."

Argen sniffed with disdain. "Thanks to Berdularion that problem is solved."

"Berdularion?"

"Yes. He's modified the gate at the dead world to take shipments of your requests directly without losing the portal's portability. He has much more understanding of my problems than Flame."

"I've talked to King Caeryl. He's sending Master Sergeant Henning with their fledging army to rebuild Realm's gate and do any necessary town maintenance. It seems Sergeant Major O'Roark wants to use Realmgate as winter quarters for both Caeryl's and the weren armies. Did you know about that?"

"No. I've got a message from Rand about visiting O'Roark and picking up Killeen. Rand claims that Mari is coming to the dead world to take Miklos' place and instructs me to be back there with Killeen before Mari arrives. Rand also dropped the news that Killeen thinks that's her position."

Now it was Argen's turn to laugh. "Some army you command. Two sergeants and two kings are running it against an enemy you can't find."

Seren growled at Argen, sounding more like Rand's bear form. "You missed the damaged Bright One calling himself the Shadowlord. The army's developing fine. I need to solve the problem that ninety percent of the troops can't breathe in space. Do you have my list of research projects for *your* professors?"

"Yes. Yes, of course. Did I mention that King Caeryl is also sending a group of his best students, several of his country's outstanding teachers and both Prince Leon and his new wife to Realmgate?"

"Makes sense. Prince Leon is the ranking officer in his army. Gets the newlyweds out of sight and provides an opportunity for higher education," Seren replied with a nod of approval.

Argen paused in thought and then asked, "Do you think Andronan is too old to run the university?"

"Andronan's probably forgotten more about educational leadership than either of us knows. Besides he has the keepers to help. Luck, Brother. I'm off to Widdershins and Sergeant Major O'Roark." Seren rose and left the room on his way to the gate.

* * * *

"Sergeant, that's an unusual group of buildings with each having an open side," Seren observed. "I can see why you want to winter at the university."

"The reverse roof canopy on that side helps keep sun and rain out. The floor is the major problem. I need a stonemason to train others and make floors."

"Did you ask Fialla to find a mason?" Seeing the look on O'Roark's face, Seren continued. "Forgot all about her, didn't you? No wonder I caught a chill coming through her gate. Take a couple days off and mend your fences. I'll carry on here with Killeen's help."

"You've got to take Killeen with you when you leave," O'Roark blurted, his face red with embarrassment.

"Why?"

"She's too good. Whatever side has her wins every time I set up any problem. The weren fight over her being on their team. I made her my aide, but that isn't good enough. She doesn't have the experience to be an instructor and she's lethal in hand-to-hand combat. Lord knows what she could do if she applied magic. Please…"

Seren laughed at the overwrought sergeant. "Relax. Rand insists I bring Killeen with me to the dead world. It seems Rand has induced Mari to take Miklos' place."

"Oh brother. Did Rand tell you Killeen thinks she's taking her father's place?"

"Yes, he included that tidbit. Don't worry. I'll handle it. Beat it. Get your overnight kit and visit Fialla." Seren chuckled, watching the sergeant scurry away. O'Roark probably wanted to be a fly on the wall when Seren talked to Killeen, but he thought the meeting with Fialla would be equally entertaining.

Seren sat in O'Roark's headquarters. One thing about the open building, there wasn't any privacy. He noticed a rolled tarp near the ceiling. Maybe they dropped that for the colder nights or in event of rain.

He called out to a passing recruit. "Could you tell Killeen I want to see her?"

"Sir, Yes Sir," was accompanied by a snappy salute.

Seren returned the salute. The recruit made an about face and double-timed away. Seren nodded. O'Roark hadn't lost his touch. Seren watched the activity. Most of the troops were building more open-faced barracks. A constant trail of men carried trees to the sawmill.

* * * *

His observations were shattered by, "Cadet Killeen reporting as ordered."

Seren almost jumped out of his chair. He hadn't heard her approach. He raised his eyebrows at her armor and the sword. "Rest, Cadet. Please take a seat. Sergeant Major O'Roark will be gone for a couple of days. He tells me you're his aide, so your job will be to keep me out of trouble as we run things."

Killeen plopped on a stool and frowned. "We have formation morning and dusk. That should be easy. All you have to do is conjure up an impressive uniform. The work schedule is made up for the next week, and the cadet officers can handle that. Sergeant Major O'Roark usually manufactures a crisis or a war game." She peered at Seren.

"I have my uniform. I suppose you want me to wear my paratrooper boots?"

Killeen nodded in agreement.

Seren continued, "We'll have a voluntary morning run instead of the war game." He paused with a frown of concentration. "You will need to come with me when I leave for the dead world. Rand has told me you expect to take your father's place, which is a good idea, but you need to rejoin O'Roark when the troops move to the university."

Killeen opened her mouth, but closed it quickly, seeing Seren's blocking hand.

"Your future troops can't be better educated than their leader. This is the time in your life that education is least painful. One reason O'Roark wants everyone in school is to discover his soldiers' hidden talents. That's also true for you. Follow up any subject areas that interest you."

Killeen frowned, but nodded silently.

"Mari, Queen of Eyre, is going to fill in for you in space. I want you to be there when she arrives. I'll put you out in front of the weren and appoint you her aide. O'Roark will have to find someone else."

"Mort," Killeen blurted. "He's like O'Roark. Mort will never be happy as an officer, but he gets things done.

"I don't want to go to school. You don't need Mari. I'm ready now," Killeen insisted.

Seren shook his head. "No, you're not. There's more to winning the support of your troops then battle logic and Cibby's provender bag. So there's no question. I'm ordering you to attend the university, and I expect outstanding performance."

Seren watched as Killeen jumped to her feet. First anger flushed her face, but he watched her get control. Resentment remained.

"Sir, yes sir," Killeen replied, saluting. Not waiting for the return salute, she did an about face and marched away.

CHAPTER NINETEEN

The next morning, only a barefoot Killeen and four cadets showed up for the morning run. Seren noticed she still had her armor and sword. He set an easy pace with stretching exercises at the midpoint.

After breakfast Seren quizzed Killeen about the four cadets and the company commanders.

"Zack isn't very bright. The other three runners are pretty sharp," Killeen reported.

"How do they compare to the existing cadet captains?"

"Jason is the best of the existing cadet officers. There isn't any difference between the other three commanders and the cadets who ran."

"Replace the cadet captains with the cadets who ran. Make sure Zack replaces Jason," Seren ordered.

The next day as dawn arrived, fifteen cadets joined Killeen for the morning run with Seren. The group included the demoted company commanders. Seren set a faster pace and added basic PT exercises at the midpoint. He carefully watched Jason.

"What are we teaching the cadets except to brown-nose the leader?" Killeen asked when she joined Seren after breakfast.

Seren laughed. "Anticipation of command prerequisites is not a bad skill. Put Jason back as company commander and move Zack to adjutant."

"Adjutant? What is that?"

"In the cadet corps, nothing. In the regular army, the adjutant handles personnel assignments and paperwork. Read the manual. The adjutant issues the call for review. Zack is going to surprise you. He reads other people's abilities well. A good independent assessment of talent is always valuable. He sees people differently from the three of us."

"You mean me, the sergeant major and yourself?"

"Correct. Zack's the one that persuaded the other three cadets to join us on the run."

Killeen's face battled between a frown and bewilderment. "How did you figure that out?"

"I cheated. I had a long talk with Mort. You made a good choice there, but we can't call him an aide. Issue written orders promoting Mort to regular army corporal. Add the instructions that cadets will give him the same military respect as the sergeant major. He becomes part of the training cadre. Also issue liberty after lunch to all cadets who participated in the morning run. You and Mort push the non-runners hard this afternoon."

The following morning the majority of the corps showed up for the morning run. Seren organized them into their normal companies. Jason's company had a hundred percent participation. Seren put the old company commander in charge of the unit with the lowest number of runners and had the present leader run along beside him. At the midpoint, Seren introduced the full PT regimen. On the way back he brought the run down to double time so they entered the base lined up in ranks.

Returning from breakfast, Seren found O'Roark going through boxes of army manuals. "What are you looking for?"

"The manual on conducting a military marriage." Noticing Seren's puzzled look, O'Roark added, "I sort of got engaged."

"Sort of? Is that anything like sort of pregnant?"

Out of nowhere, Killeen chimed in, "O'Roark did take a shower with a girl." Her long-term grievance had been rectified.

O'Roark shook his head with a growl at both of them. He grabbed a book and shook in the air. "Here it is. You can marry me and Fialla at the gate before you and Killeen leave."

"No!" Killeen interrupted. "You must do the ceremony here, before your troops. Fialla has friends in Riverville that must be invited. I'll send Mort down with the barge to help with transportation. We need a horse corral, bleachers, a stage, and we must start food preparations today. This is your chance to make the pass in review practice meaningful. I wonder if Riverville has a band...."

Seren agreed. "She's right. Not that I'm a ship's captain to do marriages. I'll have to get word to Lealor."

"I've already done that. Fialla is in the loop, too," Killeen said.

"Oh? How did you accomplish that?" Seren didn't try to hide his surprise.

"You forget I'm a Sidhe." With disgust on her face, Killeen marched away to arrange the next day's wedding.

"See what I mean?" O'Roark said. "She takes over. Where's her 'Sir, Yes Sir' or any signs of military respect? That's why you've got to take her with you."

"Relax," Seren commanded. "I don't want to plan a wedding for tomorrow yet. She's working with both Lealor and Fialla—that's higher authority. Military courtesy is partly to teach command presence and Killeen's got that. What's with the armor and sword?"

"Beats me," O'Roark snarled. "That's the way she showed up in the gate, returning from Achaea. I can understand the armor. Miklos would be unhurt if he'd been wearing any. But the sword...." O'Roark threw up his hands in disgust.

"Queen Mother Branwyn I'll bet," Seren muttered. "I don't know enough about their traditions to stick my nose in. Speaking of not knowing, are you sure I'm authorized to perform this marriage?"

"Read it and weep," O'Roark said, throwing the book at Seren. "Remember, you're the one who sent me to Fialla to 'mend my fences.'"

"I didn't say anything about getting fenced in," Seren protested. He held up his hand to stop O'Roark's retort. "Should we cancel the morning run?"

"No. Now that's started, it'll be a required activity. I've been running on the side getting ready to institute the program anyway."

"What about your knees?" Seren had noticed the change in O'Roark's walk.

"Fialla and Lealor fixed them." O'Roark's eyes got a faraway look as he remembered jumping. "I've never loved a woman enough to get married." He smiled ruefully. "To think I picked a real witch."

Seren cracked up. When he could stop laughing, he warned O'Roark. "Don't think ideas like that, or you'll end up a toad."

"That's nothing new. I kept waiting for Killeen to turn me into one, every time I made her mad," O'Roark muttered.

"One more thing. I need an explosives expert. I want to develop firing nets on the mine fields I'm installing."

O'Roark thought for a minute. "How would a legless man do in space? I know an explosive genius that isn't doing well as a disabled veteran." Reading Seren's scowl, he quickly added, "Don't worry. He got that way cleaning up someone else's mess."

"I suppose that's another Debbie procurement project? We should invite Argen to your wedding, but if I know him, he won't get anywhere near a marriage ceremony. I suppose we better find our dress blues."

* * * *

When the troops started their morning run, Killeen, Mort, the cooks and the master carpenters were conspicuous by their absence. Seren wondered what they were making now. The bleachers, corral and combination reviewing stand-marriage platform complete with wedding bower covered in white roses stood waiting. Seren was almost sure he had never seen eight-inch roses before. The whole area smelled of rose petals.

Seren kept the pace reasonable and shortened the PT at the middle stop. Rather than run back, he held the troops to double time. The obscene marching chants familiar to all armies filled the air. Seren chuckled as most were directed at the sergeant major.

As the army reached the parade ground, Seren peeled away to where Killeen stood, leaving the troops to the tender mercies of O'Roark.

She pointed to the sky where two dragons with riders soared. "Who's the girl on Sparrow with Rand? I didn't give anyone but Rand permission to ride Sparrow."

Gazing at the sky, Seren recognized Fialla and Lealor riding Fafleen. That must be Drak with Rand on Sparrow, thought Seren. Two more dragons popped into view. Fafnoddle and Ebony had also arrived. "That's not a girl. It's Rand's son Drak," he told Killeen.

Flame's still too injured to come and Berdularion won't leave his command. He doesn't see what the fuss over a witch marrying a human is anyway, Fafleen announced, not even waiting to land.

"Where's First Egg and Old Fafnir?" Seren knew the dragons could hear him, and if they wanted to, they could read his mind.

Father sleeps most of the time and First Egg is hiding from Ebony. He stole Rory's gold and disappeared. He claims he doesn't have to study *The Dragon Chronicles* anymore. Ebony disagrees, Fafnoddle reported as he landed.

As Seren went to greet Fafnoddle, he saw Killeen already hugging Fialla. He overheard Fialla's whisper.

"Why did you think Drak was a girl?"

"Look how Drak's dressed. You could have had a flower girl."

"Hush dear, that's Lealor's son, too. You've done so well. Don't spoil things."

Seren breathed a sigh of relief. Thank goodness for Fialla. He glanced at the mournful Sparrow. Killeen must have blistered him on some private channel, he thought. Seren raised his head to see Fafnoddle's amusement. Trust him to pick up all the undercurrents. Seren observed Ebony had now joined the other females.

Fafnoddle dropped his head to the ground so Seren could scratch an irritating ridge itch.

Seren felt as good scratching as Faf did receiving. It brought back fond memories. "I'm surprised Rory isn't throwing a fit."

"Oh, he's mad all right. Embarrassed, too. First Egg is a very young dragon to get the best of a leprechaun."

Seren hid his smile at the faint, but unmistakable, parental pride in his son that Faf couldn't hide.

Seren noticed Zack standing near and motioned him over. "Show Faf where the dragons will be watching. See if you can roust up a veggie snack for him." To his dragon friend Seren explained, "I have to go get cleaned up and dressed, one of the things you never have to bother with."

* * * *

Seren stood underneath the arch of roses, thankful that he didn't have any allergies. It dawned on him that he hadn't memorized what to say to marry Fialla and O'Roark. The dragons bugled a harmonious version of the wedding march as Killeen materialized into Seren's hands a white leather-bound book containing the army order of service for a wedding. "That kid thinks of everything," he muttered inaudibly to himself as Fialla and O'Roark reached their place before him. After Seren's momentary panic left him, the rest of the service went quickly.

Standing in the receiving line, Seren was pleased with the ceremony. Riverview had produced a band that could play a march. He had nightmares of a band playing a waltz, or worse, a polka, while the troops passed in review. The army had looked good. He had received many compliments on the crossed sword line the newlyweds had passed through. Now the smell of the reception goodies was driving him to distraction. Especially since he had skipped breakfast. Guests were still crowded around Fialla and O'Roark, but he was free.

On the way to the reception line, the first catastrophe took place. Seren heard Killeen say, "I'm so sorry. I tripped." Seren pushed his way forward to see Drak, his white velvet suit covered with red wine spreading rapidly, probably with magical help. Seren beckoned to Zack. "Take Drak and put a uniform on him."

"Oh my, it's going to be one of those courtships," said Fialla on her way to console Killeen.

Puzzled, Seren turned and saw that Zack had already returned.

"I found a good fit. Was he happy to be out of that outfit! He's looking for a coat. Claims dragon flight is cold," reported Zack.

Seren had only started sampling the fare when he heard the clash of swords. O'Roark beat him outside. There, they found Killeen standing over a prostrate Drak with her sword at his throat.

"Yield!" Killeen demanded.

"Cadet! Attenthut!" ordered O'Roark.

Rand rushed to his son and picked him up. He then marched Drak by the scruff of the neck in the direction of the dragons. "That's it. We're going home. Beaten by a girl."

"I don't see why you're upset. She used a trick I hadn't seen before," floated back.

"Pots and pans," O'Roark ordered a sullen Killeen.

Fialla had appeared at O'Roark's elbow. "Come, dear, that's enough. Let's return to our guests." O'Roark allowed himself to be led back inside.

Seren stood admiring the new hall the troops had built for the reception. He nearly jumped out of his skin when Lealor spoke.

"That went well."

"What are you talking about? They were sword fighting at a wedding."

Lealor giggled. "I know. Drak lost. Now Rand will take over his weapons training and spend more time with Drak. All because he lost to a girl." She sighed. "Actually, Drak is quite good. I have a hard time finding weapon masters he can't beat. Yes, Rand will be spending more time at home."

Fialla had joined them. "Are you foreseeing the same thing I am?" she asked Lealor.

"I think so," answered Lealor. "I've loved that girl since we met at your cottage, so I'm not unhappy. Their whole life will be a rocky road."

Seren shuddered. He hoped these two female plotters were wrong. Killeen and Drak were kids, for Bright One's sake. He wondered if the women could foresee every person's future spouse. Where were they when he was in love with Megan? He wouldn't have listened anyway—still wouldn't. He'd get Killeen and escape early in the morning.

CHAPTER TWENTY

Killeen was so exhausted she didn't even bother to undress or remove her sword. She fell into bed, glanced at her poor hands, and moaned. Her sword hand calluses had dissolved. The other cadets doing pots and pans had tried to do the bulk of the work, but she insisted on doing her fair share. She dozed off, dreaming of a mountain of pots and pans with Drak on top challenging her to a rematch.

Her body jerked as Seren banged on the door and stuck his head in.

"Good! You're dressed. Grab your kit and meet me at the corral. Time's awasting."

Killeen groaned and pulled a pillow over her head to hide from the early sun's rays streaming through her window. What had pulled his chain to make him want to leave so early?

Knowing the pillow wasn't going to help, she staggered to her feet, shouldered her duffel bag and with determination, dragged her body out the door.

* * * *

"Don't bother with a saddle. We both know how to ride bareback," Seren instructed.

Killeen swung onto her mount, thinking about a sore posterior. Oh no, he wasn't going to the ford. They were going to swim the river. Now her boots would be soaked. The cold water finished waking her. On the other side she urged her mount into a gallop to catch up.

Reaching Fialla's cottage, they put the horses in the corral and started for the gate without cooling the animals. Killeen was startled to see a robed gatekeeper.

"Good morning, Vigan," Seren greeted the keeper. "Got assigned here for the wedding, did you? Good. You know where I'm going."

"Will you take care of finishing the horses?" Killeen asked.

Vigan scowled at her. "I don't do livestock. Aldon's son will be here shortly. He can take care of the horses."

Seren frowned at Killeen as if she were stupid. "You'll learn more about keepers when you're at the university." He pulled her onto the gate and turned toward Vigan. "Send us to the dead world, now!"

Killeen blinked. Light glowed dim and red. The gate lay in a hollow with some kind of cover overhead. Seren had already started up the slope, sending dust over her boots.

Coughing, she hurried to catch up. She tried speaking normally, but she couldn't, so she shrugged and switched to telepathy. *When does the sun rise?*

It's up. This is all the light you get, but there's no night. This world is stationary. If you want night, you must move to the other side. Watch your step. The gravity's one tenth of what you're used to. Walking is tricky until you learn how, replied Seren. *See that ridge to your left? That's where we're going. I made that trip in a spacesuit. Actually I had a boost. Walking in that suit exhausted me.*

* * * *

He waved a small dragon away. *That's a bottle dragon, BD for short. He carries the breathing-air bottles if you're suited up. That's one of Flame's better ideas. He collected all the undersized dragons and trained them to service spacesuits. They are also his spies.*

Spies? Whatever for? She zigged and zagged for a few steps, stopping to watch Seren walk so she could mimic his movements. *What are those buildings to the left of us?* Dust billowed behind them as they walked.

The big one on the left is the dragons' sleeping quarters. Dragons can go about twenty-four Widdershins-hours without oxygen. The sleeping quarters have oxygen-enriched air, so the dragons are always ready to go. That was another good Flame idea.

A huge dragon swooped down and landed in a cloud of dust. When Killeen stopped coughing, she welcomed him. *Berdu, you're beautiful.*

Berdularion! Seren corrected. In this form, he's king of the dragons. I see Flame's spies report to you, too, he added, facing the dragon.

Of course. I came to report. Fortunately, everything was boring. His tail wrapped around Killeen in a hug.

It won't be for long, Seren asserted. *I've got rolls of cable and thousands of mines coming. They all will have to be installed, and I don't know how much help the weren will be. The weren have to wear spacesuits and are paired up with a bottle dragon,* he explained to Killeen.

Speaking of useless, don't forget Mari, Killeen added.

Oh, yes. I understand you were in agreement on the idea to get Mari, Berdularion. My aide here made sure Rand stays more on Widdershins, Seren added.

Well, I'm here now! Rand popped into view. *I've got to teach my subjects how to shift into dragon form. Arthurian gave me a spell to help. Mari is on her way.*

Oh goodie, Killeen observed. Watching Rand move to the smaller building, she added, *I guess that is the weren quarters where Mari will be staying.*

Berdularion put a talon in front of his face, vainly trying to hide a smirk.

No. She'll have quarters with us, if we ever get there, Seren snarled.

Suddenly a dragon darted out of the building toward a boulder. A bottle dragon immediately appeared. The weren dragon waved him off, showing that he was minus his breathing apparatus. Then he turned and bolted back in to the building.

Stupid weren, going without any breathing equipment, grumbled Seren.

In an eye blink all the shapeshifter dragons appeared outside their building, dancing and tumbling in obvious joy. *Now what? Killeen, go down there and find out what's going on.*

The only being Killeen could come close to was Rand. She was apprehensive about asking him, but he waved her closer. *What's wrong?*

They can breathe without equipment in this form. One nitwit sneaked out to get something while holding his breath. When the bottle dragon showed up, it startled him into breathing. Now they're celebrating. Rand shocked her by giving her a hug.

I thought you'd be mad at me.

For what? Objecting to those silly suits Drak's mother makes him wear?

For tricking him when he thought he was invincible? For finding out he really is a good swordsman? You've brought me closer to my son. Now I have a reason for staying home which allows me to save face. Besides, I never miss a chance to hug a pretty girl.

Everyone says you're afraid of Lealor.

I am. That's why nothing goes further than a hug. Come on, let's go explain things to Seren. He looks like he ate a can of prunes.

As Rand approached Seren and Berdularion, not letting go of Killeen, he saw Mari arrive in the gate. *Mari's here.*

Killeen looked down into the crater. *She's pink.*

Berdularion chuckled, letting little sprits of magical fire escape his nostrils. *So she is.*"

* * * *

"O'Roark's hotshot explosive expert is at the gate," Seren explained to Killeen. "Will you retrieve him and bring him here to the main conference room, where we have breathing air? He's never been on Dead World before. I'll start the briefing when you get there."

"Does he have a name?"

"Rudy. Uh, he doesn't have any legs."

Killeen arched her eyebrows. Hmm, I could run, but I think I'll port. She got there in time to see the space-suited Rudy ride a strange chair up the slope. A cushion of air under the chair allowed it to move over land like a hydrocraft. It was slow.

A talon touched her arm. *Radio and limited air inside,* said the bottle dragon, giving her a helmet. *Touch the red button on the collar to use the throat mike, otherwise keep your fingers off everything else.*

Killeen pulled the helmet on as she grumbled to herself. She didn't know anything about radios. It was nice of the BD to help, but she felt stupid. Maybe Seren was right about school.

"Hi," the radio crackled, startling her. "How do you like my chair? The two extra large air cylinders on the back are interchangeable, but one keeps me moving, the other breathing. There's a whole pallet of cylinders back in the gate."

She pressed the red button on the collar. "Can you carry a spare on your lap?" There was no reply. The BD used a talon to push her finger off the button. Killeen burned with anger. The human inside the spacesuit was grinning while the BD laughed outright.

"Sure," crackled from the radio.

Killeen motioned the BD towards the portal and watched him skip down to get a cylinder.

When he returned, he put a spare cylinder in the man's lap.

Send the other cylinders to the headquarters' tunnel, she ordered the BD.

Berdu, are you in the main conference room?

Ssure, but remember Seren can hear you too. He doesn't like that name here—I don't mind.

Tough! I didn't want you appearing on top of me. She punched the red button. "Close your eyes and give me your hand," she told Rudy. As soon the glove clasped her hand she ported both of them into the conference room.

"Open your eyes. You can take off your helmet in here and I won't have to use this—this radio thing. Killeen tossed the helmet to another bottle dragon and watched the BD take the contraption off the human's head.

Seren stepped forward and took Rudy's hand. The BD had already stripped him of the removable top parts of the suit. The rest would have to be done later. "I'm Seren Koenig. You've already met my aide, Killeen. He pointed to the other humanoid. That's Rand, the S1. The large dragon is Berdularion, the S3. The small dragon is Mari, the S4. Our S2, the Shadowlord, isn't here."

"Everyone but Seren is a shapechanger, so no one is what he seems," Killeen added, ignoring Seren's scowl.

"I'm Rudy, and I change things by blowing them up—including my legs," the freckle-faced young man in the chair said.

Seren grinned. Argen had prepared Rudy well. He could tell only Killeen bothered him. How did he explain a nine-year-old? "Let's get comfortable at the front of the room for my briefing." For Rudy's benefit he explained, "The whole front wall's a gigantic screen."

Walking beside Killeen, Mari said, "You and Rudy ported here. I thought you never used magic, dear."

"Mother doesn't like me to. She claims my intellect should control the situation, but there was a time problem. This way you won't have to squat like a duck so long—dear."

Berdularion's smirk returned. Little Sidhe versus leprechaun, he thought.

No! Two women in a turf battle, Seren observed, reading Berdularion's mind. We'll have to be careful so we aren't the casualties.

CHAPTER TWENTY-ONE

"The reason the screen is black," Seren explained, "is because the camera is pointed at the void. I don't know of a way to provide a defense out there. Backing the camera up, you see the edge of the asteroid belt on the left, what we call Dead World and the few other asteroids the Shadowlord managed to relocate to our right.

"This is where I propose to build a line of defense."

"What's to keep an enemy from going by to the right—or over—or under?" Mari wrinkled her snout into her version of a dragon frown.

"Right now—nothing. The Shadowlord reports he can't move any more asteroids without help from Baloo, the baby Bright One. I don't think Mirza or Baloo's guardians would appreciate us waking him. Nor am I ready for the repercussions that always go with Baloo's escapades."

"Ssso?" Berdularion queried.

"There's plenty of unoccupied junk between us and our nearest populated world. We have rocket motors left over. Let's install them on smaller planetoids, aim the rocket motors in this direction and fire them."

Mari snorted. "That's not very scientific. We should take core samples to get the body's density, measure the diameter, together with how far the object went. Those professors you've got at the university on Realmgate ought to be able to make projections."

"You have to fire the first one blind," Killeen said. "Ever fire any rocket motors, Rudy?"

"No, but it sounds like fun." Rudy's eyes twinkled, showing his enthusiasm.

"All right, Mari, that's your assignment. Fire the first object toward the gap between the dead world and the existing asteroid belt," Seren ordered. "You might want to have the Shadowlord monitor the test. Perhaps he can adjust the path with his energy."

Seren continued, "The other thing I want to do to add depth is install space mines and firing nets. Of course, space mines don't exist, but I've got the marine model. Rudy, I need to tie the mines together with cable to make a firing web. I don't want a single mine to explode and set the net off. You'll need to design a three-dimensional installation. Berdularion and Killeen will work with you."

"You realize I have to blow up a bunch of these mines. I may need oxygen for them to explode." Rudy moved his chair closer to the screen, which now showed a pile of mines on the world's surface. "They aren't all the same. Once I get them to go off, I'll have to figure out the blast zone for each one of these."

"Berdularion, see that Rudy's test zone is out past the existing beacons. In addition to your normal patrols, I want you to start experimenting with putting cable together into nets. I don't suppose you could produce enough heat at the end of a talon to do spot welding?"

"Energy at the tip of a talon? What a novel idea," mused Berdularion. All of a sudden fire erupted from his talon, replacing the hopeful look on Seren's face with panic.

Everyone not in dragon form hit the floor, or in Rudy's case, the nearest corner. "Outside, Berdularion!" Rand screamed as he rose from the floor. Facing the dragon, he growled like the bear shape evident in the aura around him that flared because of his anger. "You overgrown kid. Try new things outside in a controlled environment."

Not at all influenced by Rand's demand, Berdularion continued. "What is spot welding?"

"Rand will teach you, as he says, outside." Seren attempted to brush off the dust from the floor.

"Rand, you have to discover which Earth weapons are effective for your shapeshifters' fighting force. I imagine Rudy and Killeen can help on that project." Seren had not given up on trying to remove the dust. He wrinkled his forehead in concentration. The dust disappeared. Seren tested the spell by bending over and rubbing his hands on the floor. He beamed as his hands remained clean.

"You might share that spell," Rand requested.

"Yes, please," added Mari. "I've been covered with grime since I arrived on this world."

Seren quickly transmitted the spell mentally. Poor Rudy remained as before until Mari blinked her eyes at him to remove the dust.

Rudy never turned a hair. He was a game player and accepted everything that happened as if it were part of a game scenario. "I don't understand. Why do we have to cable the mines together?" Rudy asked as his chair glided from the corner. "In space, I thought things floated in place."

"In general they do," Rand said. "Our experience has been that a wobble effect occurs. Sometimes it is produced if a moving body passes. It makes objects shift. We found out trying to use fabric shelters. There are a lot of small moving bodies, not only big comets."

"Science fiction writers on Earth theorized there were space currents and used sails in their stories. The currents may exist," Seren said.

"Cool." Rudy looked around. "Do you have any of that fabric left?"

"Lots of pieces," replied Rand. "Most have pin holes." He frowned. "I thought those space currents were always in connection with suns?" He added in disgust, "Which we don't have."

"Killjoy," Killeen hissed. She looked as if sail designs were whirling inside her head.

"Weekly status meetings," Seren reminded them as the group dissolved.

* * * *

"I hope you're happy," Mari grumbled to Seren a few days later as she gazed out at the dark space around Dead World. "The whole void from here to the beacons is full of sails."

"At least the dragons have learned to spot weld."

"Sssail frames. They haven't found any currents. The dragons have to give the riders a flying boost."

"You're missing a big serendipity. When I first got here, I was overwhelmed by the void. All those weren playing in it will be able to work there, also. We didn't have enough dragons to accomplish our goals, so this is a big help."

"When did recoilless rifles become weren weapons?" Mari started on a new complaint.

"When they found out they could carry one," Rand answered as he came in the door and sank into a chair.

"They don't watch their back blast. I almost lost a few scales yesterday. Why are they in my area anyway? Send them out beyond the beacons to be blown up by Rudy's mines." Mari showed her exasperation.

"We need weapon targets. Those big asteroids you're planning to move are perfect," Rand told her.

"Have them blow up the mortar rounds you've left all over the place. Don't weren know enough to use a time fuse? Now there are contact rounds all over. They're worse than Rudy's mines," Mari said.

"How are the werens' personal weapon selections coming?" Seren asked.

"Mari's right. We've made a lot of errors. Flame throwers work best, but right now they are scarce. They become useless once the fuel is gone. You have to return to a world surface to resupply. We discovered one interesting thing. Contrary to what I've been taught, we can establish a position in space as if we have weak gravity force under us," Rand pointed out.

"Only in dragon form," uttered the ever-present bottle dragon. "You get that from us—like the ability to breathe. Not even the Sidhe can do this—only dragons. Shapeshifter dragons not as good, can't even flame."

"Uh, oh. Sidhe incoming," Rand warned.

Killeen stamped into the room. If it hadn't been a pocket door, she'd have slammed it. Her latest modification of Rudy's suit hadn't worked and she needed to vent her anger. "Why don't you get Rudy fixed like Rand so he doesn't need his spacesuit?"

"You don't know what you're asking," Seren replied. He didn't want anything more to do with Arthurian's contract to produce children.

"I do, too. Aren't my aunts pretty enough?"

"I know your aunts are beautiful, but I don't love them. Beside—" started Seren.

"You still love that witch that jilted you."

Seren's mind flashed white with anger.

Mari pushed her way between Seren and Killeen. "Quiet," she hissed to Killeen. "You forget Seren's a powerful mage. His line is doubly dangerous when angry. Remember what his angry father did to the priests of Sardoom."

Killeen blanched. Fialla had told her the story of how the whole order and all the temples had disappeared in an instant of Jarl's rage. She whimpered as she sank against Mari's body.

"She's a child," Mari cautioned Seren.

"What he started to tell you," Rand interrupted, "is that the spell only works on people with the ability to do real magic. Remember Prince Leon? He fathered a child, but the vacuum breathing spell didn't take because he is only a normal human."

"What's going on?" Rudy rode his chair into the room. The door sliding shut behind him was the only sound.

"I—I made a mistake." Killeen sobbed. "I was trying to change things so you didn't have to be in a spacesuit."

"Why? I feel more comfortable inside the total suit than I do now. Besides, all the improvements you've done on the suit have made it much better."

"You've been modifying his spacesuit?" Seren's voice was quiet.

"Something's wrong. Send for a healer," Rand ordered the bottle dragon.

"Are you all right?" Rand whispered under his breath to Seren. Everyone but Rudy could have heard his question if he had used telepathy.

Seren moved his hand, palm outward, back and forth in front of Rand. "I'm over it," he assured Rand.

"The weren who is called a machinist helped me," Killeen replied, still hiding behind Mari. Mari had changed from enemy to protector.

Seren asked Rudy, "Do you have schematics and suit drawings?"

Rudy scowled in concentration. "Yes, somewhere."

"I gather from that answer, that neither of you thought to mark up the drawings or record the modifications. You both need to do that now while you remember the changes," Seren ordered.

"Killeen, this may be a greater gift than your magic. There aren't enough dragons or weren to defend this battleline. I'm going to need humans. If you can help make workable suits, it may save all the worlds."

"The suits will have to be armored, too," Killeen blurted.

Mari put her finger over Killeen's mouth. "What is it they say—out of the mouths of babes?"

"It's okay," Seren assured Mari. "I'm stable and my mind's in gear."

The weren healer burst into the room.

"Check them out," ordered Rand pointing to Rudy and Seren.

After what seemed like hours, the healer explained. "Rudy's in pain, but I can't tell why. Whatever it is, it's beyond my skill level."

"I feel much better here with the low gravity. I've got a suitcase of pills for the pain," Rudy told them.

"Put on your helmet," Seren ordered. "We can still hear you. Try not to overdo until we can get help."

"I'll send for Lealor," Rand said.

"In my present mood, I'm not sure I want my sister underfoot." Seren started toward the door, and then stopped. "You're right. If you can get Lealor to leave her kingdom, bring her here."

CHAPTER TWENTY-TWO

The dragon forms of Mari and the healer made the Medlab crowded. Lealor felt the intensity of Killeen's gaze as the green glow from her hands enveloped Rudy. Lealor remained puzzled. Everything seemed normal. Following the pain led her to the blood itself. How could this be? "I've never seen anything like this before. I see what looks like knots in your blood. Can anyone else see them?"

Killeen shook her head no.

"Not me," the weren healer replied.

"I can," Mari said, "but I'm not a healer."

"I'm going to destroy the largest 'knot' to see if reduces your pain," Lealor told Rudy.

Rudy yelped and his skin paled. "Things—things are better."

"It would help if you had a transfusion. Do we have any blood?" Lealor asked.

"No, and I don't know how," the healer replied. "Aren't you supposed to type blood somehow?"

Lealor sighed. "I'm afraid we're not much help."

"Doc," Rudy said.

"Who?" asked the mystified Killeen.

"Doc, the guy who gave me the pills back on Earth. He was in MASH units in two wars and is a physician's assistant in civilian life. He could run this place." Rudy's face fell. "He's old and a wino."

"What's he want with mashed potatoes?" the weren healer asked.

"Hush," commanded Lealor. "Is a wino the same as a drunk?"

"Yes," Rudy admitted. "But he can give transfusions and knows how to use the rest of the medical paraphernalia in this facility."

"We *do* know how to handle drunks," Lealor asserted.

Both the healer and Mari nodded agreement.

"He probably would be healthier here with the low gravity," Killeen added. "How do we find him?"

"I've got his address. Send that babe, Debbie. She'll find him," Rudy replied.

"Babe?" Lealor arched her eyebrows. Her mind pulled Rudy's mental picture into a hologram in front of everyone.

"Oh, my." Mari carefully placed a talon over her snout to hide her smile.

"Rand better not know this Debbie," Lealor commented, before speaking to Rudy. "Look, I do know enough to hook you up with some tubing so you can use either a mask or two tubes positioned at your nose for oxygen instead of that helmet. Let's try both methods and find out which works best for you. Then I'll talk to my brother about Doc and Debbie."

* * * *

"How do you like it here on this dead world, dear?" Lealor frowned at the dust they were raising.

"I miss the sun sometimes, but it's okay." Killeen smiled.

Hand in hand Lealor and Killeen entered Seren's office. Lealor could feel some reluctance in Killeen as they entered. "Tell me about Debbie," Lealor demanded.

"She's Argen's representative on Earth," Seren replied.

"I'm surprised you're not chasing her instead of Killeen's aunts."

Seren shot a look at the innocent smirk on Killeen's face while replying to Lealor. "Not you, too. She's Argen's assistant. He paid the same price to get Arthurian's spell as I did. Why isn't Argen the target of your matchmaking?"

"You bullied him into the tryst...." Lealor stopped with a puzzled look on her face. "I'm having a lot of trouble with farseeing lately. Argen's going to get his comeuppance right here on this world."

"How reliable is your farseeing ability?"

"Better than Argen's. When someone else's talent reinforces it—pretty good. On Widdershins, Fialla saw the same possibility that I did. The ability fails completely when you try to look at your own future. Right now my frustration is that I don't ask for it to happen—it has a timing all its own."

Seren nodded his understanding. Argen's farseeing happened the same way.

"Back to why we're here. I don't understand Rudy's illness. I thought I'd go to Achaea and talk to Aesculapius. I'm taking Killeen with me. She needs a visit home," Lealor said.

"All right, but who is running the ship on Widdershins?" Seren asked.

"Rand's father, King Erik, of course. He gives Rand a lot of static, but he is really a great help to me. Let me get closure. Nobody knows how to run your Medlab unit. Rudy suggests we bring someone called

Doc here. This is his Earth address." She handed Seren a note. "I gather Debbie is an excellent finder."

"That would be the second human who would require a spacesuit or have to stay inside all the time," Seren protested.

Killeen entered the discussion. "You've got plenty of bottle dragons now that the weren are self-sufficient. It would give me another suited subject to study. I thought I'd go to Realm after visiting my folks. I want to find out what type of courses I'll have to take to really understand spacesuits. Isn't that what you want? I'd be getting an education and working on a major problem."

"Yes," agreed Seren. "O'Roark will be bringing his army there for school. It will be winter on Widdershins soon. I need some of his people here. My building program is in shambles with most of the weren helping to construct the mine-firing nets." He rubbed the bridge of his nose. "I'll probably see you there. By the way, the civil engineer and his wife have scheduled a visit to Realm next week.

"Killeen, I like the direction you've chosen." Seren observed her green eyes widen. He hoped it meant surprise and pleasure. If Seren hadn't known what a little hellion she was, Killeen's shy smile would have fooled him into thinking she was an ordinary little girl instead of a Sidhe who could wield magic power.

* * * *

When Lealor and Killeen came through the gate, they found a man in attendance. "Who are you? Where's Branwyn?" Lealor asked.

"I'm the son of Argus. Branwyn requires my people to serve as payment for portal usage. I've already called her. See, she's coming down the path."

Killeen ran to her mother, threw her arms around her and bawled.

Lealor sighed. "I understand the feeling. If my mother ever returns, I may do the same thing." She wiped a tear away. "Where can I find Miklos?"

The gatekeeper pointed to a cottage near a grove of trees outside the stockade.

Lealor thanked the keeper and walked down the hill in the warm sunshine. She heard both the birds and the clanging of a working blacksmith. When she reached the cottage, the door was open. "Hello," she called. "Anybody home?"

"Only us fairies. Come on in, Lealor."

Lealor found Miklos propped up in bed with a little girl sitting by his feet. The child gave Lealor a brilliant smile.

"This is my niece, Jodi. Her mother recently had twins. It was a hard birth, so Jodi spends the days with me," Miklos explained.

Lealor felt puzzled, something about Jodi was nagging her memory.

"Jodi's going to be Seren's next aide after Killeen," Miklos proudly announced.

Lealor frowned. That wasn't it. "You sure start them young. Do you mind if I check you out?"

"Be my guest," Miklos answered.

Jodi hopped off the bed and stood beside Lealor holding her skirt for support.

Lealor raised her hands and the green glow spread over Miklos. She waved one hand and it disappeared. She looked down at Jodi. "Take your thumb out of your mouth, dear."

"Well?"

"Everything looks cured except your legs and one shoulder. Aesculapius has done a good job. Can you call on him for help?"

"Of course. I see you're still a healer," Miklos said.

"Not really. I used to want to work with animals. Humans, weren and Sidhe were never part of my plan. Being Regent of Widdershins keeps me busy. I get emergencies and things the other healers can't handle, whether I want them or not."

"I never thanked you for saving me. For a few days I wasn't sure I wanted to live like this, but Jodi makes life worthwhile. Thank you."

Lealor was embarrassed. She waved her hand, trying to brush away his gratitude. "Actually, I'm here because of one of Seren's people. I'm stuck and I thought Aesculapius could help me. Could you call him for me?"

"Sure." After a moment's pause, Miklos grinned. "He must like you. He's on his way."

"Killeen's here with me. Right now, she's with Branwyn. I never knew they were close."

"Branwyn is not one to let motherhood interfere with ruling her kingdom, so the relationship is unusual. It suits me. I get to monopolize my daughter's time. How's she doing?"

Lealor paused. Her initial meeting with Killeen, Fialla's wedding, their foresight vision, the spat with Seren and Killeen's dedication to Rudy, all raced through Lealor's mind. "Overall, excellent. She got in a tiff with Seren."

"Is Seren all right?"

Lealor was shocked. "What do you mean is Seren all right? Mari got between the two for Killeen's protection."

"Killeen is the most powerful Sidhe alive. If she lost control, she could hurt Seren."

"How can this be? Killeen's only three-quarters Sidhe."

"Doesn't matter," Miklos replied. "It's the way the genes got stacked. I knew the outcome before she was born. I didn't like the current situation with a male being born with that power, so her mother and I agreed on leaving her a girl. Of course, Branwyn, being a warrior queen, thinks that's the way it should be anyway. My brother, Arthurian, was furious. My foresight sees the next time genes stack that way, is for Argen's son. Arthurian will be too old to control him. Besides, his mother Ithanel will make mincemeat out of Arthurian, but that's wrong." Miklos frowned. "Seren and Ithanel were paired."

"I really don't want to get into a discussion of visions or Arthurian's plots. Those involving my own son are disturbing enough."

Miklos smiled. "I caught your and Fialla's vision of Drak and Killeen in your mind. It rings true. Will that be a problem for you? I thought you didn't like me."

"I—I resented the time Rand spent with you. It was never dislike," Lealor stammered. "I love your daughter."

Aesculapius entered the cottage. He held out his hands to Jodi and gave her a gentle hug. "What's wrong, little one? Are they boring you?

"Well, what do you think of Miklos' progress?" he continued, releasing the child before she could answer him.

"Better than I thought possible," Lealor said. "I came about another. He has no legs, but he has a wondrous chair. Maybe Miklos should try one."

"Actually, I was going to ask you about that wyvern mud where Flame is healing. Could the wyvern springs rebuild his legs?" Aesculapius asked.

"I don't know, but we could try. The chair could help in the interim. This other patient is called Rudy." Lealor flashed an image of his blood on the wall. "Have you ever seen anything like this?"

"No," mused Aesculapius. "Does he have anemia? You should watch his spleen and lymph glands."

"He has a lot of pain. I destroyed one of those knots," Lealor explained. "Seren has a modern medical facility, but we don't know how to use it. We sent for someone who knows how to give a transfusion."

"I would like to see that. Send for me when you're going to do it. I can examine the patient then. Also, I can see the marvelous chair."

A gentle knock on the doorframe preceded "Can I spend some time with my father?"

"Certainly," replied Aesculapius. "Lealor and I will continue outside." He put Jodi on the bed and they left.

Killeen frowned, watching Aesculapius and Lealor walking down the path. Both were waving their arms as they talked. Killeen turned around in time to see Jodi stick her tongue out at her. Killeen laughed.

Jodi started creating hollyhock dolls, acorn toys and colored leaves by having light shape them between her hands. They covered the bed.

"Stop that. Make that clutter go away," Killeen demanded.

Jodi stuck her thumb in her mouth and blinked her eyes.

Miklos found himself on the floor with Jodi sitting on his crippled legs. The bed, mattress, frame, coverings and toys were gone. "I'm beginning understand my brother's viewpoint on female Sidhe," he said with a chuckle as he reversed the spell.

CHAPTER TWENTY-THREE

Lealor couldn't believe she'd bought into taking Killeen to her first day at school. Coming through Realmgate with Killeen, the keeper was a surprise. "Why, Guardy, I thought you were in retirement."

"So did I. Your mom and dad have returned. Mirza took one look at the gate and started asking questions. Argen and Librisald forgot she talks directly to gates. Those two have been avoiding her ever since I got called to duty."

Lealor couldn't help it. She giggled. "What about Seren?"

"He's here, too. Got some Earth visitors he's showing around. Your mother would never embarrass him. It's like when you were kids. Trouble sort of slides off Seren's back."

"Thanks for the update, Guardy." Lealor tiptoed herself higher and kissed Guardy softly on his cheek, avoiding his beard.

"We've got a little walk," she told Killeen. "The portal used to be right at the center of the university, but mother moved the gate when the keeper applicants stopped."

* * * *

"She's having a full-course banquet at dusk," Guardy called after the two.

Lealor raised her hand in acknowledgement but kept up the pace toward the spiral towers. She clasped Killeen's hand and urged her gently onward.

Killeen didn't exactly drag her heels and bray like a donkey, but her reluctance was evident. "Will I have to take tests?"

"Of course. That's the only way the instructors can determine what courses you need. Keep reminding them you want to design spacesuits. If they're like my professors, they won't remember anything you said." Killeen stopped dead in the courtyard close to where the gate once dominated the landscape. "Everything has changed. I don't know where they register students."

"Lealor, is that really you?" Prince Leon hurried across the circle, his academic robes billowing behind him.

Lealor frowned. "Who else would I be?" She looked him over brief-ly," I've never seen you in university regalia." Noticing his boots, she added, "You won't be riding in that outfit."

"I couldn't believe you left your kingdom." Noticing her eyeing his clothes, he said, "The robes slip off easily. My riding outfit is under-neath."

Killeen's tug on Lealor's hand reminded Lealor of her purpose. "Where do new students sign up?"

"You're here for Killeen, aren't you? Leon winked at the girl before offering, "I'll take her to the proper place so you can visit your mother." He beamed with enthusiasm. "Killeen can stay with us. We have plenty of room. No small cubbyhole for my wife's niece."

Killeen gestured to his boots, visible under the hem of his robe. "You're riding horses instead of dragons?"

"Scales, yes. Arafel and I have a whole stable filled with Oromon's colts and fillies. The problem is finding someone brave and skillful enough to ride them. They only have one speed—fast. They zip over fences and gates as if there were no obstacles at all." He noticed the flare of interest in Killeen's eyes when he mentioned speed.

"Is there time enough to ride when you are a student here?"

"Surely. Early, before breakfast and later in the afternoon when classes are finished for the day. I wouldn't be surprised if Sparrow ap-peared here, too."

"If I stay, may I ride your horses?"

"You'd like that, would you? You would be doing us a service if you would help train and exercise my children." Seeing the puzzled look on Killeen's face, he clarified. "My horses think they are four-legged people—my children. No one tells them they are animals. It would break their hearts."

"I'd like to help," the girl volunteered.

Mentally Lealor heaved a sigh of relief. Killeen wouldn't be home-sick. Out loud she said, "That's a nice set of offers. Killeen's here for your people. She wants to develop armored spacesuits for them so they can survive in space."

Killeen broke in. "Tell me about the tests."

"Expect eight one-hour interviews with eight different instructors. Some will include written work, but it's fun," replied Leon. "You can't fail. All they want to do is determine what level you're currently on. If you start on a level that's too low, you'd be bored and get into trouble."

"How will Sparrow know I'm here?" asked Killeen, still unsure.

Leon chuckled. "Ebony's always around. She teaches a course on *The Dragon Chronicles*. You should see the students' faces when they find out a dragon teaches the course. I'll stay near to guide you and take you to our home afterwards. We'll go to Mirza's banquet together."

"See," Lealor chided. "You didn't need me after all. You can tell me about the fun of testing tonight." She gave Killeen a hug and watched Leon lead her away, waving his arms as he described the campus. She felt a little lonely. Killeen had been stimulating company. Lealor's face brightened. Now, it was her turn to see her mother.

* * * *

A few minutes later, Lealor, rushing toward Mirza's study, literally bumped into Arafel and a strange woman. "Pardon me. I'm acting like a little girl, but I can't wait to see Mother."

Arafel's laugh tinkled like a little bell. "This is Seren's guest, Nell. Her husband is busy talking engineering with Seren and Jarl, so we escaped to view Realmgate."

Lealor grabbed Arafel. "I'm doing a lot of hugging today, but it feels so good to be home." She offered her hand in greeting to Nell. "Arafel, mind-buzz me if you two get lost."

"Are—are you really a queen?" asked Nell, looking at Lealor's green sweatshirt and brown slacks.

Lealor snorted. "More correctly, a regent. I'm having a great time playing hooky." With a brief wave goodbye, she continued rapidly down the hall.

When Lealor barged into her mother's study, she found her father, some stranger and her brother Seren, all looking at maps and photographs. She ran into her father's open arms. "Where's Mother?"

Jarl put a finger across her mouth, "Hush. Mirza's studying *The Book of Worlds*," he whispered.

"That's at the gate and I just came from there," protested Lealor.

"This isn't any good. I can look at photos and maps back on Earth. I want to go there. See things first hand," demanded the stranger, ignoring the whispered conversation.

"It's dangerous, and you have to wear a spacesuit," Seren cautioned. "Maybe—Lealor, I noticed you were unsuited on the battleline. You must have used a spell to fix yourself. Miklos indicated he thought you could."

Jarl turned to Seren, "Son, the kindest thing you could call that mess you have strung out in space is a skirmish line," he said with a chuckle.

"Yes, yes—I see it as what it will become," Seren acknowledged impatiently. "Well, how about it, Sis?"

Lealor was put out. She didn't like that nickname, and she had come to see her mother—not change some stranger. "Yes, I studied you and

Rand at Fialla's wedding and tried the same changes. They worked for me, but someone else? Remember Leon."

"Nothing like having your own arguments turned on you," Seren grumbled, recalling the confrontation with Killeen. "Arafel claims Leon has some space breathing ability, about thirty minutes. So worst case, the change gives some protection."

"I'd like to know how she found that out," Lealor wondered out loud.

"She had Ebony and Faf give them a ride outside Realm's atmosphere. The dragons keep a shield around their passengers. Getting them to drop the protection was the difficult challenge. Then she timed how long he could stand it."

Lealor snorted. "As Mari would say, 'Not very scientific.' What other tidbit are you keeping from me?"

Seren frowned as he tried to remember. "Arafel claims Leon can do some magic now. She believes that mastering spells increases your ability to work magic. She's making Leon practice because skill improves the more you use it. She plans to retest Leon when he makes an ability jump."

"That means Rand has been holding out on me. Wait till I get home."

"No, no. It means you'd be giving Jack, here, some protection. Jarl needs the changes, too."

"He'd probably prefer your method of securing the change," Lealor replied sweetly.

"What's that?" asked Jarl.

"Lealor! Not now. This isn't the place for that discussion," Seren pleaded.

Lealor walked over and shook the stranger's hand. "I'm Lealor. You must be Jack. Please excuse my brother's bad manners." She looked at Seren. "I'll do both Jack and Dad at the same time, but Jack has to wear a spacesuit until we know more about the spell results." She motioned to Jack and Jarl. "Here, one of you on each side." Lealor put one hand on each man. "Close your eyes," she demanded. A green glow encased both individuals.

"You can open your eyes now."

"I don't feel any different," Jack said.

"Good!" said Lealor and Seren in unison.

"Dad?" Lealor asked.

"I'm fine. I'm tracing the changes," Jarl replied. "If Jack relocates here, he will have to be monitored for the ability to do magic. On Earth, that's no problem. Even Leon would be helpless there because people don't believe in real magic. They think illusions are magic."

"I need to get an x-ray machine on Realm to see if the changes show. We may have a different method to recognize magical ability. I haven't been too impressed with the present system," Lealor replied.

"I wouldn't tell Mother that," Seren cautioned.

Lealor shut her eyes. *Mother, where are you?*

On the platform overlooking the gate as your father told you.

You weren't there when I came in.

You weren't looking for me then.

Don't you have a dinner to plan?

All done, dear. The staff will make it happen.

Stay put. I'm on my way. Lealor opened her eyes and, without a word to anyone, left the room normally as a courtesy to Jack who probably wasn't used to people winking in and out using magic.

Lealor grumbled the whole time she climbed the steps. Turning the corner, she saw her mother push out a chair for her. "Do you climb those steps or float up here?"

"Depends on how I feel. If I'm mad or upset, I climb."

"They look well worn," Lealor joked. "What are you doing anyway?"

"I'm searching for the first battle Miklos and Berdularion had with our enemy. Ebony's doing the same research with the *Dragon Chronicles*. Males!" she grumbled. "We asked them to remember something else that was important at that time. You wouldn't believe their answers. It's good thing they had no ballgames on these worlds."

Lealor chuckled. "If I remember your view of football, you found both teams offensive."

Mirza gave Lealor her not one-more-word-out-of-you look.

Lealor quickly changed the subject. "Have you found anything?"

"No, but I never tried going back in time before. I'm usually looking for a place or a gate."

Lealor sighed. "I sure wish you could put a mini-gate at the palace. Porting to Fialla's cottage gate is hard."

"The Shadowlord is the only one that builds mini-gates."

"I'll do without then." Lealor still didn't care for him.

"I don't understand. You're the one who figured out he was a damaged Bright One."

"Yes, but I don't trust him, or even like him. What about Ebony? Did she find anything?" Lealor asked, intent on returning to the search.

"References that we think apply to the future. Nothing on the original battle. It's so frustrating. We know that the conflict was recorded, but when in time and where in the books…" Mirza sighed.

Librisald marched around the corner, ready to serve his time slot as keeper. Seeing Mirza instead of Guardy, he tried to back up.

"Be careful, or you'll fall off the platform," Lealor warned. "Why doesn't it have hand rails anyway?"

"I don't need them, nor does any keeper. You're safe tonight, Librisald. Well, Daughter, let's port to our rooms and dress for dinner."

"You kept my room all this time?" Lealor was touched. She hadn't thought her mother was sentimental.

Mirza laughed. "I had to. I certainly didn't want to trigger those nasty privacy spells of yours."

They both vanished. The old librarian tiptoed to the table as if stealth could protect him. Interrupting two powerful mages was not a policy he wanted to start. He was too old to spend the rest of his life as a frog.

CHAPTER TWENTY-FOUR

The feast completed, only close friends and family remained in the large serving hall. Fafnoddle lay against one wall, his eyes closed, with one ear slit cocked. Ebony sat on her haunches, leaning against Faf. Killeen was curled up in front of Ebony, positioned so she could see. Most of the men had found Andronan chairs or sofas and were reclining to imitate Faf. The women still sat at the table.

"Boy, I never could understand how the Romans could stretch out to eat, but afterwards makes sense," said Sergeant Henning, who had learned to come to these affairs with his belt loosened a notch. No TV dinners here. The taste of freshly prepared food was, in Henning's opinion, one of the best reasons to live on Realm.

"You don't need a couch," O'Roark observed. "I've seen you sleep standing up."

Seren moved to a chair beside Jarl. All conversation ceased. "We've had a wild time while you were gone, Father. Let me recap the situation. Berdularion, Flame and Miklos got into a battle with an unknown horde of creatures that killed a Sidhe. They misdirected the enemy away from us. I've started preparations to stop this threat from sweeping across our worlds. How are we going to transfer command?" Seren asked Jarl.

"We're not," Jarl replied. "I don't have your military experience. I'll take back the other Dragon's Knight duties, but Argen's been doing those anyway. You started the defense of our worlds. You may keep right on managing the army."

"Now, wait a minute," Seren protested. "The proclamation wasn't a life-time commitment. Berdularion claims this enemy has been turned away by trickery twice now. We must install a defensive barrier to stop them at the edge of our galaxy."

Jarl scowled, but after a minute, nodded. "That's your new goal, Seren. Stop the probable enemy invasion."

"At least you can help with discovery. We don't know who or what we're fighting. Trying to utilize Dead World and add to the space junk around it is time consuming." Seren was already looking at alternatives.

What is it you call that place you're building?" his father asked.

"Battleline," Seren told him.

"Dead World," Rand and Argen said together.

Jarl laughed. "Let's call it the Battleline. We all agree it's not that now, but that is what it must become. In this case the 'line' is three dimensional."

"It would help if we were all consistent." Seren agreed with his father. "I don't know if I have much foreseeing ability, but I can visualize what it must become. You're assigning me a long term problem with tremendous cost."

"We—Ebony and I—see it, too. It will happen," insisted Fafnoddle.

"Show me," Killeen, now standing, pleaded.

Faf, Ebony and Seren focused their vision on Killeen. Mirza made the vision expand so everyone could see the future.

"Wow!" The look on Jarl's face showed his amazement. The group silently agreed.

"I made several errors making the proclamation. One mistake I made was underestimating Argen. He's done a good job with routine Knight duties, helped Seren with supplies, and provided the university with a great staff," Jarl observed.

"That doesn't mean Argen's off the hook for messing up my gate." Mirza gave him 'the look'.

"I was never trained how to modify a gate. Not even Andronan knew how," Argen complained. "You should forgive Librisald. It's hard enough to get his cooperation, without you terrifying him for following orders."

"What about Seren's civil engineer, Jack? Will he stay?" Rand asked.

"His wife likes it here. Nell's a teacher. She can instruct at the college. She's happy because the class her children attend at underschool is small." Arafel was enthusiastic.

"Speaking of children, that's another thing," Mirza added. "I don't like my grandchildren being raised on Eyre where I can't spoil them. It's hard enough to see Drak."

Both Argen and Seren visibly squirmed in discomfort.

"That makes another good reason for putting a mini-gate at my palace," Lealor said.

"Sparrow is getting worn out ferrying everybody to and from the portal at Fialla's cottage," put in Killeen.

"That problem's solved." Everybody stared at Prince Leon's Sidhe wife.

"Not the gate. The grandchildren," Leon explained. "The Sidhe foster their children as soon as they can walk. Arthurian has agreed. Arafel and I are going to foster them here on Realm."

"I need Jack." Seren hoped to change the subject's direction. He didn't want to explain his part in the recent Sidhe population increase.

"I'm worried that taking him to Dead World in a spacesuit tomorrow will scare him off."

"Have Rudy show him around instead of all you spell-modified humans," Killeen blurted. She ducked down out of sight behind Ebony's scaly legs.

Rand laughed. "Good idea." He slapped the arm of his chair.

"How is Rudy doing?" Lealor was concerned about his health.

"Great," Rand said. "I checked him out at Dead World. To him the whole experience is a lark. Air-chair and all, he's a natural in space. Nothing scares him. He can't wait to start blowing things up."

* * * *

"I don't see why this is necessary." Rand grumbled as he fitted Killeen into a spacesuit. "Finding small size items is proving difficult here on Realm."

"How can I improve something that I haven't experienced? You ought to try the instructions you give weren."

"Amen," Lealor agreed. She received a dirty look from Rand and laughed. She didn't feel it came close to a Mirza 'look'. She didn't know that the Lealor 'look' would become legend in the future.

Jack was trying to pay attention to Seren's instructions, so most of this went over his head. All he knew was that the trip with a young girl was to meet another man in a spacesuit.

Seren continued his explanation. "When you get there, a bottle dragon will be waiting. If the bottle alarm goes off, turn this switch and stop. The bottle dragon will change your air cylinder. If the alarm goes off again, turn the switch back and stop. The routine repeats itself. The bottle dragon has six spare canisters. Counting the two you're carrying, that gives you eight. After using six, you must start for the conference chamber.

"The gravity is one tenth what it is here. That makes walking awkward. Follow Killeen to see how she does it. We'll meet you at the chamber. Both Rudy and Killeen know Dead World completely. They'll take you anywhere you want to go."

Seren looked Rand. "Is Killeen ready?"

"Perfectly," Rand assured Seren. "Okay you two. Walk into the circle and have a safe journey."

Killeen took Jack's glove in hers and led him into the gate. They vanished.

"That's dirty pool," Lealor said. "The image is—if a young girl and a man without legs can survive—I can, too." She shook her head. "Nobody finished answering me last night. How's Rudy?"

"My fault," Fialla replied. "He's holding his own. I could see the knots in his blood, but Mari had to be the one to destroy the largest growth. That made me more sympathetic to the useless weren healer." She scowled. "Claimed he was a combat medic or corpsman, not some healing witch."

O'Roark frowned behind her at the disrespect for his wife's abilities. Seren was surprised. He seldom saw O'Roark's Irish temper flare.

"Hush, I've heard and been called a lot worse." Fialla gave O'Roark a pat. "Hurry home as soon as Seren lets you."

Seren added more information. "Debbie's found Doc, but she had to put him into a detox hospital. She got his signature on a contract while he was still high. He'll be along in a couple of weeks."

"Who gets to cure his problem?" Lealor glared at Seren's grin. "Don't tell me. I can guess."

"I hope you don't mind me leaving with Lealor," Rand said. "It's easier if we go home in one trip."

"That's what sergeants are for," O'Roark offered. "Covering your—" he paused abruptly, seeing Fialla's frown, "ah—posterior."

It was Fialla's, Lealor's and Rand's time to disappear into the portal.

* * * *

Seren and the two sergeants gathered in one of the many conference rooms in the Realmgate castle. "Where's Prince Leon? He should be here," Seren demanded.

Sergeant Henning went to the door and ordered a waiting private to find and bring Prince Leon.

Jarl knocked and entered the room. "Mind if I join you?"

"Bright Ones no," Seren replied. "All of you feel free to comment at any time."

There was another knock on the door. Sergeant Henning opened the door and went into the hall. He came back shortly. "They found Prince Leon. He's training horses. The Prince wants to know if he should get cleaned up or come as he is."

"As is," Seren snapped.

The sergeant went back outside and returned quickly.

"I gather this a common problem for you, Sergeant?"

"Yes sir. The Prince only likes the ceremony. Otherwise, I run the army."

"Tell us about the prince's army," Seren ordered.

"I came here with four hundred men. Two hundred are now keeping the university running. Of the remaining two hundred, ten are good enough to be officer candidates and one hundred are noncom candidates. The rest will always be grunts," Henning reported.

The door opened and a pouting Prince Leon, smelling like the stable, entered and plopped in a chair.

Jarl chuckled. "Mirza will have your hide if this odor stays."

"Prince Leon can have his *daily* staff meeting here." Seren turned to the sergeant. "Does it take two hundred men to keep the school running?"

Prince Leon had scowled at the word *daily*. Now, he shrugged and looked at Sergeant Henning.

"The school had been idle for so long that there is a lot of maintenance. I haven't been included on progress," the sergeant reported.

"Who's running these men?"

Prince Leon shrugged. "Not me. Maybe Andronan."

"Starting now, Prince Leon, you are. First try to reduce the numbers. If there are any officer candidates, I want them back in school. Next, the same thing goes for NCO candidates. Replace these men from the sergeant's list of grunts. Even the maintenance troops should have part time or evening classes as fitting."

"But some of these men are my friends," the Prince protested. "They asked for these jobs."

Seren rose and leaned across the table, his face pushed close to the Prince. "You don't have any friends. You're running an army. If you're lucky, Sergeant Henning will save your ass many times over."

The Prince drew back in shock. "You sound like Arafel."

"Maybe she should be in charge," Jarl observed.

"No." The Prince rose and drew himself up. "I'll learn."

"Good!" Seren snapped. "You're next, O'Roark."

"I'm bringing five hundred weren, consisting of one hundred officer candidates, two hundred NCO candidates and two hundred grunts. In the spring, Rand will have one thousand weren reporting at basic training camp. I see where you're going. You want my grunts and NCO candidates now. I'll use Henning's NCOs and officers to run my operation."

"You're right, Sergeant. I've got only fifty weren at Dead World. Promote all the prospective noncoms to corporal and brevet the twenty-five best prospective officers to second lieutenants. Rand and I will have to continue their formal schooling on Dead World. I need construction troops now."

Both sergeants O'Roark and Henning jumped to their feet. "Consider it done, sir," O'Roark replied.

They saluted and left.

"What if the grunts don't have the skill to do the maintenance work?" worried the Prince.

"Bring in civilian craftsmen from your father's kingdom," Jarl replied.

"You're dismissed. Report to the Dragon's Knight if I'm not available." For the first time since the meeting began, Seren relaxed.

The Prince got slowly to his feet, gave Seren a half-hearted salute and wandered out.

"He's young," Jarl remarked. "I bet Henning's been tearing his hair. I'm not military, but I can help. I'll get with Andronan and explain the changes. I'll bet he can show military command presence, too."

"Thanks. I can't spare the time to help train him." Seren laughed. "You really got to him with that crack that maybe Arafel should be in charge.

"Please talk to Mother about modifying both gates to take a large number of men. One at a time is not going to cut it. I'm off to Dead World to see how many new weren we can accommodate now. We'll take the grunts first and let the others get as much formal schooling as possible."

"What will you use for NCOs?"

"Rand will have to promote some of the weren already there." Seren rose and shook his father's hand. "Thanks again." Seren left the room.

Jarl drummed his fingers on the table. Which was going to be the bigger problem? Andronan or Mirza? Prince Leon was a piece of cake.

CHAPTER TWENTY-FIVE

Flame rose from the mud hole and trumpeted his good health to his mate. Great gobs of mud dropped off as he staggered toward a steaming gusher.

"There's a hot pool nearby," offered Seabreeze, the only wyvern in sight. All her subjects had disappeared with Flame's first roar.

"No! Want sssteam. The hotter the better," Flame bellowed.

"Is he fully cured?" asked a worried Fafleen, watching Flame standing in the center of the steam eruption.

"Physically, yes. Mentally…" Seabreeze paused. "I'm concerned. Why don't you take him to the Ancient One?"

Fafleen drew her head back in alarm. "She dislikes males more than the wyverns. The only way I'd take Flame there would be if he showed me he was completely out of control."

"Seren will have to deal with him then. Strange thing, Seren and Flame are a pair like you and Lealor, but neither will complete the bond," Seabreeze mused.

"What are you going to do about Lealor's request that you allow Miklos to heal his legs here?" Fafleen asked.

"Another alien male," Seabreeze hissed. "I wasn't going to have two underfoot at the same time. It might be too late for a complete cure. Timing is important."

"Are you going to demand a female of his race attend him?" Fafleen understood Seabreeze had accepted the request.

"Jodi will do."

"Jo—Jodi's a small child." Fafleen sputtered in alarm.

"She will be a gatekeeper on this world a long time in some of the futures we see. It would be good for her understanding if she spends time here as a child. Besides, Miklos will work to blend in."

"It is time to go," Flame trumpeted.

"His muscles are weak. He'll never make Realmgate. Try and persuade him to rest at Fellkeep." Seabreeze warned Fafleen.

Flame was already flying when Fafleen leapt into flight.

* * * *

On Dead World, Rand sprawled over several chairs in the conference room half asleep while Seren doodled on a large easel. Seren told Rand, "I want to move the weren to this cave for barracks and abandon those surface structures. Look at this sketch. We can put one hundred twenty-five in here using this design."

Rand moved enough to see the plot plan. "You've done away with our conference room."

"When we get that first fissure structure finished, I'll get it back. I need construction workers more than a fancy conference room. I am surprised that with the weren being larger in dragon shape you haven't been in trouble for lack of quarters."

Rand stretched. "We would have been, but the dragons moved out. Mari split up the weren. Put construction workers in one shelter and net-makers in the other. I suggest you leave the netmakers where they are."

"Are conditions crowded?"

"Not really. This arrangement gives you fifty additional spaces," Rand pointed out.

"You're telling me netmakers don't mind those cruddy structures?"

"Correct. It's closer to where they work and play."

Seren nodded. "Okay, but you and Mari have to generate some rank structure before the new weren arrive."

"I'll delegate the task to her. She has to live with the mistakes."

"Where did the dragons go?"

"The bottle dragons and world sentries are here in this cave." Rand pointed to a spot on the photo of the world's surface. "Berdularion took the others to the new asteroid. They moved in on the right side. It's full of caves."

"How do they get the necessary oxygen?"

"I haven't a clue." Rand shrugged.

Jack burst through the door, followed by Killeen and the bottle drag-ons. As soon as Rand took his helmet off, Jack started talking. "You didn't tell me it was cold."

Rand scowled. "Your suit has a heater. You should have told the BD if something was wrong."

Behind Jack's back, Killeen was throwing pieces of her suit at the BD as she disrobed. The BD looked like the local washerwoman with too many clothes in her arms. Another BD popped in and started redistribut-ing the load. Killeen was down to her shift.

"Killeen, please add some clothes," Seren requested.

She scowled, but a jacket and pants appeared.

Seren didn't want to know where her shift went.

Jack turned and stared. "You promised to go sailing with me!"

He's hooked, Rand sent to Seren. "Killeen doesn't need a spacesuit. She's a Sidhe."

Jack looked puzzled. "What does being female have to do with needing spacesuits?"

Seren laughed. "S-I-D-H-E. It's a Gaelic fairy race. Look them up when you're back on Realm." He watched while Jack nodded agreement. "Returning to your cold climate question, we use a two percent calcium chloride solution as an admixture to the concrete."

"That's not good enough," Jack insisted. "You've got steam and that sail covering here. I want a heated structure for the first seven days. I didn't have a corrosion allowance for the rebar. Do you have cylinder data on your previous pours?"

Rand was lost. "Cylinders?"

"They're small test cylinders poured the same time as the structure and cured on the job site," Seren explained. "How many?"

"Nine. I'll break them at three, seven and twenty-eight days. The rebar placement was excellent. Maybe I'll use 'High early' for that ground slab. I really wish we had some data on your previous pours."

"I poured some small concrete blocks for holding things off the ground. We don't have any wood. I must use concrete or steel items for everything. Will they help?" Rand asked.

"Yes," said Jack eagerly. "We can do the math."

Killeen broke in. "May we go sailing now?"

"Certainly." Seren gave her a big smile. "We can always answer questions back on Realm."

Rand started putting Jack's helmet on.

"How do you communicate without a radio?" Seren asked.

"Rudy and I have a set of hand signals," Killeen responded as she bounced out the door.

* * * *

Flame's shoulder muscles ached as he and Fafleen flew toward Realmgate, but he wasn't going to tell her. He would keep up.

Fafleen, like all better halves, could sense her mate getting weaker. Spotting Fellkeep, she spiraled down to land in a clear area close to the woods. While Flame settled, she moved into the trees and kicked kindling into the clearing. Dragging a dead tree, she saw Flame had already started a fire and was close to extinguishing it as he tried to sit in the middle of the flames.

"Putting only your tail in will have the same warming result and give the fire a better chance to grow."

Watching her mate stagger to the side, she flamed the tree into manageable hunks and pushed them into the brighter fire. Fafleen returned to the forest for more dead wood.

Always impatient, Flame torched the tree hunks into active burning as Fafleen reappeared with a smaller tree in her mouth, dragging another large one with her talons. By dusk they had a roaring bonfire.

Inside Fellkeep, alarms were finally penetrating the mind of the hibernating Shadowlord. Half awake, he sorted things out. At least the problem wasn't inside the castle. It was outside. Trying to clear his mind of cobwebs, he made his way to the nearest turret. "Dragons," he spat. What were they doing here? This was *his* place.

Fafleen and Flame were both startled when the Shadowlord appeared in front of their fire. Flame immediately blasted the intruder with all the fire energy at his command.

The Shadowlord stood there, absorbing the flames with a smirk on his face.

By now, Fafleen recognized him. "SSStop it, Flame. He's friendly." I hope, she added to herself mentally. She felt too exhausted to do battle. Poor Flame, she thought as she watched him sag. That energy outburst had destroyed all the gain made by the bonfire.

Fafleen addressed the Shadowlord. "You didn't use to be able to absorb fire like that."

"True," the Shadowlord agreed. "See the new silver area on my right shoulder? I've learned to convert the energy. I'm learning more of how a Bright One functions, but it's slow."

"Can you give the energy back? Flame has need of strength. Today was his first day out of the wyvern's healing springs."

"In the morning, I can do better than that. I've learned how to channel the sun's energy into others, but alas, not into me. It makes great roasted deer. Maybe Flame would make a good relay. I could channel energy into him and he could blast me."

They both heard a weak negative snort from Flame, instead of his usual roar.

"Being exhausted is no excuse to trespass on my land," the Shadowlord continued.

"Your land indeed! The woods belong to the dryads." Fafleen extended her talons. "I'm not exhausted, and Mother and Father are but an eye blink away."

"Save your fury for the enemy out there, silly dragon." The Shadowlord nodded in the direction of the void. "I can read how tired you are."

"Why aren't you in the void, helping, instead of threatening us?" Fafleen stuck her snout inches from the Shadowlord's face.

The Shadowlord pushed his nose against Fafleen's snout, unafraid, but not balanced. "Nothing to do. Seren's building. The weren are making wire nets for mines and have been using them to catch the asteroids Rudy gets moving by firing rockets. Very discouraging." The Shadowlord pulled himself up in disdain. "So I have been enlarging Fellkeep and my property." He pushed a finger into Fafleen's nose. "This is cleared land, not woods. Mine."

Fafleen showed her teeth in the dragon equivalent of a smile. "Poor baby. You're sulking here at Fellkeep because you can't be important. Mirza needs help in configuring gates for troop transport, and Lealor needs a mini-gate. There are things you can do." Fafleen snapped a talon at him, backing him up. "Go away while we rest. Get yourself back here in the morning to show us your energy channel trick."

The Shadowlord vanished much as a magnesium strip ignites in air.

* * * *

On Dead World, Seren finally got himself stretched out for a nap when Killeen's frantic yell blasted into his mind. *Jack's been caught in a current and is headed for the mines. We can't catch him.*

There aren't any currents, Seren protested.

He found one, Killeen shrieked.

Seren teleported to the top of the weren barracks, forgetting to stand. He appeared flat on his back. Quickly he rose. Spotting Berdularion, Seren yelled mentally, *Do something*!

What do you suggest?

Have the dragons teleport back to where they were working on the web.

They can't teleport. They're weren shapeshifters, Berdularion replied, rippling his scales in aggravation. *That does give me an idea.*

Now what? Seren thought as he felt himself dissolve.

CHAPTER TWENTY-SIX

Fafleen and Flame spiraled down to stand on the gate. "Permission to go to Dead World," Fafleen said sweetly.

Mirza snorted. "As if you had to ask. Of course, dear." She gave Fafleen an indignant look before speaking to her mate. "You're looking good, Flame."

In silence, Flame drew himself up regally and puffed a smoke ring at Mirza.

With pride Fafleen laid her head over Flame's neck. "Don't be surprised if the Shadowlord pays you a visit. I told him about Lealor needing a mini-gate and your problem of configuring the gate for troop movement."

"Jarl won't be thrilled, but I could use help. Maybe I was too hard on Argen. I can't figure out how to enlarge this gate any differently than he did. The gate on Dead World is the Shadowlord's anyway." Mirza stretched the tension of the problem away.

"The next trip Lealor makes to Dead World would be the time to have the Shadowlord install the mini-gate at the palace," Fafleen added.

The two dragons vanished.

* * * *

Sardoom's Priest, Rand swore, untangling himself from jangled wire, looking at a mine six inches from his nose. *How did I get here?*

My fault, Seren explained. *I suggested to Berdularion that dragons might catch Jack from here. He sent us. We're both too far away.*

Killeen's in the net, too. What's she doing?

They both watched in horror as Killeen dove from the net and slammed into Jack, knocking him loose from his kite.

Seren saw Flame and Fafleen emerge from the Dead World gate out of the corner of his eye. *Great! That's all I needed.* His horror increased as Killeen and Jack plunged into the still-open portal.

Rand, you're going to have to take over here. Keep Flame and Berdularion from killing each other.

Seren followed Killeen's example and dove through the open gate. The surface solidified after he disappeared. Except for some holes in the camouflaged netting, the Dead World gate looked normal.

Thanks a lot. You know how I dislike command, Rand complained to the empty void as he ported to Dead World's surface. As he landed, he noticed Mari had joined the group of dragons.

You look good, Son, Berdularion told Flame.

What are you doing here and what isss this imitation? Flame demanded, poking a talon in Mari's pink dragon belly. Smoke curled from his nostrils.

Mari was changed into a dragon by Arthurian himself. She's taking Miklos' place. Rand hoped the mention of the Sidhe king would cause Flame to pause.

Mari didn't wait. She looked down at Flame's talon and her eyes blazed. Flame's talon disintegrated, leaving a bloody quick.

Fafleen hurriedly pushed herself between Flame and the other two dragons. *Let Rand explain the changes,* she cautioned Flame.

Rand nodded his thanks. *My subjects have shapechanged into dragons thanks to a spell from Arthurian. The change allows them to operate about eight Widdershins hours in space without air tanks. Then they have to be reoxygenated like dragons do after twenty-four hours. As I said, Mari commands the weren as Miklos did. Your father took your place.*

I have returned! Flame seethed, interrupting Rand. Small jets of fire joined the steam from his nostrils.

I haven't finished. Rand was angry. *When Seren's gone, you take orders from me. We've moved in more asteroids to make our position wider. We've added a network of mines, as well.*

Most of the dragons have caves on one of the added asteroids. Wait until you see your new quarters, interrupted Berdularion. *You can have your command back immediately. I would be happy to ssshow you and Fafleen the changes Rand has mentioned.*

Thank you. Fafleen hooked her tail around Flame's neck in restraint. Her hind foot was carefully positioned on Flame's front foot. *I have never been here before.*

Yesss, agreed Flame, dismissing Rand and Mari from notice. *We will allow you to give usss a tour.*

As the three dragons lifted in flight, Mari asked, *Am I always going to have to put up with that overstuffed ego? He's worse than Arthurian.*

Flame behaves better when Seren is here, Rand assured her. *Explain to me how, after all this time, Jack is the one who finds a current.*

Mari shrugged. Beats me. Everyone is having a good time riding it now. Do you want Rudy to open a hole through the minefield to see how far it goes?

It sounds like a good idea. We might want to send a surprise package that way some time in the future. Now that we've found one, can we locate others?

Mari threw out her arms is resignation. *I don't know. Maybe we should get Jack back.*

Fat chance, Rand thought.

* * * *

Killeen managed to control the landing at Realmgate so both she and Jack stayed on their feet, only to be bowled over by Seren's arrival.

"I thought trained skydivers could land on their feet." She put her nose in the air and sniffed. "*We* did."

Seren ignored her, helping Jack stand and take his helmet off.

"What happened?" asked Jack. "That was fun."

By this time Mirza had made it down to the portal. "Really, Seren, you know better than to arrive helter-skelter like that."

"Not now, Mother. You don't know half of the story. Thank you for having the Dead World gate anchored to Realm."

"Killeen," Seren continued, "You can't dive into a gate like that. Add gatekeeping to your course of study. The two of you could have ended up anywhere."

"Well, we didn't dive, we fell. At least I used the passage to slow down and get here feet first." Killeen was unrepentant.

"I want you here at the university in a course of study. You make outstanding decisions with a complete lack of knowledge. I need your abilities augmented, though I'm apprehensive as to what you might do with knowledge."

Killeen stalked away in a huff after throwing to the ground the parts of Jack's spacesuit she had removed.

"I think you need my help with that young lady." Mirza smiled as she watched Killeen stamp off.

"Please, be my guest," Seren replied as he got the rest of Jack's spacesuit off. "Shall we return to your cottage, Jack?"

"I really enjoyed kiting in space. What caused all the commotion at the end?" Jack asked while they walked toward his Realmgate home.

"Two things. You were getting near the minefield and nobody could catch up in time. That's why Killeen knocked you off your kite. Then she did something equally dangerous, diving into an open gate."

Jack saw Nell running towards him with open arms. "We won't mention being in danger, right?"

Seren nodded agreement. By this time, Nell had her arms around Jack.

"You know, there isn't enough engineering work here to keep me busy. Maybe I should move my consulting company to Illinois. That would be near enough to a gate to handle your requirements."

Nell had backed away and was glaring at Jack. "I want to teach here at the university. Also, the children will get a better education on Realm. We can return to Earth for high school."

Uh, oh, thought Seren. "You still have a month before the end of the semester. Maybe you could explore Wilmington and Clear Lake as a home site. Spend the week at Realm and the weekend on Earth."

"You'd let's us do that?" Nell asked.

"If Jack doesn't want to teach, what other choices are there?"

"Too bad that warehouse doesn't have an airstrip," Jack mused. "It would help to explain all the trips to and fro."

"That sounds like a good idea. Why don't you talk over your plans with Argen? He's the devious one." Seren grinned. "You still have time to arrange things."

"I think you're going to have a hard time getting the children back to Earth on this weekend," Nell said. "They like Realm."

"I want those concrete samples," Jack was eager to change the subject. "That's one thing that will be easier to handle on Earth. I'll send you a new mix design after we break them. I'll return for the pour."

Jack put his arm around his wife. "I'm sure we can work something out so we'll both be happy." They started toward their cottage.

Seren double-timed it back to Realmgate. He'd seen enough. Even happily married couples had trouble. He could picture Megan's responses to that kind of problem. She'd display all the give you could get from a chunk of granite.

* * * *

Mirza took Killeen with her when she visited Andronan in his office at the University. "Which one of you came up with the gate expansion?" she asked her grandfather.

"I wasn't any help." Andronan shook his head. "Even Ebony couldn't find anything in *The Dragon Chronicles*. Nothing showed in my gate histories either. Why are you talking to me instead of Argen?"

"He's avoiding me. I can't get the gate any larger than truck size. Since the weren have to change into dragons first, that cuts how many will fit into the back," Mirza complained.

"Make long wagons," Killeen suggested. "The weren can sit back to back. The truck's no good on Dead World anyway. Have the train of wagons be pulled by a crawler."

"That would work." Andronan gave her an approving smile. "It would get Seren his workers quickly."

"I suppose if we put a tractor at each end, we could bring the trailers back and forth rapidly. I'll set Prince Leon to work building wagons right away."

"You'd be better off talking to Sergeant Henning," Killeen quipped.

"Yes, you're probably right, dear. Why don't you stay and talk to grandfather about gate dangers?" Mirza vanished.

Andronan looked down at Killeen. "You're wondering what an old duffer that can't even stretch a gate knows about anything. Right?"

Killeen did something she never had done before—she blushed. Nailed, she thought. He had figured her reaction to a tee.

Andronan took off his glasses and polished them on the cuff of his robe. He paused briefly and his eyes took on a faraway look before he smiled at Killeen. "Gate safety, is it?" he murmured as if to himself.

Killeen dutifully nodded and said, "Yes, sir," politely as her mother had taught her. She had seen Andronan at a distance, but never up close. As a Sidhe, she knew she, like all her race, was a powerful magic worker. Usually humans didn't wield magic—not real magic, she thought. All of those spell books and years of studying to do things she could achieve with a blink of an eye, almost without any thought. Some humans couldn't sense magic, didn't believe in it! No wonder Arthurian and his court had a poor opinion of humanity.

It was Killeen's innate awareness of magic that made her so respectful toward the silver-bearded old man wearing the snow-white robe. He was the most powerful magician she had encountered, human or not. Mirza's abilities, impressive as they were, became as nothing when compared to this old man's mastery of the arcane arts. With a start, Killeen returned to the present, abandoning her train of thought. Andronan's eyebrow was raised in inquiry. Evidently he had asked her a question. She inwardly cringed, waiting for the punishment she knew she deserved for not paying attention. Arthurian would be scowling by now, a suitable chastisement already prepared and ready to inflict. Andronan, however, was smiling! Killeen couldn't believe it. All of the master magicians she knew of would have blasted her before now for her inattention.

"Wool-gathering, eh?" Andronan chuckled.

"Sorry, sir," she managed through dry lips. Her shoulders were tensed, prepared for whatever he chose to do.

"Relax, child." He knew what she was thinking. "How can I be angry with you when I, myself, have a tendency to wool-gather?"

At that moment, they heard a tap on the door. "Come in. Come in," Andronan commanded.

"Here you be, exactly as ordered," the servant said, putting a silver tray containing two large banana splits, complete with three cherries each, on the oval oak table, which he gave a swift polish using a rag he took from his belt.

"How does it get so dusty in here?" he murmured, obviously expecting no answer. He stepped back to admire his handiwork, asking, "Will that be all?"

Andronan gave him a friendly nod as he said, "Perfect, Martin. Exactly what I ordered."

"Of course. Have I ever failed to give you perfect service?"

The servant's voice didn't sound very respectful to Killeen. Arthurian would have toasted him on the spot for his insolence. Martin was through the door and gone in an eye blink.

"Did I make the right choice? Ice cream used to be the children's favorite," Andronan told her with a gesture to be seated.

Killeen was impressed with his perspicacity, and a little awed to realize the children he spoke of were Mirza, Lealor, Argen and Seren. Imagining the regal Mirza as a child was a stretch for her imagination.

Killeen felt comfortable enough with Andronan to ask a question. "How did you know I liked banana splits?"

"I believe it was Seren who told me. Basically, he's a nice person, under that war-like demeanor he forces himself to wear to impress everybody. He left here to go to Earth as a nice boy, but when he returned, he was a stern man. I have never asked, of course, since it's none of my business, but I am sure something happened there that changed him forever." Andronan shook his head sadly. "Forever…"

CHAPTER TWENTY-SEVEN

* * * *

This was the first time an adult had talked to her as if she were a grownup. No wonder everyone liked Andronan. Killeen did herself.

"May I ask you something?" she ventured.

"Certainly," Andronan assured her. "Nothing like a question to find out something you want to know."

Killeen gestured to their rapidly disappearing banana splits. "Uh, why didn't you…" she gestured with her hand, forming a million silver motes in the air.

"Magic, you know, takes energy. That's why I trained myself to let others do what they can, although a blink of an eye probably would be more expedient."

Killeen realized she had been given an important piece of advice in the nicest way. She made a mental note to remember it. As she thought about it, she realized she did have a tendency to zap items into existence without waiting for anyone to help her. It was a Sidhe trait. Probably part of her natural makeup, but not especially endearing to anyone who was incapable of magic. Was that why so many mortals feared magic users? People took pleasure in being part of things. She resolved to be more sparing in her use of magic—at least while she was among ungifted humans. This decision was to make her one of the most beloved Sidhe leaders in years to come.

Andronan took the last creamy bite into his spoon. He gazed at it in appreciation. "Didn't have any bananas here years ago," he told his guest. "Jarl brought a few rhizomes from Earth and started a small grove in the university gardens. Marvelous fruits, you know, filling and loaded with all sorts of good stuff. I think everyone here in the university likes them." He paused, considering bananas for a moment. "The peels are good for the roses, you know."

Her mother, Branwyn, would be interested to find that out, Killeen thought. She would have to send her mother a rhizome or two to try in their garden, once she figured out what a rhizome was.

The clink of Andronan's spoon in his empty glass dish brought her back into the present. Andronan, with a gentle gesture of magic so slight that Killeen almost missed it, removed a fleck of strawberry ice cream from his beard.

His eyes twinkled as he used a finger in a shooing motion toward Killeen. Immediately, the ice cream on the corner of her mouth disappeared.

"That was sure good," she said.

"Now that we are discussing good," Andronan said gravely, "I am supposed to talk to you about gates and their safe use."

I should have known, Killeen thought to herself. Adults are all the same. Here comes a lecture for sure.

"Not a lecture, dear child. Let us say I need to give you some information you do not have as yet, which you will need any time you travel anywhere using a gate."

He was so gentle and matter-of-fact that Killeen didn't resent his words. She pushed her dish to the side of the table and leaned forward, indicating her readiness to listen.

"Let me begin by telling you a story."

Killeen was surprised. Most adults of her acquaintance simply tore a strip off her when she had done something wrong. Andronan was telling her a story? She was curious.

"A long time ago when Mirza was a child herself, although it seems like yesterday to me, my son, Ciban—made up of his mother Cibby's name and mine, it was,—and his wife—Star, her name was—were in a hurry to go exploring and jumped into a gate without proper safeguards."

"What happened?" Killeen asked, realizing that she had never heard of these two people before. She had never thought about Mirza's parents. Indeed, it was difficult to think of adults as children and having parents themselves.

"They had no gatekeeper present when they left. Although we searched for months, we never found a trace of either of them. My only hope is that they landed together somewhere. I'm certain they are still trying to find their way home," he added sadly.

"That must have been terrible—especially for Mirza. She was only a child then, wasn't she?"

"Yes, she was. Cibby and I reared her."

"She was fortunate she had such nice grandparents," Killeen offered, sensing the deep sorrow of Andronan.

"Thank you."

Killeen watched silently as he blinked back tears.

He managed a smile. "Don't you grieve, child. It all happened long ago. They could walk through that door any time. At least that is what Cibby and I have been telling ourselves for lo, these many years." He brushed his hand across his eyes. "Didn't use to tear up like this. Sorry. It goes with being ancient, I think."

"That's all right," she told him. "I never thought about losing my parents before. It's a pretty scary idea."

"Not nearly so frightening as the idea of losing young people through their carelessness," he informed her. "When you use a gate, you need to remember that the Old Ones who first built them were in contact with thousands, perhaps millions, of worlds. Never enter a gate without making sure where you will come out."

Killeen nodded her agreement.

"After my son's disappearance, we set up the system of keepers so no one else would suffer the same fate."

Killeen looked suitably impressed. "I hadn't actually thought much about the gates. They were always there."

"I understand you are militarily inclined right now, but remember that gate travel is a marvelous thing. It would make an interesting field of study for you after you finish your soldierly phase."

"Aren't you going to give me the lecture about being ladylike?"

"A soldier is a wonderful person, willing to offer his or her life for others. Women have as many heroic tendencies as men. Over the centuries, while women heroes have been relatively few, there have been some great ones."

Killeen was just getting ready to ask Andronan to tell her about some of them when she heard a knock on the door.

* * * *

Mirza scowled as she noticed Jarl's packed bags. "Where are you off to?"

"I'm going to Dead World. It's time to start reconnaissance again."

"I don't like the sound of this. Don't you enjoy living with me?"

Jarl sighed. There she went again. If he was impatient, it was, 'Don't you like spending time with me?' Now, that he had a mission to perform, this was the variation. "I'll jump in the gate and return every evening." Mirza couldn't see his crossed fingers behind his back.

Mirza pondered. "There's a lot of that going on. O'Roark goes home to Fialla. Jack plans to come here to spend the evening with Nell. Rand assures me that if the palace had a mini-gate, he'd return nightly to Lealor. I'm not sure the ancients had this kind of use in mind."

"It shows how much we love our spouses." Jarl tried to pour oil on troubled waters.

"If you don't show up, I'm coming after you," threatened Mirza. An evil thought jumped into her mind. With him gone it would give her a chance to review gate problems with the Shadowlord.

Jarl gave her a kiss and ran to jump on one of the wagons lurching toward the gate. He pushed his body between two stoic dragons, placing a bag in each one's lap.

A few moments later, a shimmer of silver motes announced the Shadowlord. "He's finally gone, is he? Jarl and Lealor must be related. They are so unforgiving."

Mirza shot him a look. Had he been hovering unseen, waiting for the coast to clear? Was that crack about her husband and daughter supposed to be a joke? Mirza sighed. The Shadowlord was right about one thing. Neither of those two liked or trusted him.

"I've given a lot of thought to this gate enlargement problem," the Shadowlord continued. "A larger size requires more energy. The ancients must have designed a limit on the energy usage to protect the sun. Remember, every time I tried gate modification the sun became unstable."

"What's your suggestion?"

"Wake up Baloo. Seren needs him anyway."

"No!" Mirza frowned. "What does Seren need him for?"

"He wants Baloo to bend the frame of this universe on the right side of the battleline."

"That's impossible," Mirza protested.

The Shadowlord shrugged. Silver energy danced in all directions. "Who knows what a baby Bright One can do? I find in dealing with Baloo, you tell him what you want and he does it. Tell me making a tunnel between the planes of the universes was possible. I didn't even suggest that one."

Mirza felt her face flush. She knew Baloo had done that looking for her. "You're back to being deceitful. I thought you were changed."

"I don't see Oron or Cronal helping me or Baloo. They promised me the—I was going to say moon, but my case it was a sun," the Shadowlord said bitterly. "They are too busy to care about our growth."

"I agree you both have been neglected, but I'm not waking Baloo. Not yet anyway. There's too much history between us for me to give you motherly advice. Why don't you talk to my Grandmother Cibby?"

The Shadowlord drew himself up into a scarecrow's caricature. "Are you throwing me at an older woman?" He looked down his nose at her. "I'll find my own way."

The Shadowlord vanished.

Oh my, thought Mirza. I forgot to ask about the mini-gate. Maybe I should talk to Cibby to see if we can get help for Baloo and the Shadowlord from the Lady.

* * * *

As they glided over Dead World, Jarl sat astride Berdularion's back. *What's Seren going to do with that second sub?*

It's already filled with explosives for an unpalatable sandwich, the amused dragon replied.

What about the space capsules?

Stripped of everything except the breathing air and modified for an external oxygen tank. I believe Seren plans to use them as observation platforms. The dragon shook slightly as if that amused him, too.

Is it true you can return to the exact battle spot, Jarl threw out his hand, *out there in the void?*

Yes! Some material there remains uneaten by the monsters. Plastic, Seren calls it. I can locate myself using that scrap.

What are we waiting for? Let's go. Berdularion and Jarl vanished.

Flame and Seren had watched from the ground. *Well! Did they ask our permission for wherever they're going?* Flame demanded.

Seren laughed. *Why should they? We are only the children.*

Mari stamped up. *The ground slab is poured without Jack being here. What am I supposed to with all these weren? There are wagonloads of them pouring through the gate.*

Start laying ground mines on Dead World. I want the entire surface covered with them. Rudy has the plan. If you get this world finished, start on the asteroids, Seren told her.

Not mine! Flame punctuated his instruction with a sheet of fire.

You're going to get somebody blown up, Mari grumbled as she stamped away.

Seren chuckled. *That's the idea.*

She's not very nimble, is she? Flame observed.

* * * *

Wow! Jarl was shocked. I didn't anticipate anything this desolate.

You can make out the asteroid belt if you look that way. Berdularion pointed with a talon. The enemy will follow the edge of the belt right to our defenses.

Can you jump blind the same distance in the opposite direction as the belt?

Yes. Let me pull this plastic together in one glob first.

I've got a better idea. Let us move one of the larger space capsules here, suggested Jarl.

Berdularion's eyes whirled. *There isn't any us. I'm the one doing all the work, but taking the capsule will upset Flame. Here it comes!*

Great! Do it again. Bring another one.

The next space capsule appeared with a passenger holding on outside—the Shadowlord.

What are you two doing? Flame is going berserk. The Shadowlord chuckled in glee.

Climb on, the dragon invited. *We are going to make a blind jump— that-a-way.*

Where had Berdularion seen a western? wondered Jarl inside the capsule with the others hanging on outside as the vehicle and three disappeared.

The other capsule sat empty in space marking the departure spot.

CHAPTER TWENTY-EIGHT

* * * *

Martin stuck his head in the door. "Argen is in an uproar. He doesn't know how to put the spacesuit on this Earth human named Doc. He seems to be black like Ebony. There's quite a big crowd of onlookers."

Martin started to close the door, then shouted, "Andronan, you're late to your class."

"A black human? Neat. No one ever told me they existed. Can I come back later?" Killeen asked.

"Drat!" Andronan grumbled. "That class will keep me from seeing this wondrous thing, unless we take a field trip. Go, child. We'll catch up."

Forgetting everything, Killeen ported directly to the gate. She could see Argen was in a snit.

"What's all the fuss? The Shadowlord's black, or he was in the beginning. Earth humans come in yellow, brown and red, too—like dragons or wyverns," Argen complained.

As Killeen started putting the spacesuit on Doc, the crowd booed.

"Are they going to kill me?" the nervous Doc asked.

"No," Argen said with a sigh. "Right now, you're a novelty and they're unhappy because we're sending you away." He glanced around. "Where is Mother when I need her? She could disperse this crowd."

"We had better hurry. Andronan's coming with his class," Killeen added.

"Great. Killeen, you'll have to go along. Something's wrong on Dead World. It's as if nobody's watching the gate."

"No way. Seren was angry with me. Told me to stay here. I'm not getting into more trouble."

"Will I be a novelty at the next place?" Doc asked as they got ready to put on his helmet.

"I doubt it. The weren are more civilized. These yokels belong to Prince Leon. They live a very rustic life," Argen assured him. "Killeen, I'll take the heat if Seren's mad. I promise."

"Actually, with all the dust, you'll soon be gray like everyone else," Killeen told Doc as she dropped his helmet on. She pulled him into the gate and they vanished, as first Mirza, then Andronan, complete with his class, arrived.

Mirza frowned. "Grandfather, what is the meaning of this uproar?"

The mob and Andronan's class disappeared faster than the gate travelers, leaving a bewildered old mage facing Mirza and Argen.

* * * *

There's nothing here, the Shadowlord complained, jumping off the capsule to float in space. *Let's return.*

Not yet. Can you bring the second space capsule? Jarl asked Berdularion.

Yes, from where we left the spare though, not from Dead World, the large dragon answered.

Another space capsule appeared underneath the Shadowlord. *Are you happy now?* Jarl asked.

No! Flame's right. You—you two are insane, sputtered the Shadowlord.

Can you sense Dead World enough to bring a capsule half way here from there? Jarl gave his mount a friendly pat.

I don't have sufficient energy, Berdularion replied. *Maybe if we took some from the Shadowlord.*

The Shadowlord physically recoiled and moved behind the capsule. *You haven't the skill. Besides, I'm short myself.*

Oh, I don't know, the dragon mused. *You're forgetting Jarl's a perfect channel.*

Jarl grinned. He was enjoying the Shadowlord's discomfort.

A blinding light suddenly appeared. *What's this, a dragon threatening a Dim One?*

Since when did you become a babysitter, Drakon? Berdularion asked. He adjusted the lenses of his whirling eyes so he could see the golden energy plume in dragonoid shape.

The baby whined to Mirza. She told Cibby. Cibby complained to the Lady. The Lady caught me first. Oron and Cronal are nowhere to be found, so here I am.

Jarl chuckled. The Shadowlord considered a baby—he would never live this down. *I don't suppose you could move a capsule halfway here?*

Quiet, human! Drakon ordered. *I suppose if I have to replenish the baby's energy, I can boost yours, Berdularion.* Light flashed from Drakon to both the Shadowlord and Berdularion. *Be careful, brother,* Drakon warned the dragon. *You've never had this much power before.*

What about bending the universe's plane to seal the end of the Battleline, Jarl persisted.

I'm beginning to understand Oron's viewpoint about humans. Drakon glowed so brightly Jarl had to look away. He looked at Berdularion who nodded agreement to Jarl's request. *Very well. It's done.*

Now Lor, I'll take you to the nearest sun for lessons, Drakon told the Shadowlord, using his Bright One name.

I don't use that name any more, the Shadowlord protested.

Drakon blasted the Shadowlord with an energy explosion that tumbled Berdularion and his rider head over heels. *Quiet. Are you human-contaminated, too? First you whine, now you talk back to me? Enough!*

The tumbling dragon and his rider found themselves alone. Berdularion spread his wings slowly, breaking his roll.

Jarl, you do have more nerve than sense, talking to Drakon that way, the dragon observed. *Although he looks like a dragon, he is a Bright One.*

Got what I wanted though. Now bring a capsule halfway up this path we're making.

* * * *

When Killeen and Doc arrived on Dead World, no one was at the gate, not even a bottle dragon to protect Doc. *Blast!* Killeen sounded more like O'Roark than a young Sidhe maiden.

She teleported into the conference room only to find herself and Doc standing on a sleeping dragon. In fact, snoring reptiles surrounded them.

Mari, help! She screamed telepathically.

Mari appeared in mid-air. Doc moaned and fainted. The sight of a pink dragon floating in air was too much for the recovering alcoholic.

"What's wrong, Killeen?"

"I tried to teleport to the conference room and ended up here," Killeen explained, removing her grip and letting Doc drop on top of the sleeping dragon.

Mari chuckled as the door to the room splintered. Rand and Seren each tried to get into the room at the same time, causing both to tumble to the floor. Mari's chuckle exploded into laughter.

"Okay," Seren said as he brushed himself off and tried to look official. "What's the problem here?"

"Killeen ported herself and this guest," Mari pointed to the unconscious Doc, "into this den of dragons, not knowing you changed the conference room into weren sleeping quarters."

"There's no one watching the gate either. Not even a bottle dragon for humans in spacesuits," Killeen challenged.

"Don't look at me." Rand defended himself. "That's Berdularion's responsibility."

"He turned everything over to Flame," observed Seren. "Do we want Flame in charge of the gate?"

Rand pointed to the bottle dragon that had appeared. "Be careful. His spy is here. We don't have any weren gatekeepers."

"You do, too. I saw some in Andronan's class. He would welcome a practical training assignment for his students," Killeen interrupted.

Seren had heard enough although she was right. "What are you doing here?"

Mari interrupted the planned tongue-lashing. "Don't you think we should deal with the unconscious spaceman first and find a better venue for our accusations?"

Seren nodded his head in agreement, but he wasn't ready to quit everything. He pointed at Rand. "You get some gatekeepers from Andronan or man the gate yourself." He turned and stomped out of the sleeping quarters, raising a cloud of dust.

Mari picked up Doc. "Come child, the dispensary is still in the same place." Both females and the bottle dragon vanished.

"Great, go-fer or commander, whichever suits our glorious leader. Seren needs a sergeant," Rand grumbled as he closed the door on the still-sleeping weren.

* * * *

Doc opened his eyes to see Rudy trying to help Killeen get his space-suit off. Doc moaned. "Usually I see pink elephants. I haven't been near the sauce in weeks, and I still saw a pink dragon."

Rudy laughed. "She's real enough, and our boss, too."

As Doc sat up, one of the dragons grabbed his hand. The sight of talons along his wrist caused Doc to sweat.

"I'm a healer," the dragon announced. "All my problem cases are lined up outside the door."

Doc stumbled to the door, cracked it open and groaned. "They all look the same."

Rudy broke up in laughter again, ignoring Doc's scowl.

Doc tried again. "I'm a human physician's assistant, not a vet."

"You'd better learn to work on weren fast in case of battle damage," Mari announced. "I'll have them shift back to human after you examine them as dragons. You start learning how to treat dragons."

Doc, who hadn't noticed Mari, jumped a foot. He sank onto a stool. "I don't suppose you have any whisky?"

Mari stuck her snout in the air. "I'm not Rory," she said with disdain as she disappeared.

"What - What did that mean?" Doc stammered.

Rudy shrugged his shoulders, "Beats me."

Killeen giggled. "Her consort is named Rory. One of the things he's famous for is wheedling drinks of whisky."

"I suppose I might as well get started," Doc grumbled. "Thanks, Killeen, for getting me here alive—I think." He watched her grin in reply and dart out the door. He was shocked to see a hand grab her by the back of the neck.

Seren's voice carried through the open door. "Not so fast, my little aide."

* * * *

Rand was trying to explain things to Mirza. "I need a weren keeper from Andronan's class even if it's only a trainee. Would you please ask him for one?"

Mirza frowned. "It sounds like an idea he'd like. Why don't you ask him yourself?"

"I need to run down O'Roark. Seren is driving me crazy. I think a good sergeant would help. Where is O'Roark, anyway?" Rand frowned.

"He's on Widdershins running a surprise inspection on the skeleton crew he has securing his training base."

"Good. After I persuade him, I can get Lealor to Dead World. That human, Doc, is there. She wants Rudy to have a transfusion and several cronies plan to attend. Please get that mini-gate installed while she's gone."

Mirza wasn't satisfied with the information Rand was giving her. "Who's manning the gate?"

"Killeen."

"She's not a trained keeper."

She's better than nothing. Besides, she's being punished," Rand told Mirza.

"Punished?"

"For not staying at the university. Boy, is Killeen mad at Argen. Says his guarantee of protection from Seren's anger is useless.".

"Where's Jarl?"

"Out in space," Rand answered. He watched Mirza's face go white with shock, then flush with anger. "He's with Berdularion, so he's safe."

Misunderstanding, she shook her head in disgust "Like his last rider, Miklos?" *Librisald, front and center.*

The old dragon appeared on the platform.

"Watch the gate," Mirza ordered.

She gave the 'look' to Rand. "See Andronan yourself. I'm going to Dead World."

Mirza floated down to the gate and vanished.

CHAPTER TWENTY-NINE

Killeen shivered as she gazed into the ebony sky. Looking toward the void, she saw total blackness. When Killeen turned toward the known worlds, she could see the stars, dimmed by the vast distance between them and Dead World. Never before had Killeen felt so alone, so bereft, so miserable.

How long would she have to sit here waiting for Seren to come and release her from her assignment? Acting gatekeeper in a Sidhe's eye, she thought with a mental snort. Punishment defined this job. Dead. That's what this part of the universe was and that's what her chance of replacing Mari was. Considering the university and her goal to design space armor as a personal solution to her problems seemed dull.

The Sidhe, by their very nature, were involved with life in all its myriad forms although they were prone to using illusions when it suited them. No Sidhe would imprison a living being in a dark, cold place like Dead World without first bespelling them into a long sleep. Killen could not sleep. Seren had assigned her to tend this seldom-used gate.

A tear made its icy way down her cheek. Hadn't some earth poet —Shake-something-or-other—said, "To sleep, perchance to dream...." Killeen flicked the small ice crystal onto the frozen ground.

It would be easy to set the gate for the center of a sun and jump through it. No one had tested whether a Sidhe's powers were greater than a sun's heat. She sighed. Who would miss her? Perhaps her mother and father would finally notice she hadn't been around for a long time and wonder where she had gone. One of the things she envied the humans was their close family ties. With her father injured, Prince Leon took more of an interest in her than anyone she was related to in her Sidhe family. She thought briefly about Drak. His aura attracted her. She overheard Fialla say something about a vision of Killeen and Drak together. Would he miss her? Probably not, she thought while blinking back more tears. Having frozen teardrops on her face was really unpleasant. She sniffed despondently and kicked a rock, which overturned the chamber pot Seren had outfitted her with before leaving—so much for all Fialla's lectures about modesty.

The knocked over chamber pot called the bottle dragon. He listened to Killeen's thoughts and fled. Who to report to? Flame was out of range. Maybe Mirza?

Killeen thought of her mother's palace and shook her head. If her parents found out about this stint of gatekeeping, Argen and Seren had better watch out! Argen, she thought, as if his name were a curse. So much for a human's promise! Hadn't Argen said she wouldn't get into any trouble with Seren if she accompanied Doc to Dead World? She would never forget the look on Seren's face when he spotted her. He hadn't even given her time to explain!

A Sidhe with any sense wouldn't have trusted a human. Some of the Sidhe hated humans. Even Arthurian only allowed them around when they could help him. Strange, the humans made friends with all kinds of creatures, including Baloo, the Bright One, and the Shadowlord, a damaged and now abandoned Bright One, who had made so much trouble for the humans by creating gates that destabilized suns. Jarl's family, in particular, had suffered. While Argen and Seren had forgiven the Shadowlord, they abused and punished her.

At least it was interesting around the humans. The young Sidhe were so cold and proper. They never wanted to do anything that was fun. And the adult Sidhe! They treated everyone—even their mates—with such disinterest it was no wonder few Sidhe were being born.

She wiped her eyes on her hooded robe. She was tired of materializing tissues and handkerchiefs. The ground around her was littered with used tissues. Her pockets were full of soggy handkerchiefs. She looked down the path formed by the gate.

Nothing. No one.

Maybe she should run away and join Arthurian. She closed her eyes and thought. Should she? He might even marry her and they could rule together. What of her plans to be the best warrior of the known worlds? She had already mastered the sword and all the other weapons commonly used in battle. Berdu had taught her dragon tactics. She wanted to learn about human tactics as well. Although Seren had been cruel and unfair, she had to admit he really understood warfare even when he was fighting another species. Actually, his knowledge was all that stood between the worlds of the gates and the enemy. Killeen was sure of this. Was it worth sticking around to see how things worked out? Maybe…

* * * *

As Mirza came through the gate she saw the huddled figure of Killeen. Quickly moving to her side, Mirza knelt and covered the little girl with her cloak. Mirza found herself seized by an outside force as Killeen broke down in tears.

Is this what is meant by sobbing women? The thought blazed into Mirza's mind.

Angry at the tone and irritated at the interruption, she turned her head to be blinded by a brilliant light. Turning her face back, she shielded her eyes with her hand. Mirza peered through the natural gaps of her fingers. *Shadowlord? What happened to you?*

Your meddling is what happened. The Lady sent Drakon to instruct me. I got a dose of revitalization and instruction on how to tap uninhabited suns.

I would think you'd thank me for my 'meddling', Mirza snapped. *How about making yourself useful and creating some kind of cover in that rock surface?* Mirza noted Killeen had become still and had moved her head so she could peek at the Shadowlord.

Never one to miss an opportunity to show off, the Shadowlord's eyes blazed as they acted like lasers cutting a square out of the rock surface. He levitated the perfect cube and hurled it into the void in the direction of Flame's home asteroid. *Let's see that blowhard explain that,* the Shadowlord gloated.

Now, a smaller second room farther in would be nice, instructed Mirza.

The Shadowlord snarled. *Women!* Never satisfied, he thought to himself as he cut out the smaller room. He threw the small rock cube after the first. *Anything else, your Majesty?*

Well, pocket doors would be nice. That requires magic, not energy reserves.

Your wish is my command. Circular doors for both rooms rolled out of the walls. Before the last one closed, a flash of energy shot into the room. The Shadowlord's attitude conveyed his belief that he had done enough. Before Mirza could think of anything else, he vanished.

Mirza calmly rolled the doors open and marched into the first room with Killeen trailing behind. *I think some wall tapestries would be nice.* They instantly appeared, followed by weren-sized chairs and sleeping pallets. More furniture materialized until Mirza was satisfied. *There, basic keeper comfort has been established.*

What was that last flash of light? Killeen asked.

Look at the far ceiling corner. Both light and heat—a small damper is required. There, that's better, Mirza exclaimed in glee.

A bottle dragon appeared in the room. Under one arm he carried a new chamber pot, the other held a container of water. His eyes whirled at the changes.

In there. Mirza pointed at the next room.

The bottle dragon deposited his load. He hurried outside to gather up the knocked over chamber pot and fled.

The antics of the bottle dragon caused Killeen to show a small smile.

Must have been a male, Mirza observed. *They are all afraid of us when we are adjusting our living conditions.* She smiled at Killeen. *Sit and explain to me how you got mistreated while we wait for the weren keepers.*

* * * *

Seren joined Jarl and Berdularion in his newly opened section of the main cave complete with breathing air. "Rand isn't back yet. I'm not going to wait. Explain to me what you two have been up to," Seren began.

Mari lay curled up by the door. Her snort represented her opinion of waiting for Rand.

"Where are Flame and the Shadowlord?" Jarl asked, stretching.

Berdularion pointed a talon at the bottle dragon. "This one serves Flame's wishes. Flame wouldn't be caught dead in my home."

"I've been here for some time," the Shadowlord murmured, perched high on a cliff in the cave. Only his eyes blazed in the dark. His body remained covered by a black-hooded robe.

"Currently there are two capsules sitting where the sub was eaten. We leap-frogged them out into space doing a search, but returned. It's quite obvious the space capsules can be used both as markers and as observation or listening posts. They can be manned by young dragons who sleep most of the time anyway," Jarl began.

I'll make the assignments, Flame interrupted mentally. He blew a smoke ring in his own asteroid home. The link to the bottle dragon was strong, and the BD coughed.

"The only thing left to decide is where to place the subship," Jarl continued.

"One space capsule is left," Seren pointed out.

"Oh, I planned to use that to search for the enemy"

"Mother won't like the idea," objected Seren.

"You've got bigger problems with Mirza." The Shadowlord's eyes danced with glee. "She has taken Killeen back to Realm."

"Who's watching the gate?"

"Weren from Andronan's class per your instructions, Seren," Mari said. "The Shadowlord's right." She added as if surprised at agreeing on anything with him. "Mirza isn't happy with your treatment of Killeen."

"Killeen disobeyed."

"Argen required her to." Berdularion joined the conversation.

"She didn't tell me." Seren shrugged.

"Killeen tried to, but you wouldn't listen." Mari blew three perfect smoke rings in Seren's face.

"Oh boy, and I missed going home several nights." Jarl moaned, thinking about Mirza's promise to come and get him.

"If we can get back to business and leave the subject of wedded bliss," the Shadowlord suggested. "How close are we to being able to kick in the hornet's nest?"

Mari reported. "We poured the walls on your underground mansion. They have to cure before we can start the roof forms." She curled her tail around her front feet like a cat. "Next time, find a crisis for Jack back on Realm or Earth. He's a real pain during construction."

"The minefields are placed on Dead World and seventy-five percent of the other bodies in the Battleline," Seren added. "Of course the space mines have been in place for some time."

"The weren are armed and practice daily. Enemy contact will tell us if we did the job right," Mari observed.

"See, you old fossil. You're not needed. Go home! Flame ordered his father. Put the subship out in the middle between the observation stations. I'll start dragon patrols between the stations in addition to manning the stations when Jarl leaves.

"You need to complete your underground module and finish laying mines before you locate the enemy," Berdularion advised. "But I agree. Flame's right. My presence is no longer required. I'll use up my extra energy by moving another large space body up to the right side where Drakon bent the universe. Then I'll return to Widdershins. More killing I don't need." Berdularion closed his eyes in resignation.

Mari jumped into the planning. "We have lots of details to complete. For example, Rudy still needs a transfusion. What's the order of battle? Where are we going to house more troops?"

"Boring," the Shadowlord said. "Don't call me until Jarl goes on reconnaissance. Maybe I'll court his widow."

* * * *

On the surface of Dead World, Flame was sitting beside Seren trying to raise the subship. He could get it about a foot off the ground, then it crashed down to settle deeper in the gravel. Both were covered by rock dust. Flame's tail, beating the ground in frustration, added still more dust. Neither heard Berdularion land behind them.

Berdularion cocked his head, and threw both Flame and the subship out in the void to the spot preselected by Flame.

Flame's mental shriek of rage penetrated back to Dead World.

He doesn't sound too happy, Seren observed.

Gives him something to remember me by, Berdularion said, vanishing.

Did he pun? wondered Seren. One thing was for sure. He didn't bother using the gate.

Where is he? Flame slid to a landing.

Gone! Before you get your talons tangled in an uproar, consider you couldn't lift the ship he threw out with you, Seren warned.

Flame belched fire at Seren and disappeared.

A chuckle behind him froze Seren in place. Turning, he saw a gleeful Mari.

Relax. Flame went back to his asteroid cave to sulk. He's not dumb enough to chase after his father. What did you want to see me about? Mari asked.

Seren pointed back toward Eyre, Realm and Widdershins. *That closest world—what's it called and is it occupied?*

It's Sierra—nothing there but mountains and ice. It's the dwarves' home world. Why?

Seren hesitated. *I need you make a treaty with the dwarves so we can pull our troops back there in safety. Also figure out how the dragons can pull multiple weren through space. I could use some dwarves here to do some tunneling, if that helps negotiations.*

CHAPTER THIRTY

As Killeen stepped out of the gate, Arafel threw her arms around Killeen in a gigantic hug. "How could you think none of your Sidhe relatives love you?"

Killeen felt a warm glow inside. "How—How did you hear me here?"

Arafel patted her stomach. "I had help. He heard you and kicked me until I listened. I think Arthurian is wrong again. This child is special."

A neglected dragon bugled from the courtyard.

"Sparrow," Killeen shrieked, running to throw her arms around his neck. "You came to greet me, too. I've missed you so."

Mirza had been silently watching the welcome. "See, child, you are loved. Go home with Arafel and Sparrow, though I don't know where he's going to fit. Tomorrow, get together with Andronan for some more gate instruction. Prince Leon will have to straighten out your class schedule."

Seeing Killeen's less than delighted look at the thought of school, Mirza added, "Think of all the horses that have been neglected while you've been gone."

Killeen grinned and skipped off towards Arafel's home with Sparrow waddling behind waving his tail in the air, keeping time to inaudible music.

Mirza gave Arafel a hug. "Ah, the resiliency of youth. Thanks for coming. Your and Sparrow's presence was a needed boost."

"We love her more than she realizes. Will this experience damage her relationship with Seren?"

"I doubt it. Killeen's whole goal in life is to earn Mari's position. Now she's learned that Seren doesn't listen well. I may do some damage to both Argen and Seren. First, I have to run down my wayward husband."

Arafel giggled. "They do get to be a pain sometimes—don't they?" She nodded and started after Killeen.

Mirza waved a greeting to the stoic Librisald standing on the platform above the gate.

* * * *

"Well, how did you like being a gatekeeper?" Andronan asked as he and Killeen resumed their session on gate safety the next morning.

"Boring."

Andronan chuckled. "That's what Mirza thought before a rogue gate pulled her to your world of Achaea. Then, Lealor got sent to Widdershins on a gate malfunction. The right word is *dangerous*."

"Everyone knows Baloo caused that malfunction."

"True, but the mishap did take place." Andronan paused. "Do you see a pattern here? Mirza's parents gone, Mirza snatched to Achaea, Lealor ending up at Widdershins, and this happening to experienced gatekeepers? Does it make sense why Seren doesn't want you diving into open gates?"

"Seren!" Killeen spit out the name like O'Roark would a curse. "I'm sorry, but I don't want to be a gatekeeper."

"Fair enough, but you must respect the gate system. You should learn how to look through the gate and entertain yourself with what's happening on the target world. Let's go to Realmgate and look through at Widdershins. Then I'll consider my duty completed. If you ever change your mind, my class is always open to you." Hand in hand, Andronan and Killeen walked toward the portal.

* * * *

"When were you going to tell me?" Mirza asked, giving Jarl 'the look'.

Jarl glanced around frantically. What had she discovered? "The space capsules are all safely positioned."

"That was bad enough. I'm talking about your plan to search for the enemy. It's called reconnaissance, right?" Mirza's foot tapped in short little bursts of energy.

Jarl was relieved that her tapping foot and arms folded in front of her were the only signs of her wrath. "Who else can do it? Flame certainly proved he hasn't the right disposition. Berdularion has gone back to Widdershins, Killeen's too young, and neither Rand nor Mari is willing." Jarl kept his voice very reasonable and conciliatory.

"That isn't the question." Mirza took a deep breath. "Let me repeat myself. When were you going to tell me?"

"I can't go until Seren's bunker is finished. He's introduced a re-lationship with the dwarves. I have no idea where that's going. It may cause further delay."

"Since you won't answer my question, I assume the mighty Dragon's Knight was going to sneak off like a grounded teenager. Remember, if you don't come back, I'm coming after you." Her sigh signaled her ire was spent. "Meanwhile, let's concentrate on some quality time with each other."

* * * *

Mari and her guest entered Seren's temporary office. "Meet Prince Johan from Sierra."

Seren rose and held out his hand in greeting. "I'm surprised you responded so rapidly."

"My father, Teuton, understands that you are what's between us and an unknown enemy. He would never require a fee, but if you persist, one barrel of German beer per weren would be welcome."

Seren chuckled. "How much per dragon?"

"They stay outside. Dragons definitely are free. We have plenty of caves. Inside, there is an atmosphere, but not quite like what the weren are used to."

"Do you have a gate?"

"Probably, but we haven't used it for so long no one knows where it is."

"Mari, see if some of the weren gatekeepers can sniff out the portal. If that doesn't work, get Mirza to search. It will make receiving barrels of beer much easier," Seren explained. "We'll send over some of the dragon oxygenators. You'll wonder how you ever did without them."

"I'm your liaison, so I will stay here," Prince Johan told them. "I can't wait to try this flying around on contraptions—kiting, I think you call it."

Rudy's chair glided into the office. "My cue, right? Follow me, Johan." The air-chair spun and left, Johan trailing behind.

"I want all the weren moved to Sierra except those necessary to finish construction on my building and the ones you classify as berserkers. Tell O'Roark that his new troops are also going to Sierra."

* * * *

"I hope Argen buys a beer factory." Mari snickered. "You do realize Sierra is a long way from Dead World and the battleline? You're not going to get any timely support."

"Find that gate. Remember, I asked you to come up with weren carriers that the dragons could pull. Also I want a space-mine net on the back side of the battleline. Send Flame to me. That's all. You're dismissed."

When Flame appeared, he looked around in surprise at his father's quarters. "This isn't too bad for a has-been."

Seren shook his head in disgust. "That 'has-been' did a good job here in addition to saving your life. Now it's time for you to measure up. I want you and your dragons to find fallback caves on Sierra."

"We will never retreat."

Seren went red hot with anger. He pushed his face almost into the dragon's large whirling eye. "You will do what I tell you, or I'll blow you up myself. The enemy won't get the chance."

Flame pulled his head back in alarm. Could he do this? These Koenigs were full of surprises. After all, they had bested the Shadowlord. Their father was the Dragon's Knight. Maybe he'd better be careful. "We will do what you say."

"Good. Also, I want space-mine cages around the space capsules. That's too far for weren, so the dragons will have to set them up. See Rudy for instructions."

"Rudy is getting weaker. Maybe you hadn't noticed?" There, thought Flame as he stalked away. I can play this silly game because you don't have eyes in the back of your head. Flame vanished.

* * * *

"I don't understand," Doc complained. "Why can't I do the transfusion back on Realm or wherever we're going?"

"Realm doesn't have a facility like this and Rudy needs it now," Mari explained. "Also, I've invited guests."

A knock on the door announced Lealor and a tall old man in a shining white robe. "Hi. Where's the patient?"

Doc looked up at the distinguished old man. "Who do you think you are? Aesculapius?"

"Why yes, I am, and this is Queen Lealor of Widdershins."

Doc was saved from further embarrassment by the appearance of Rudy. "Hi, Lealor. Do I really have to go back to Realm and leave space?"

"Now, you know, Rudy, I haven't a clue about military planning. That's Rand's expertise. Let's see how you're doing." A picture of moving particles appeared on the wall.

Doc knew he was seeing Rudy's blood. He had no idea how.

"There aren't any large knots, so the pain must be less. The number of knots has doubled. How do you feel, Rudy?" Lealor asked.

"You're right, not much pain, but I get tired so quickly."

"What do you think?" Aesculapius asked Doc.

"A transfusion is part of the standard treatment, but it's not a cure."

"That's what we came to watch," Lealor agreed.

"It's pretty simple. Rudy, get out of the chair and on the table."

Lealor gave Rudy a boost of energy to help him.

Doc inserted the tubing and rigged up the bag. "Now all we do is wait."

Lealor put Rudy's bloodflow up on the wall again.

"It spreads the knots out, but there's no reduction," she said, pouting.

"I think Doc would like a more scientific term than knots," Aesculapius suggested.

"Nah," Doc said. It works for me." Doc completed the transfusion, and warning Rudy to rest, sent him on his way.

"No modern cure?" Aesculapius asked.

"No, he's my friend, but there's nothing I can do," Doc replied with a grimace. "He's terminal. Taking him out of space will kill him more quickly."

"I'll talk to Mother," Lealor promised as she and Aesculapius left.

Discouraged, Doc stood there scratching his head. Who was Mother, and how would talking to her help?

* * * *

Seren looked up in surprise as his mother and Argen barged through his Dead World office door.

Mirza shoved Argen in the direction of a couch. "Sit there," she commanded. She turned and faced Seren. "I don't like the way you're treating my granddaughter."

"Granddaughter?" Seren was lost.

"She means Killeen," Argen volunteered.

"Oh. You're buying into that farseeing of her and Drak. I thought farseeing was very inaccurate," Seren observed.

"Mine is," Argen offered helpfully.

Mirza drew herself up in a righteous position. "In this case, three of us are seeing the same future, although there is a small chance of my being wrong. No one has treated a keeper like you did."

"Killeen isn't a keeper. I sent her out to watch the gate as punishment."

"She is a natural keeper, better than any being Andronan's got in his current class. Unfortunately, she wants to be a warrior. Why are you trying to punish her when Argen guaranteed you wouldn't?"

Seren glared at his brother. "You did what?"

Argen shrugged. "I told her that if she took Doc to Dead World, I'd protect her from you."

"As if you could. When were you going to tell me?"

"I thought you'd listen to your own people. I'm not scared of you like they are."

Seren sat back and pushed his fingertips together. "So I made a mess. The little minx had a false promise of protection. She's a gatekeeper in disguise, and all the females project her as a future relative."

"Don't forget you didn't listen," Argen added.

"Quiet," Mirza snapped at Argen. "Your hands aren't clean on this.

"Actually it's worse," Mirza continued. "Seren, when was the first time you saw Killeen?"

"At Argen's famous subship meeting. She sat on Flame's tail."

"How much real time has gone by since?" Mirza inquired sweetly.

"About a Widdershins year, but she's bigger, older." An odd look passed over his face. "Bright Ones in a bucket, she's been bespelling me into thinking she's older." Seren groaned. "Think of all she's accomplished and she's only a kid."

"Well, she'll be protected now—from both of you."

"Wanna bet?" Argen muttered under his breath.

"What was that?"

"Nothing, Mother." Argen fumbled with his hands. "I merely observed Killeen has a mind of her own and a will of iron."

"While we are on unpleasant subjects, Rudy is terminal. Bringing him out of space to Realm will accelerate his illness. Why don't you keep him here?

"Anything else, Mother? You're full of good news. I can use Rudy here. If nothing will save him, he can help save us."

CHAPTER THIRTY-ONE

Berdularion, you shouldn't be here at Eastpoint, Jarl admonished. *Flame is still furious about being flung into space.*

Who is going to know? I didn't use the gate. I've put the sentinel dragon here in the other capsule to sleep. Let's move his spare oxygen container on to the one you're going use as a ship.

Why? I already have a spare.

We don't know how long you're going to be searching out there. Having spare oxygen never hurts. One of the bottle dragons will replace this container anyway.

I was trying not to leave tracks

A missing space capsule isn't a track? Who are you kidding? Everyone has agreed with the need for your reconnaissance mission anyway.

Not my wife. That's why I'm sneaking off. The capsule being gone is so obvious, Flame might not notice it.

Berdularion snorted smoke. *I don't doubt it, but the bottle dragon assigned here will spot the change instantly.*

Okay, Jarl agreed reluctantly.

Are all the Earth systems Argen installed working correctly?

Yes, I've got air-jet steering, rockets fore and aft for movement, and air-to-air missiles for protection.

The giant dragon shook his head. *No metal or heat radiates from that enemy. The missiles will be useless.*

That's not correct. I can direct them and blow them up mentally. I may let the enemy take a bite out of the warhead first, Jarl joked.

You'll change your attitude when you're face-to-face. I found them frightening. If you're ready, get inside. I'll fling you into the void, saving your rockets.

Jarl melted into the ship, gradually being absorbed by the ceramic tile, and prepared the space capsule for his adventure.

That's a neat trick, Berdularion thought. *Jarl's spending too much time around the Shadowlord. That's the kind magic he's famous for.*

Berdularion fixed the second spare oxygen container to the ship. He concentrated on the magic necessary to anchor himself in space, then picked up the ship between his talons. He lifted the spare capsule over his head. Utilizing as much of Drakon's energy boost as possible, he flung the vessel out into the void. He enjoyed being able to access all that power. It was like being young again. Brushing his talons along his scales, he faded from sight.

* * * *

The chief bottle dragon knew something was wrong by the way his underling was approaching. The BD looked ready to bolt. "What's the problem?"

"There's no spare oxygen tank at Eastpoint."

"We have spares. Replace it."

"The other space capsule is gone."

"That explains everything. Jarl's left on his mission. He took the spare oxygen tank."

The BD wasn't through. "I can't raise the watch dragon."

"Is he alive?" his supervisor asked.

"Yes, but he won't respond. Somebody has to tell Flame."

Ah, there is the problem, thought the chief bottle dragon. Flame's temper has been out of control. The BD doesn't want to be blasted. "Thank you. I'll check it out."

The chief bottle dragon appeared at the Eastpoint lookout and materialized inside the capsule. He sniffed. He could smell the enchantment. Who was capable of this? Fafnoddle certainly, but the odor wasn't right. No stale vegetables. He could smell steakfruit—Berdularion. It had to be. The chief BD ported back to Dead World.

How to tell Flame? That was the problem. The chief bottle dragon hurried toward Seren's office. Maybe he could 'accidentally' bump into Seren or Mari. He'd have to explain why he was in a hurry. Let one of them tell Flame. Rounding the corner he saw he was in luck. Seren, Mari and the Shadowlord—all in one place.

Mari hunched her pink dragon form down to bring her eyes level with the others. "The only weren left on the Battleline, beside the berserkers, are those constructing the second shelter. They are also working on a structure to hide the turbo generator prior to shutting it off. The old sub batteries are all charged. You'll only have power for three days once the generator stops."

"What about some old-fashioned torches?" Seren asked.

"Won't work. The only wood on this world comes from shipping pallets. All the wood disappears as if by magic. No one knows where it goes. You'll have to use those Earth gadgets called flashlights."

The chief bottle dragon deliberately ran into Mari, knocking them both sideways.

* * * *

"Whoa, what's the rush?" The Shadowlord grabbed both dragons, using his augmented energy to stabilize them.

"I've got to get information to Flame," the bottle dragon explained.

"Balderdash," the Shadowlord said. "Flame doesn't reside on this world and you can use telepathy. What information are you afraid to give him?"

"The—the spare capsule is missing." The bottle dragon stammered.

"That's not upsetting. We knew Jarl was going sometime," said Mari. "What else?"

"The Eastpoint dragon is bespelled and snores like he could sleep forever." The little dragon whispered. "The whole area reeks of dragon magic."

"Ah," Seren observed. "Jarl had dragon mage help. Since you're afraid to tell Flame, it must have been Berdularion."

"I'll take the place of the watch dragon, if Flame can remove him," the Shadowlord volunteered.

"Great, but first give me a chance to visit Flame in his asteroid cave," Seren agreed. "At the very least, Flame will have to select where we dump his dragon sentinel."

"I wouldn't want to wake up in Flame's clutches," the bottle dragon murmured with a shudder.

* * * *

Seren had never before visited Flame's asteroid home. The rock walls weren't smooth like the cave on Dead World. Seren touched the jagged wall and pulled his hand back with an oath. He looked at the cut on his finger and wondered how the enemy could eat asteroids.

Stop! Be recognized, the sniffing sentinel demanded.

Open your eyes, Snare.

The dragon cracked one eye. *Oh, it's you. Should I tell Flame you're here?*

Please. Seren continued down the corridor, finding Flame on a glowing bed of coals, his tail in a roaring fire. His oxygenator must be redlining, Seren thought. *Now I know where all the missing wood goes.*

Yesss, I get cold in space. Here, touch my talon.

Seren reached out carefully, not knowing what to expect. The talon was ice cold. Seren released it quickly. *Do you ever get warm?*

Flame shifted deeper into his bed of coals. *I'd like to learn Drakon's secret of capturing energy from unoccupied suns.* His eyes whirled backward, the dragon equivalent of a chuckle. *Drakon loaded my father so full of energy, he leaves sparks when he walks. Berdularion will have to stay in dragon form for some time until his energy level lowers.*

Do I detect that you're not angry with him?

Flame blew a puff of smoke at Seren. *I can respect him when he's in dragon form. It's the Berdu form that angers me. That and taking charge when he thinks the situation's dangerous.*

Seren nodded. *I can relate to fatherly presumption. Jarl has taken off to locate the enemy without giving me a word of warning. That's one reason I'm here.*

Flame snorted. *I gather the second reason is what's got all the bottle dragons hiding. When I get warm enough, I'm going to shake them for being cowards.*

Your father evidently helped mine. The Eastpoint watch dragon is bespelled.

Flame lifted his head and shook it. *The relationship is very unusual. Jarl is teamed with Fafnoddle and Father is teamed with Miklos. I've asked Fafleen to research if secondary bonding ever happened before. The other strange thing is that the male dragons are magi, but the female humans are magic wielders.*

Seren was startled. *You mean Ebony and Fafleen aren't magi?* His mind spun. Was Flame claiming to be a mage?

They are dragons. Remember Ebony could not break free from the Shadowlord herself.

Seren marveled at Flame's attitude. Next time he needed cooperation, he'd make sure the dragon was physically warm. *As I remember the story, Mother couldn't handle the Shadowlord without help. Can you remove the bespelled dragon from the Eastpoint space capsule so the Shadowlord can take his place?*

Flame smacked his tail in the fire, causing Seren to duck flying embers. A sleeping dragon appeared in a corner of the cavern.

How are you going to wake him? Seren asked.

Flame replaced his head back on the coals. *It's a time spell. We'll sleep it off. The Shadowlord is in place.* Flame's eyes closed. Two dragon snores rumbled in the cave.

Seren figured he'd been dismissed.

* * * *

Jarl jerked against the restraints and then banged his hand against the side of the ship. He struggled to get awake and find what caused the jarring noise. He felt like it was pureeing his brain. Finally realizing the cause, he shut down the alarm and looked out the hatch window at a sun. Further inspection showed three worlds in orbit in the distance.

He checked his instrument panel. He had recorded the vector he'd come here on so he knew what direction to follow home. A series of numbers appeared on the distance dial, but Jarl didn't know the measurement they represented. He started fooling around with the optics. One of the worlds jumped into focus. He could see that it was covered with strange bug-like beings, which were eating everything.

Another alarm went off. Jarl changed the picture to find a horrible scaly face occupying his screen. The large mouth was gruesome with vice-like jaws. A white maggot wiggled from one eye. Worse, the creature was rushing toward his capsule. Jarl realized that one of the reasons the monster was closing so fast was because his capsule was still moving forward. Too late, he slammed on the braking jets. The apparition, which didn't inspire in Jarl a desire for closer contact, filled the screen. Jarl fired a missile that refused to track. He guided it mentally right into that ravening maw and detonated the warhead. The capsule shuddered as remains buffeted the ship. Berdularion had been right on both counts. Jarl's attitude had changed, and he found the enemy frightening.

Jarl scanned the area around his vessel—nothing. He returned to the optics that let him view the worlds below. Uh-oh, hundreds of the creatures had taken flight. The way their wings moved reminded Jarl of beetles or Texas tree roaches, but they were sufficient to get the monsters airborne. Leaving his observations, he marked the distance numbers in his log, reversed the azimuth to return home and fired his rocket motor.

The trip back exhausted Jarl, but he felt too worried to sleep. He kept the instruments focused behind him. His heartbeat picked up speed and pounded like jungle drums as his worst fears were realized.

Hundreds of monsters were chasing him—and gaining.

CHAPTER THIRTY-TWO

A surprising, but welcome voice, entered Jarl's head.

This is the Shadowlord. I'm at the Eastpoint watch capsule, but space mines have been placed around it since you left. Brake long enough for me to hitch a ride toward the Westpoint capsule and the asteroid field.

What about that lookout capsule near Drakon's dimensional warp? Can we save that one? Jarl asked, braking the ship once more with its air jets.

Maybe. I'll try to put that capsule behind the second maze of world mines. The Shadowlord's landing made Jarl's vessel rock. *I'm aboard. Let's go.*

Jarl noticed the time spent had been costly. Three of the lead monsters from the chasing pack were upon them. *Watch out!* he cried.

Two dragons appeared out of the darkness and flamed the two closest creatures, but winked out as more arrived.

Will you get this ship in gear? the Shadowlord demanded, ducking the third attacker. *I'm on the outside, remember? For that partial rescue we can thank Flame and his dragon patrols. At least they're alert.*

Jarl fired the maneuvering jets toward the asteroid belt. Looking back, he saw the watch capsule vanish and space mines surrounding Eastpoint explode, killing more monsters. *The capsules are recovered. It looks like someone had the same idea about saving them.*

What is all over this ship? It's bad enough to be ducking monsters and globs of goo from that explosion, but it's so slick I can hardly hang on. Besides, that third attacker will get turned around sometime. Move, for Bright One's sake.

Jarl started to grin, remembering when the remains of the first creature he killed with a missile hit his ship, but he instinctively ducked as several monsters made a pass at the capsule.

The Shadowlord used his eyes like lasers to destroy the two closest attackers. *I'm going to be the main course in a monster meal. Can't this thing go any faster?*

Not on steering jets. We're almost at Westpoint. I couldn't navigate between the asteroids if I fired a rocket. How far into the field should I go?

The Shadowlord blasted a couple more creatures. He watched two dragons flame several more and vanish. *Flame's using his dragons wisely this time. They appear, flame some of these monstrosities, and then disappear. Good tactics.*

We're passing the space mines that protect the Westpoint station. Do you think those things will be attracted to the steel of the cables? Jarl asked.

Think I can't see the cage? I'm outside, remember? Go into the field about a hundred Earth yards. Slow down, the Shadowlord ordered as the capsule tipped, dodging an asteroid, almost throwing him off.

Make up your mind. First you demand speed, now I'm going too fast, the angry Jarl replied.

Stop here. I've got a good field of fire. The Shadowlord ignored Jarl's outburst.

Jarl applied the braking jets and hurried to a viewport. He could see the creatures climbing the empty space mine cage. It went off in a blast of energy, which made him flinch. *Are you all right?*

Of course. I need to figure out a way to collect the energy from blasts like that. I'm going to hold my fire and see how the enemy approaches the asteroid field.

Jarl took the time to watch the horde. He turned his head in disgust as they ate fragments of their blasted comrades. One monster collided with an asteroid, which meant he instantly became part of the food chain. Another landed and started nibbling on an asteroid. It spit out chunks of rock, lost its perch on the asteroid and rolled over, apparently dead.

The Shadowlord quickly destroyed the other enemy close to the field. *Do you have anything to bind that dead monster?*

There are some nylon slings aboard.

Get out here with them. Hurry.

Jarl and the Shadowlord bound the dead creature. *Now what?* asked Jarl.

Attach yourself to the body and teleport yourself to Realm. Seren wants a dissectible specimen.

You're kidding, right? Jarl felt nauseated. I don't have that kind of energy.

You bragged how you could channel energy from me earlier. Do it. I'll make it easy for you, but hurry. Company is approaching.

Jarl climbed under the webbing. Even in space, contact with the dead being made his skin crawl. He opened up energy channels to the Shadowlord and vanished.

The Shadowlord chuckled as he passed into the space capsule. Better be careful what you brag about, he thought. He settled in to watch the enemy attack develop.

* * * *

"I'm only a physician's assistant, for Pete's sake, not a forensic expert. I've never assisted in a morgue," Doc complained, standing in the middle of the university's new operating room.

"Right now you're a royal pain the rear," Argen said. "You're the best we have, so get with it."

"You didn't give me healers to help me dissect this monster. These guys actually run a meat market. They are butchers."

Argen made a feeble attempt at 'the look'. "That's why you have them. They're experienced at cutting things up."

Doc stopped trying to reason with Argen. At least he had an assistant manning a tape recorder. Maybe he could make Argen sick. "The subject is short of eight feet long. The wings start right behind the head and are also eight feet long."

Doc paused. "Turn him over," he instructed the butchers before he continued. "The six legs are four feet long when fully extended. The front two don't look much good for walking since they have pincers. The body is uniform, with no visible segments. It has no ability to bend. It seems armored."

Doc nodded to one his assistants who hit the body with a large knife that bounced off the chitin that encased the creature. An assault with an axe resulted in a glancing blow that sheared off a leg at a joint.

"Hold it. There's a tricolor, greenish, yellow-brown liquid flowing from where the leg got cut off." Doc looked around for Argen, but he had already left. Too bad. Varicolored blood would have made Argen sick.

Doc continued. "The front pincers are unusual. They have an opening on the top. I can see a tube as part of the front leg or arm running back into the body. The head, ugh. It looks like something I'd imagine after a week's drunken binge. The eyes are large, insect-like with no eyelids. I notice three holes where a nose might be located. No visible ears or antennae. As to the maw, it's large, about two-thirds of the face. Unfortunately, the maw is closed and won't move."

Doc motioned to his assistants. "See if you can cut off the head."

They were able to wedge a knife between the head and body, but couldn't widen the gap. Axes also proved ineffective. A large saw with a butcher laboring at each end eventually did the trick. Now the floor was covered with the strange-colored fluid from the body.

"Move the head to this table," Doc requested. After working with it for a few moments, he said, "I can't force the jaws open very far. Get me a hydraulic jack."

"That's not a standard butchering tool," one of his assistants complained.

Doc threw up his arms in disgust. "Do it," he ordered. Walking over to the body, he peered inside the opening. "The body appears to be one gigantic stomach. No visible heart or lungs. The smell is horrendous. The fluid color inside is mainly green." Doc took a long metal rod and poked the residue in the stomach. The mess crumbled like play sand.

A sullen assistant entered and announced, "Here are some hydraulic jacks. I brought several sizes."

"Good. Let's force the mouth open." Doc continued his monologue. "The jaws look like what you might see on a vise. It appears they could crush anything. Evidently the pincers cut up objects and feed the maw, which crushes the pieces. There would be no way to get loose from this mouth. Again, most of the head is mouth."

"Let's see if we can get an eye out," Doc ordered.

After a lot of effort, the eye came out in three pieces. "Ah, an optic nerve which goes up to—spaghetti? Nothing I recognize as a brain, only this mess of white pasta. Damn, that stuff moved. Smash it quick, but save one strand."

The butchers responded with mallets.

"Get some drills. I want to determine the thickness of that head and this body." Doc turned back to the main carcass. He traced the tubes from the pincers up to sacs inside the stomach. When he cut open a sac, a bolt of energy discharged from the new opening, causing him to jump back.

The butchers, having better reflexes, hit the floor that was awash with bug fluid.

Doc couldn't help but laugh at the results. The yellow-greenish-brown goo covered them. "Get cleaned up, but turn this carcass over first."

Doc found the wings broke off easily like the legs. There was no armor down the dorsal surface under the wings. He frowned, looking at the ten-foot tail. What value did it have?

Using a butcher knife, he cut lengthwise along the exposed back and discovered two intestines and two orifices. Doc experimented moving the tail. He found that it would seal one orifice at a time. By then his two assistants had returned. "Drill holes every three inches on the head and body and record what you find. Put that white pasta string in a glass jar. I've seen enough." Doc left to get cleaned up.

When he came out of the shower, he sighed. "Now if I could only contact that leprechaun, Rory."

"You called?"

Doc stared at the leprechaun floating in the air. "I'm told you can produce Irish whiskey."

Rory held out a flask.

"Ah, detox, here I come. Would you care to join me in a gigantic bash?"

Rory nodded, and the two got down to serious drinking.

* * * *

When Argen opened the door to Doc's room, he found two drunken bodies littering the floor.

Rory cracked one eye open, but at the sight of the furious Argen, he vanished.

Argen got Doc into a chair. "What's wrong with you? After all the money we spent to get you dried out, why start drinking again?"

"Fell off the wagon before. Hic. Real monsters this time, full of strange, multicolored goo." Doc fell back to sleep.

Argen shook him. "I need answers now, not when you get sober."

"Okay." Doc belched. The sour smell drove Argen back. "Theories only. I can't prove anything. Better use armor-piercing bullets. Regular ammo won't get through that shell. Never found a heart or ears. Most nerves, breathing apparatus, are inside the shell. The beast is flatulent. It moves through space by farting. First one side, then the other. The tail works as a stopper. The jaws can crush anything, the pincers can cut anything and it has a dormant ability to fire energy from the pincers. Rip off the wings and the creature is vulnerable.

"Now I'm going back to my nightmares, which don't come close to that monster."

Argen hurried. He gathered up a copy of the audiotape, took photos and wrote down Doc's conclusions. He met Killeen on the way to the gate. "Can't talk now. I have to send this information to Seren."

"I'll take the packet to the gate for you, if that would help," Killeen offered.

"It sure would. I've got to check whether we have any armor-piercing ammo." Argen stormed away.

Killeen smiled when she approached the gate. Librisald was on duty. Unauthorized use of the gate would be a piece of cake. She waved Argen's documents. "Urgent information for Seren," she said, passing through the gate with a smile. How easy it was to fool humans!

Seren watched a large screen showing huge numbers of the enemy increasing in front of the space mines. "Have they found the spacesub yet?" he asked Rudy.

"That blew up an hour ago. It took about a hundred of them with it. Sometimes I think what one knows, they all know. Then they do something stupid."

"Explain."

"We installed space mine cages around the watch capsules. When the enemy appeared, Flame removed the capsules, leaving the cages," Rudy began. "They charged all three cages, so we blew up another hundred. They should have changed their approach after the first one. Another example is the time-fused bombs the dragons are throwing into their mass. There's no reaction—except death."

"Okay, I see the case for stupid. What's your case for shared knowledge?"

"Leaving the Shadowlord alone in the asteroid belt, for one. He's only a threat if they attack him. Second is how they approach our main space minefield after hitting it the first time. They stay well back. My guess is they will try to blow a corridor through the field."

Seren grunted his agreement. "I was surprised that your crews could replace the mines triggered by their first contact. Your recognition of that opportunity and the dragon cover were excellent."

Mari joined the two of them. "I've got Doc's report on the enemy body. Shouldn't we give those things out there a name?"

"Watching them travel in space, they look like snakes with that tail whipping back and forth. It's amazing how they move in unison without getting tangled. How about Slithiz?" Seren asked.

"You're the boss. Anything is better than enemy," Mari said. "Doc has a half-baked theory as to why they—I mean the Slithiz—move like that."

"What's bothering you?" Seren noticed her unease.

"Doc's report. It wasn't in the usual transmission case. I found it stuck between two boxes of armor-piercing ammo with a red ribbon to attract attention."

"Maybe somebody read it before you did," Rudy suggested, still glowing from Seren's praise.

Mari shook her head. "No, the report had never been disturbed. You can tell when something's been read. There's always a smear, a turned corner, a page out of order—something." She gave her dragon equivalent of a grin. "That's how it is now, Seren. I read the report."

"Are the armor-piercing munitions all distributed?" Seren scanned the conclusions, more interested in practical aspects.

"Your berserkers have them. We're ready to leave. The gate is shut down and covered with twenty feet of gravel. The turbo-generator is off. You've started your seventy-two hours of battery power. The generator's cover has been installed and there's a gravel layer over it. It looks like a small hill. That's the best I could do. My weren on the back side of this world are ready to leave. When we're gone, only you, Rudy, two space mine-setting weren, and the berserkers remain. The bottle dragons have left."

Seren took one of her talons in his hand. "Excellent. Thank you."

"Oh, no, you don't. I'm not saying goodbye in this shape." Mari changed into her leprechaun form and, ignoring the chain of command, gave Seren a kiss, then vanished.

"She didn't have any clothes on," Rudy gasped in shock.

Seren chuckled. "No, she didn't. Isn't that the dream of every warrior? To be kissed goodbye by a naked female?"

"Certainly not mine." Rudy was embarrassed. He knew Seren and Mari didn't have a romantic relationship. Who would with a pink dragon or foot-high leprechaun?

"We don't need all these lights for two of us. Can you cut everything off but the screen? That should give us longer on the batteries."

"Sure. It's done. How are you going to finish reading Doc's report?"

"I've got my trusty flashlight." Seren took out his light and clicked it on.

"I don't. Do you have any spares?" a female voice asked out of the darkness.

"Kill—Killeen," Seren sputtered in anger. "You're back again. I thought you were grounded. Does Mirza know you're here?"

"Of course not. I've been delivering mail."

"You brought Doc's report." Seren put the pieces together. "Where have you been hiding?"

"Visiting the weren berserker groups. They're my troops, too. Now they know somebody cares about them." She flashed her new light on the list of teams that would be sacrificed to defend the line's surface.

Seren felt embarrassed. He should have visited the berserkers. "None of us left on the Battleline plan to survive. I don't suppose ordering you back to Realm would work?" He reflected his anger by the red glow from his eyes that lit his face in the dark room.

"Nope. I'm going provide a Sidhe protective shield for you and Rudy. I hope my magic will save your life."

"Or cost you yours," Seren grumbled.

Killeen kissed Rudy on the cheek. "There. Now you have a kiss, too. From what you said, I guess having my clothes on is acceptable."

"Yes!" Rudy and Seren replied in unison.

While Seren read Doc's report again, Rudy and Killeen watched the screen view of the thousands of gathering Slithiz. Rudy knew Killeen would not understand, but he now knew how Custer felt seeing all those Indians.

* * * *

A couple of days later Rudy observed the horde begin moving. "It's starting," he yelled.

Seren roused himself awake to see the leading Slithiz hit the front field of mines. They didn't take the time to eat their dead, but poured through the hole in the space minefield. "Where's Killeen?"

Rudy shrugged. "Out with the berserkers, I guess."

Killeen, get back here, Seren ordered telepathically, hoping she'd pick up the command. He banged the flashlight on a chair arm in frustration.

"I'm here. Why the uproar?" Killeen slid into Rudy's light beam.

Seren pointed his red light pointer to the picture on the screen.

"Impressive," Killeen muttered. Hours later as the onslaught continued, she changed her opinion to boring.

Typical warriors, Rudy and Seren slept.

CHAPTER THIRTY-THREE

"Flame says about three-quarters of the Battleline is covered with the Slithiz, and all the dragons are exhausted to the point that they can't flame," Rudy reported as he observed the screen.

"I didn't know you could hear dragons. How long have you been able to do this?" Seren rubbed his eyes from the strain of reading by flashlight.

"Since I got here. When you or Mari talk mentally to them, it's strange because I only get the dragon side of the conversation."

Seren shined his flashlight around the empty conference room. "Where's Killeen? Some aide—she's never here. Maybe one of the magi will put a locator on her so I can keep her in view."

"She's been rescuing injured berserkers. Once the enemy was on the surface, the berserker mission of not making things too easy was complete."

Before Seren could explode, Killeen entered the room. "Boy, is Argen going to be mad."

* * * *

"Not as mad as I am at you putting yourself at risk." Seren rose to his feet and leaned over his desk. "What possessed you to go out there on the surface with those monsters?"

"It wasn't that bad." Killeen took one step back before she remembered she was a soldier. Soldiers didn't retreat at the first salvo in a battle. "Flame always created a distraction for me. Besides, Sidhe aren't very high up on the Slithiz food chain. Metal is number one, eating their own is two. Concrete block, particularly mortar, is three. Rock is four. Ammunition is item five." Killeen giggled. "I had fun blowing some of that up once they ingested it." She returned to the menu. "Weren are next on the delicacy list."

Seren was not relieved. He sat with a sigh. He couldn't seem to stay angry with Killeen. Could she cast a spell that made people like her? Seren wouldn't put anything past her. She was a little rascal that made good things like rescuing the berserkers happen. "What is going to make Argen mad?"

"Because the weren survivors are cutting off the ends of his precious cement mixers. They are going to hide in there when you blow the place up. Most of the berserkers are hurt. I sure wish we had kept some healers. I don't have much skill in that direction. Is there time to port the wounded before we blow this place?"

"Probably not. We didn't plan on survivors. How long before the weren are inside the mixers?" Rudy maneuvered his air chair closer to the red destruct button.

Killeen wrinkled her brow as she concentrated on mental images. "They are all inside now."

Seren sent the disengagement order, *Flame, retreat to Sierra. There's fifteen minutes on the clock before everything explodes.*

"Sparrow is on the other side of the rear space mine-field. He says the Dead World coverage by the enemy is now seven-eighths. The occupation of the other asteroids is about fifty percent," reported Killeen, communicating with her favorite dragon.

"Put up our protection shield, Killeen. Rudy, give us a two minute warning before you push the button," Seren ordered.

"It wouldn't hurt to get under the desks in the front of the room," Killeen suggested.

"What? Your big shield, the reason you disobeyed and came here, isn't good enough to bring us through this without a scratch?"

"I've been experimenting with the shield in the berserker fighting. It gets dents, sometimes."

"This, from the young lady who was playing it safe? What about Rudy?" protested Seren, who wasn't happy with the idea of hiding under a desk. Leaders did not hide.

"I'll be fine. I'll direct my chair to a corner. I've put the lights back on. No sense saving batteries now. Two minutes until I push the button," Rudy said.

As they found their way to the front, Seren observed Killeen materializing two wads of cotton, which she stuffed in her ears. Noise protection, he thought, or she had found another way to ignore everybody's orders. He watched Rudy push the red button on the wall.

In the split second between Rudy's pushing the button and the explosions, Rudy's life force went free.

The room shook. The noise was tremendous. Shield or not, the force of the explosions threw Seren and his desk against a wall. Seren lost consciousness.

* * * *

The surface of Dead World was gone. Rocks, gravel, enemy parts, and building materials hung above the surface. The heavier items slowly settled in the weak gravity while dust and small particles flew into space. Asteroids disintegrated, broke in two or crashed into each other as the explosion went outward in all directions. Simultaneously, the blast of the front space minefield riddled everything nearby with shrapnel. Rudy's design masterpiece painted destruction along the Battleline.

* * * *

Seren slit one eye open and quickly shut it. The bright light made it impossible for him to see.

"Back among the living, are we?" A voice sounded from far away.

Seren forced both eyes to open. He hadn't expected to survive, even with Killeen's Sidhe shield. "Doc? Where am I?" his voice croaked.

"In the new university hospital on Realm," Doc replied. "It's a hospital in name only although Argen is pouring equipment in here right and left." He gently placed a friendly hand on Seren's shoulder. "You weren't in prime shape. You had two busted eardrums, which your sister, Lealor, fixed—not me. Bruises over ninety percent of your body, which time will fix, and a severe concussion."

Seren weakly waved one hand to quiet Doc. "Killeen?"

"Didn't you hear Sparrow, her pet dragon, bugle when you woke? She'll be barging in here shortly. She's fine. She's got a few bruises like you. Remember, Killeen wadded cotton in her ears. She is smarter than you, senior commander."

True enough, Seren saw Killeen rush through the door. He could hear Doc, but didn't hear any dragon bugle. He saw the door slam against the wall, but the noise was faint.

Killeen slid into the side of the bed, grabbing Seren's hand as the bed shook. "I'm sorry my shield wasn't better."

Doc removed her hand. "Back off. He's too sore for your touching and rambunctiousness. Seems to me your shield was pretty good—you're both here." He grinned. "Next time stuff his ears with cotton, too."

"Rudy?" Seren asked.

"Didn't make it." Doc's voice broke. "Not a mark on him. He was hanging onto life to push that button. Must have died right afterwards with a grin on his face. The undertaker won't have to fake that smile."

Killeen wanted to have this discussion later. "My weren in the cement mixers all made it," Killeen said. Her tone indicated how proud she was that her idea worked.

"Enough talk. You're too weak," Doc ordered. "This shot will put you back to sleep."

"I just woke up," protested Seren, trying to wave Doc away.

"Too much company," Doc declared. He ignored Seren and administered the shot. Seren's eyelids closed.

Mirza stormed into the room. "You knocked him out again? Before I could talk to him? I knew I should have ported." Mirza glared and took out part of her ire on Killeen. "Back to pots and pans, little girl. You weren't released to come here."

Killeen scowled, but remembering how powerful Mirza was, refrained from sticking out her tongue. Killeen's glamour to make herself seem older never fooled Mirza.

"He's going to be fine," Doc assured Mirza. "Earth medical rules are in force here. He needs to rest."

Killeen left the room and skipped down the hall. She had seen Seren conscious and his mother hadn't. Pots and pans were a small price for getting one up on the witch. She allowed herself a rather fiendish grin.

* * * *

When Seren woke the second time, Mirza was pacing the room.

At his stirring, she darted to his side.

"Mother?" he said weakly.

"I wasn't going miss talking to you again. Besides, it's the only way I can keep that minx out of here."

Seren tried a smile. It hurt, but not as much as a frown. "Killeen?"

"Who else? I did go into a rage when I found out she'd sneaked off to be with you again on Dead World. Librisald spent a little time as a toad until Jarl made me reverse the spell.

"After the earlier gatekeeper incident on Dead World, Killeen's Aunt Arafel was worried about your relationship. Bah! If Killeen was older, I'd worry about it, too."

Seren sat upright. "Mother!" He groaned and eased himself down. "You've already married her off in your visions—remember? She saved my life. The bunker wasn't sufficient."

"I know it, but I will teach her to obey. I've invited her mother for a visit. Branwyn picked right up on why. The three of us are going to rein in that filly."

"Three?"

"Oh, I forgot to mention Fialla, our recently-wed gatekeeper. Let's change the subject. This one makes me angry."

"I understand, but it wasn't that long ago you were giving me the lecture that Killeen's only a little girl. A little girl that the whole weren nation adores, not to mention Berdularion and Sparrow. Be careful."

"Don't worry. All three of us love her, too, but she's going to finish school and learn discipline. Even Ebony will help."

Seren chuckled, then grabbed his side in pain.

"Now, what's funny?" Mirza asked, folding her arms across her chest.

"The last I heard, First Egg had disappeared over a small matter of discipline. Doesn't sound like Ebony brings much to the party."

Mirza glared at her son for a moment, then dissolved in laughter. "You're right. First Egg and Killeen are winning, but we have to try. This generation is so powerful."

She heard a small noise in the hall. "Rand is outside, eager to bring you up-to-date on the battle. Why don't you talk to him for a while?" Without waiting for a reply, Mirza rose and motioned Rand into the room.

"I need to check on Killeen's whereabouts," trailed back through the door.

Doc stuck his head in the room. "Ten minutes."

Rand looked perplexed.

"That's when he gives me a shot to put me back to sleep," explained Seren.

Rand shrugged. "It seems like a sleep spell would be better." He paused. "Where to begin... After you blew up the Battleline, Berdularion led a flight of older dragons and magi against the remaining enemy. The explosion of the front space minefield was masterful. It blew up thousands of Slithiz in space at the same time as the Battleline erupted. The enemy survivors drew back to the area where the space capsules used to be. So all Berdularion and his army had to do was mop up those stunned by the explosions."

Rand shook his head and continued. "I'm around dragons all the time, but I forget how mean they can be in battle. Even the magi like my wife scared me. When they were done, nothing alive was close to Dead World except some Slithiz in Berdularion's old cave. The weren took them out with flamethrowers.

"Jarl rode Fafnoddle, I got Sparrow, and Prince Johan rode Flame, of all things. Did you know that Flame could sense where you were located? Besides, he wasn't good for fighting by then, because his fire energy was exhausted. About all Flame could do was smoke and hiss. The other two dragons were nasty enough to make up for him. Boy, can dragons dig. Once the dragons uncovered your bunker, Jarl and Prince Johan piled into that concrete structure. They found the weren in the cement mixers first, then dug their way in to you and Killeen."

"How many Slithiz are left alive out in the void?" asked Seren.

* * * *

"Maybe twenty to thirty thousand. You destroyed seventy percent of their force."

Seren sighed. "Too many still live."

"They'll never get past the Battleline. Let me tell you what's going on now. The weren have rebuilt the front space minefield. Prince Johan and Jack - I'm surprised that a Scotsman and a dwarf can agree on anything—are designing and building an underground fortress. We know what weapons work now and the world's and asteroid's surfaces are full of pillboxes with anti-aircraft weapons. If the Slithiz all came at once, they couldn't get by, even if the dragons weren't there."

"That's it. Time's up," Doc announced, shoving Rand out the door.

When Seren saw what looked to him like a foot-long needle, he said, "I can manage a sleep spell." Seren pushed the needle away. "Tell me how long you want me out."

* * * *

When Seren opened his eyes again, he found Killeen in the chair next to him, her knees drawn up to her chin. "Hi, kid. I thought you were grounded."

Killeen stuck her small nose into the air. "I am not a kid, I'm a royal Sidhe. Your witchy mother has gotten mine to come to Realm along with my used-to-be best friend." Her face fell. "They are plotting against me."

"Best friend? Oh, you mean Fialla."

Killeen sniffed. Didn't Seren care if they plotted against her? She'd thought after that explosion they would be buddies, even if he was the big cheese. "What do you want me to do?" she asked, realizing she would get no sympathy from Seren.

"What I said the last time. Get both a military and engineering education. I need humans in space. The maximum number of weren available for military duty is five thousand. Add a couple hundred dragons and that's what we've got to take on thirty thousand Slithiz. We must have a spacesuit that doubles as protective armor for humans to fight this enemy. I'm not comfortable with that mass of enemy alive out there. I don't care how good our fortifications are." Seren gave her his version of his mother's look.

"Okay, I'll be the perfect little lady. I'll go to school and study hard. I'm interested in spacesuits because of Rudy, so I'll design a good one."

Seren smiled. This time it didn't hurt as much. He must be healing. He couldn't see Killeen as a perfect little lady—at least not for long.

Killeen hesitated. "Speaking of Rudy, the weren have a request."

Seren scowled. That still hurt. "The ones at school?"

"No, the ones on the Battleline. They would like to name Dead World after Rudy."

"Not now. Let's table the idea. It's too painful. Maybe, if Doc or O'Roark know his last name… When were you in contact with the weren on Dead World?"

"Yesterday. I don't need a gate anymore." Oops, she thought. Maybe I shouldn't have told him that. Better change the subject.

"You're losing the conference room where we were. It's being made into barracks again." She held up a small hand to quiet Seren. "Don't worry. They're building a fancy new one."

"Do you think visiting Dead World is a part of being a perfect little girl?"

"That was yesterday before I promised." She decided not to give in too easily. "I'll have to think about it." She ignored the expression on Seren's face and rushed into speech before he said anything. "By the way, Dead World is worse than before. It's flattened. A six-inch layer of dust covers everything." She paused at the sound of footsteps in the hall.

"Uh, oh. The wicked witch is coming." Killeen vanished.

Mirza entered the room and sniffed. "She was here."

"I wouldn't know, Mother. I woke up moments ago." As Killeen's senior officer he felt he had to cover for her.

"Fibber! The two of you are thick as thieves. You could help."

"I am, Mother. I am." He hid his amusement with a long-suffering expression.

* * * *

Later, as his daily exam was underway, Seren asked Doc, "What do I have to do to get out of here?"

"You know where the fountain is in the center of town?"

Seren nodded.

"The fountain is one mile from the hospital front steps. When you can run there and back, you're free to leave. Begin by walking."

As soon as Doc left, Seren found a pair of fatigues and started dressing. His bruises were changing to a light shade of green. His skin looked like a frog's. Getting dressed proved painful. Amazingly, the boots didn't touch any sore places.

When he made it out the front door, he found Arafel with a baby stroller waiting for him. "Can you walk two miles?" he blurted.

"I walked farther than that each day before I had him." She pointed at her sleeping son. "If I can't make it, you can join me on a park bench."

Seren enjoyed the walk. Arafel knew a lot about what was happening on Realm. She didn't gossip, but kept up a running commentary. Seren wondered if she would have the time to print a small newssheet. He was exhausted when he returned to his room and fell into bed to sleep, still dressed.

* * * *

The next morning when he went out, Nell and her children greeted him. Seren got tired watching them scamper back and forth on the lawn. During the walk Nell brought him up-to-date on the university. It was obvious his company was being carefully selected. This time when he returned, he got the fatigues exchanged for the typical gaping hospital gown before dropping off.

The third morning, Killeen was waiting. She rattled on about her courses until they were halfway back from his daily trek.

"Don't you think you could do the rest at least double time?" she asked, breaking into the gait.

No little spitfire was going to best him! When he returned to bed, Seren repeated his first day's performance by falling asleep in his fatigues.

He could hardly wait to see who had been lined up for him the next morning. It was Henning with a squad of men.

"This is the obese squad," the sergeant explained. "We will be with you every morning until you make the run. Won't we, fat squad?"

"Sir. Yes sir," they shouted in unison.

That morning, Seren double-timed all the way back. By the end of the week, everyone was running the two miles. Seren pointed this out to Doc.

"Okay, you're released tomorrow morning."

The next morning Seren dressed in khakis so he could still wear jump boots. The hospital was strangely deserted. When he came out the front door he found Killeen and a beautiful woman who looked vaguely familiar. He scowled at the way Killeen was dressed. From the lack of skirt length, Debbie must be her new role model.

"Hi, I'm Killeen's Aunt Ithanel, in case you don't remember. I brought our daughter here. I wanted to introduce you to your child before you left Realm."

* * * *

Seren's discomfort at being greeted by someone he had a forced one-night-stand with rose as he became aware of the crowd lining the steps and route to the gate. He drew back.

"Oh no, you don't," Killeen said, grabbing his arm. "They came to see their hero and thank you. If I have to behave, you have to walk this gauntlet of praise."

Ithanel took his other arm and the two females walked him down the stairs and onto the roadway to the cheers of the onlookers. Now, he knew where the hospital staff was. They were all on the front steps. He twisted so he could see Doc's beaming face behind him. Seren knew who set this parade up. "Remember, Doc," he called. "Paybacks are hell."

After a couple of blocks he saw Arafel with two strollers. Ithanel left his side. She picked up one baby and presented her to Seren.

"This is your father, Kerrigwen," she told the child she had brought for Arafel to foster.

Seren tried to figure out the correct holding procedure. This wasn't included in his army manuals. When their eyes met, the baby smiled. Seren heard the mental voice of his daughter. *"Da-da."* He was lost. She loved him. Now he would have to spend time on Realm. This wasn't in his plans. Awkwardly he returned the youngster.

Ithanel took back Seren's daughter and kissed him on the mouth. The crowd loved it. She returned to Arafel's side to be replaced by Henning. The crowd continued cheering.

"Is it true you've rejected that gorgeous creature?" Sergeant Henning asked.

"Not my child." At Henning's surprised look, Seren said, "Oh, you mean the Sidhe. Yes," Seren replied with a scowl.

"Mind if I chase her?"

"Please do." Seren was flustered.

Killeen's giggle interrupted his thoughts. He thought she sounded relieved about his feelings. Half a block down, Seren stopped by Sergeant O'Roark and Fialla. He knew instinctively this was where Killeen would leave him. He turned his cheek for a kiss.

"Oh no you don't," she repeated. Killeen twisted his face by his chin and kissed him full on the mouth, then laughed at his expression, skipping to Fialla's side.

"You're too young to know how to do that," Seren bellowed over the laughter of the crowd.

"She's eight going on twenty-eight," O'Roark agreed. "No male is safe."

His wife, Fialla, shook her finger in O'Roark's face. "I'll keep you safe."

"What about me?" Seren tried to look defenseless.

"You live in interesting times." Fialla felt glad she was only a simple Widdershins gatekeeper.

The crowd whooped again.

Seren looked at his two sergeants. "Can't we double-time to the gate through this mob?"

Both sergeants nodded agreement, so they double-timed down the street to the increased roar of approval. As they neared the gate, Seren saw both of his parents and Andronan. Good grief, was that Cibby beside him? She almost never left her woods cottage to come to Realmgate.

It slowly penetrated that the obese squad was decked out in their dress uniforms as an honor guard. He gathered enough fat had been knocked off them for Sergeant Henning to give them this duty honor.

His mother hugged him and wiped his eyes with her handkerchief. "Mother," he protested. "Those two sergeants must have photographers posted. I'll be blackmailed for years."

"Hush. Hold me tight. I still want to be one of the women in your life. Now greet your great-grandmother."

Seren bent over to give Cibby a kiss on the cheek.

* * * *

"No way," she said. "I want a proper kiss like all those young hussies. I'm proud of you, Seren, even if you are mentally unbalanced. What possessed you to blow yourself up?"

"It was the only way to stop them, Grandmother."

Seren straightened. Arm in arm with his father and Andronan, they approached the gate. He hugged both before stepping onto the portal surface, vanishing to Dead World.

CHAPTER THIRTY-FOUR

In that short period, Seren had forgotten how dim and red the light was on Dead World. This wasn't the original gate. If he hadn't seen Rand waiting in a tunnel entrance, he'd have been worried. He walked up the slope and gazed at the surface of the world in shock.

It was a desert. A Sahara without an oasis.

Behind him, the weren in dragon form were replacing a removable rail beside the gate. Finished, the concrete cover on the rails slid over the gate. The noise startled Seren. The weren were now shoveling sand on top of the cover.

Seren walked to the lighted tunnel entrance where Rand was sitting on a golf cart. *What's wrong with the old gate?*

Nothing. Let's go inside so we can close this thing and talk normally, Rand urged.

The large vertical hatch slowly closed, leaving a whitewashed, well-lighted corridor. "You ought to be able to hear me now. We try not to do anything that is in the Slithiz's visual line of sight. Johan did dig down and expose the old gatekeeper's room that the Shadowlord made. He and a crew are tunneling toward it as we speak. It's slow work. They have to pour concrete walls, columns and roof beams frequently."

Seren climbed into the golf cart, which started along the tunnel. "I'm surprised by the surface of Dead World."

"Why?"

"I thought there'd be carcasses lying around, other signs of the conflict," Seren replied.

Rand scowled. "That's right. You didn't know. We gathered everything in nets—carcasses, expended war material, ammunition, and garbage—then fed the Slithiz."

"What?"

"Argen read in a book that humans attack when they're hungry. Maybe it's true for the Slithiz. It got rid of the surface mess and they're fed. We've been bringing in excess garbage from other worlds once a week. It's sociologically expedient."

Seren was horrified. Feeding the enemy? What next? "I might have known that you and Argen would have another crazy idea like using submarines in space. The two of you are beyond belief."

Rand turned the cart into a large, cavern-like straightaway.

Seren groaned. Troops were lined up on both sides of the passageway.

"Hand salute!" rang out.

Seren raised his hand to return the salute. The music for "Pass and Review" blared from speakers.

"Much more efficient riding in a golf cart than marching," chortled Rand, pleased with himself.

They turned another corner and Seren put his hand down. The cart stopped in front of a massive doorway. The whole underground area was large to provide dragons easy access.

"We can use the small entrance over here," suggested Rand. He gestured towards a closed door, which opened to reveal a massive conference room. His entire staff was present, including Flame.

Seren raised his eyebrows when he noticed the dragon was sitting on a gray panel.

Understanding Seren's unspoken question, Flame answered, "Sssteam coils to keep me in a good mood."

"Seats." Seren ordered the rest of his staff. "Do you all support this feeding program?"

"We had a little trouble with Flame at first," Mari replied. "He kept trying to smuggle a time bomb into the garbage." She glared at the unrepentant dragon.

"A lot of worlds are benefiting," Rand added.

"Not to mention yours and Argen's pocketbooks." Seren grumbled. "Environmentalists must love the program."

"It is probably too late to change feeding cycles without triggering a battle," the Shadowlord told him.

"What about communication? Have we been able to talk to the enemy?"

"Doc never found any ears or slits like the dragons have. Battle analysis confirms that they have no sense of hearing. An explosion out of their line of sight doesn't cause any reaction." Rand shrugged his shoulders.

"How do you know? You weren't here." The Shadowlord leaned forward.

"I tried to communicate mentally." Mari, tried to defuse the tension between the two. "All I got was a high-pitched squeal and a vision of a ball of wiggling white worms. Ugh. The effort was very painful."

"We created a simplified Rosetta Stone out of plastic—the only thing they refuse to eat—and included it with the garbage. The Slithiz threw the plastic disk out of their feeding area," the Shadowlord added.

"The disk is moving very slowly toward the asteroid belt," said Johan. "I had Flame add a position marker nearby when I noticed the change. The space marker isn't moving."

"That disk bothers me. We are still running attacks out of the asteroid belt on non-feeding days. In addition to attrition, I'm trying to force them to face two directions," the Shadowlord explained. "How could the Slithiz physically hide in the belt?"

Seren nodded approval for having two fronts. "It's obvious to me that they'll never try to land on this desert world again. Which means they'll try to go through us to Sierra." Seren pointed to the screen, viewing the space between Sierra and Dead World. "I want an additional space mine screen in front of Sierra and dragon patrols in between the two space mine fields. In addition, I want to create a complete void between Dead World and Sierra. I don't want anything for the enemy to infiltrate, hide on, or eat."

Seren's eyes focused on the dwarf. "Johan, will your father need weren troops to set up defensive positions on Sierra?"

"I don't think so, but I'll have to check. He will want military training."

Seren turned to Rand. "How is the troop situation on Dead World? How many weren are stationed here now?"

"About five hundred." Mari broke in. She was in charge of the weren on Dead World, not Rand.

"Five hundred!" Seren exploded. He glared at Rand. "You promised me five thousand."

"Not exactly. All the weren have to spend a year in a nonhuman shape to become full citizens. As their king, I've decreed the only shape acceptable is dragon form. After the year, they can revert to any form they choose. I said five thousand would get military training and spend the year in dragon shape. The most I can get here at any one time is about two thousand."

"Right now, it doesn't matter," Johan observed, pointing to the model on the table. "We don't have the facilities built for many more bodies. I'm sorry, Seren, but it takes time to do construction underground, even using the fissures, which we now have to dig out. We also need an underground set of turbo-generators." His pointer indicated their future position. "It will require patience."

Seren watched Flame snort sparks at the word patience. It was good that the dragon was warm. He appeared relaxed, maybe a little sleepy, much easier to deal with. Then Seren snorted, sounding almost dragon-like. He didn't handle patience well either.

"We can stop any attack or attempt to break through," the Shadow-lord insisted. The rest of Seren's staff nodded in agreement except for Flame, who somehow managed a shrug.

Seren scowled. His whole posture radiated skepticism. "A couple more points. Johan, increase the human facilities quickly. Humans can do the inside work. That way I can maximize the weren we have outside."

Johan touched his bushy eyebrow in a salute of agreement.

"Everybody, bring your second in command to these meetings. We have plenty of room and we'll get more ideas that way." Seren gazed around the room, judging acceptance.

"Now, if someone would show me my quarters…"

"I'll do it," Mari volunteered. After a short walk, she pointed out his office. She gazed upward. "That's a five foot reinforced concrete ceiling overhead."

"Useless. Blowing up this world won't work again. Let me stop here for a minute." Seren opened the door and entered. He felt discouraged. True, a major battle had been won, but the enemy still threatened. He was short troops, facilities, and probably the material he needed to destroy the Slithiz. In his mind, the Slithiz sitting out there in space was a stalemate, for Bright One's sake. He hated stalemates even in chess because you had to begin again. This situation wasn't any different. The staff meeting reports proved everything had changed.

Seren promised himself he would get what he needed and finish the job. Stalemate - he hated the concept. Seren still couldn't believe they were feeding the enemy horde. He kicked an empty wastebasket in frustration. It flew against the wall with a satisfying crash.

* * * *

"You shouldn't be upset," Mari said. "You did what was required. All Jarl asked was that the Slithiz be stopped."

"Berdularion claims nothing can occupy space. The Slithiz appear to be doing it. If he's right, they're going attack sometime. Our forces are out-numbered. I don't consider the Slithiz stopped."

Picking up the basket, he noticed the wall it had slammed into was lined with pictures. He walked over and grinned. That O'Roark! Some of these were from this morning. He took down the one of him holding his daughter.

"Mari, Killeen claims she doesn't need a gate anymore. Can I travel without one, too?"

"Maybe. You'll have to try short hops first." Mari's eyes danced with her amusement. She had noted the look on Seren's face when he saw his child. Good, the child would keep Seren balanced. Mari had no intention of telling Seren how lively his life would be as the father of a half-Sidhe baby daughter.

EPILOGUE

The pounding on his door forced Andronan to lower the footrest and lever himself out of his chair. Shuffling to the door, he had barely cracked it open when Killeen swept in. He peered down the hall in both directions. It was hard to believe she had caused all the commotion by herself. Closing the door, he asked, "Did you change your mind about being a keeper?"

"Bright Ones, no! I came for advice because you're ancient and wise."

"Anc—Ancient." Andronan sputtered, then smiled. To Killeen, he probably was ancient. "Wisdom is a glamour. Age means you see more possibilities—not necessarily which one is right."

"I promised Seren I'd be a perfect little lady." Killeen, ignored Andronan's attempt at humor. "It's so hard. O'Roark says it's because I live by 'Ready—Fire—Aim'. So I came to you for help on aiming first." She put her hands on her hips. "Besides, you know Seren and Mirza well and can help me figure out the consequences when I do what I want."

Andronan chuckled at her idea of being a perfect little Sidhe. His great-granddaughter Lealor had approached life the same way as a child.

* * * *

Flame paced back and forth in his cavern, emitting short bursts of fire. Stalemate! He hated the word. No dragon worth his scales would accept anything but complete and final victory. Human weaklings like those back on Realm and Widdershins might be pleased with the cessation of hostilities, but not a dragon prince. He burrowed into his bed of coals, sinking until only his snout and eyes were exposed. Now, how could he prod the Slithiz into a battle? He gave a deep groan of ecstasy as his body absorbed the heat. He would definitely plan a few strikes, not the piddling guerilla sorties the Shadowlord was doing. After he took a long nap, of course.

He closed his eyes and dreamed of glory.

www.ingramcontent.com/pod-product-compliance
Lightning Source LLC
Chambersburg PA
CBHW031415250626
47155CB00004B/1499